Possessed

By

Love

Books by Kay Brooks

The Row Series:

Spicer's Challenge
Dreams Fulfilled
Newfound Love

Persistent Intruder
Love Again
Shadows of Déjà vu

Victory Hill Trilogy:

Northwest to Love
Journey Back to Love

Biographies:

The Dancing Couple
I've Still Got Sand in my Shoes

Possessed

By

Love

Enjoy!
Kay Brooks

By Kay Brooks

Published by KDB Manuscripts, 2022

Front Cover Design by SelfPubCovers/Frina

Possessed by Love

This is a work of fiction. Similarities to real people, places
or events are entirely coincidental.

First edition, November 19, 2022
ISBN: 978-1-7354278-3-6

Published in the United States of America

To: Kitty

Cousins by birth, sisters in our hearts

CHAPTER ONE

"Don't be late!" Brooke O'Connor punched the words on her cell phone to Levi Matthews, pressed the send arrow, then proceeded to plait her ginger red hair into a long single braid. Twenty-four, soon to be twenty-five, she managed the family's B&B – *Victory Hill*.

She'd grown up in the expanded mansion as a child, always dreamed it would be hers one day.

Today was an important day, she thought as she twisted the first section over the second. Part of her dream was finally coming true, and Levi Matthews needed to be there. She continued to twist and tug, quickly moving to the ends of her hair.

Brooke couldn't believe she had let her brother and parents talk her into hiring Levi to do the renovations to the restaurant and B&B. He wasn't even from Williamtown. A believer in giving back to the community, she preferred to use a local contractor. Levi was from the state capital, Richmond.

But Cameron, her brother, had checked Levi's references, raved about how Levi worked with several historic preservation groups in Richmond, even had pictures and newspaper articles of his accomplishments.

1

Victory Hill was a family-owned business, and she was out-voted.

Brooke had so many plans for their home place. Originally a boarding house and tavern, *Victory Hill* was now a four-point-five-star bed and breakfast with a separate five-star restaurant that would be celebrating their centennial next spring.

The original six room structure had been built in 1780 by William Donovan, founder of Williamtown. Succeeding Donovan's expanded it into a mansion until the War Between the States when it was used as a hospital. In 1864, James Donovan, William's great grandson was killed in the battle of the Crater near Petersburg, Virginia. It was believed James' wife, Chelsea, died of a broken heart while awaiting her husband's return.

After remaining empty for almost twenty years, the Donovan family sold the mansion at the turn of the century, and it served as an orphanage until it was quickly closed in 1915 when the headmaster was murdered.

Her great-great grandparents, Edwin and Wilma Comfort bought the abandoned mansion for five hundred dollars in the spring of nineteen twenty.

Wilma named it *Victory Hill* because of the victory gardens she and the community tended in the back yards during the first World War and the tragedies associated with the orphanage.

Someone haunted the house – a wounded soldier, James Donovan's widow or the murdered orphanage victim – Brooke wasn't sure which. She preferred to think it was Chelsea Donovan. That was certainly a more romantic promotion for the B&B's website.

Victory Hill's centennial was coming up next spring and Brooke had big plans. But first, there were much needed improvements – updated bathrooms, an enlarged kitchen and remodeled attic. Improvements that would increase the B&B's marketability and earn her that extra half point.

Improvements she wanted done yesterday.

Levi Matthews on the other hand, preferred to take his time. According to him, true historic preservation was best when done slowly and meticulously to preserve the integrity of the building.

Brooke jumped when her phone signaled Levi's response.

"Nag, nag, nag. They're not even here yet."

That was beside the point, she fumed, then breathed a sigh of relief. If Levi knew they weren't here, that meant he was somewhere on the two-hundred-acre property. Not in town, or Richmond, ordering supplies he always seemed to be needing.

She applied a hint of Caribbean green shadow and a thin brown line above her eyes, brushed her full lashes with mascara; finished her make-up with a stroke of pink powder to her cheeks and apricot balm on her full lips.

Brooke reached for the wreath green Cassia tunic with asymmetrical crinkle chiffon hem she'd decided to pair with her black leggings and dressed quickly. Turned a half circle each way to study her reflection in the mirror and smiled. Professional and comfortable, she thought.

"Just be sure you're here on time." She texted before grabbing her favorite loop earrings.

If she could get up at the crack of dawn to help Connie, her co-manager with breakfast for their guests, then work the lunch and dinner shifts in the restaurant, why couldn't Levi Matthews hammer a few more nails? Put up a wall? Be on time for a meeting?

Each generation of Comforts had expanded and improved the mansion and she was simply carrying on the tradition.

Her great, great grandparents – Edwin and Wilma Comfort – had purchased it. Rejuvenated it, ran it as a boarding house. Wilma's delicious hot meals made it a popular tavern.

Her great grandfather, William Comfort enclosed the detached kitchen and enlarged it to better serve their customers that flocked there for his wife Elsie's good cooking.

Her grandfather Harry built the separate, larger restaurant for the popular eating spot. He also added the wing to the back of the house - bedrooms for his expanded family while enclosing the back porch, installing stairs to the two-room loft above the kitchen and laundry room.

When Brooke started managing the B&B last year, she had moved out of her parents' house into the loft. Connie lived in the converted laundry room downstairs, off the kitchen.

Like her ancestors, Brooke was upgrading the mansion, but the renovations were important on a personal level too. She was tired of sharing a bathroom with Connie and wanted a bathroom of her own in her own living quarters.

"I thought you said they'd already committed to the project. What's the hurry?"

Levi's text interrupted her perusal of the corner of her loft where she envisioned her own personal bathroom.

Brooke blew out a breath. Hated that one simple text seemed to stretch into a long string of conversation.

"I just want to make a good impression!"

Young Investment, based in Houston, Texas, had agreed to fund the renovations to the B&B and restaurant, and Aaron Young, grandson to the financier, would be arriving within the hour to discuss the project and meet the contractor in charge.

Aaron also owned the *Streaming Syndicate* an online newspaper and had visited the B&B two months earlier. Unbeknownst to her, Aaron had been on a mission to recruit Piper Richardson who was also staying here on her way to an Alaskan cruise. Piper wrote the popular blog – *On the Move* – and her two blogs about her stay at *Victory Hill* had been a big boost for business.

Brooke smiled as she recalled Piper's latest blog announcing her engagement to Aaron who had followed Piper onto the Alaskan cruise.

As if the renovation project wasn't enough, Jake Carmichael with *Jacob's Foundation* would also be here to discuss the Victory Hill Community Garden grant his foundation was funding for the town and schools. Jake and Aaron grew up together and he'd been impressed by her family's pay it forward involvement with the community.

Williamtown would be the first pilot program and the foundation agreed to match whatever funds the town raised. Brooke had been unable to attend the Foundation's Awards Banquet so Jake and his fiancé, Cilla Graham decided to bring the funds to her.

Jake and Cilla had been high school sweethearts that drifted apart then reconnected at the restaurant on their way to celebrate her grandmother's ninetieth birthday last month. Cilla worked for *Jacob's Foundation* and wrote the grant to fund the community garden project.

Jake had just assisted with another of his Foundation's projects – Operation Renewal – which provided housing for disabled veterans and their families.

Brooke had arranged for the two couples to have the B&B to themselves for the weekend. She also hoped to convince them to add their pictures to the *Wall of Love* in the restaurant. Images of ten other couples who met at *Victory Hill* and married within six months were already displayed on the wall.

"Do I need to wear my tux?"

Brooke inhaled deeply and threw her head back as her eyes shot sparks at the ceiling. Why did he have to be such a jerk?

Making *Victory Hill* a wedding venue was another of Brooke's centennial goals, and all Levi Matthews had to do was convert the third-floor attic into a penthouse/bridal suite.

5

And add a bathroom to her loft, she repeated to herself as she stepped out of her bedroom into her office and sitting room. She stared at the door in the far corner that opened into a small storage room.

Perfect place to add a bathroom, she smiled. Above Connie's small bathroom downstairs, adjacent to the bathroom in *Harry and Rita's* room next door to her loft and below the designated bathroom for the honeymoon suite on the third floor.

Her phone pinged a new Facebook post.

"So excited! My puppy will be ready for pick-up at twelve tomorrow. Can't wait to give it a new home!"

Brooke smiled. Anyone would think her friend, Melanie was adopting a new puppy in time for an afternoon visit to the dog park. Not smuggling an abused friend out of town at midnight.

She and a small group of friends had created a private *Free Spirits* Facebook group. They weren't about ghosts or alcohol spirits, but rather a network of angels spread across the country with the mission to help women and children escape abusive relationships. In a little over a year, they had relocated twenty women.

She looked at the door to the attic. Another reason she needed a private bathroom. She had secretly sheltered several of the women on their journey to freedom. Once the B&B had been full and bathrooms were a must for women.

"So happy for you and hope the puppy adjusts to his new home!" Brooke replied to Melanie's post before she headed down the steps.

Ten minutes later, Brooke plumped the bright yellow pillows on the sofa and two lounge chairs on the side porch. She'd already swept the few stray leaves that had blown through the wide arched openings that offered spectacular views of the long front drive and the tall Magnolia trees, gardens and gazebo on the side of the house.

She kept her eyes and ears tuned to the white-fenced lane that curved past the front of the house around to the back entrance for any arrivals.

She brushed a damp cloth across the top of the bar for the third time, turned the bottle of champagne chilling in the wine chiller and checked the mini fridge beneath the bar to be sure the extra bottles were cool.

Where was the jerk? she fumed as she looked across the lawn one more time.

"You'd better be on your way," she texted Levi Matthews.

*L*evi Matthews leaned against the stainless-steel counter in the kitchen of the *Victory Hill* restaurant. Six foot two, with a long face, pointed chin, straight nose, thin mouth, deep-set gunmetal gray eyes, he'd been working here for two months now. He'd double majored in college – business and architecture, masters in historic preservation – but continued to be self-taught. Researching to learn how to do whatever needed to be done the best way possible. He preferred to work with his hands, patiently transform houses, or antiques, to their special charm.

Chiseled arms crossed over his chest, long legs crossed at his ankles, he watched Angelina Comfort-O'Connor's long fingers prepare a tray of canapes. She was average height, little leggier than her daughter. Short auburn hair with a hint of gray was cut short around her oval face, wispy around her long slender neck.

Levi shook his head at Brooke's text.

"I'd be willing to bet that your daughter was a handful when she was growing up?"

Angelina and Finn O'Connor reminded him of his parents who lived in Richmond. Both were easy going, easy to talk to, easy to be around. Hard workers, he was amazed at the sense of coordination they shared.

The kitchen was tight, grill and work counter sandwiched between the walk-in refrigerator and dish-washing sinks on one side and path to the back door on the other. There was a drink station at the swinging doors to the main restaurant and bar. Somehow, they had managed to work around each other for twenty years.

He'd hoped to discuss a couple ideas he had for the restaurant's kitchen remodel, but everyone seemed to be more focused on the important guests who would be staying the weekend at the B&B.

Tall, with long legs capable of big strides between the grill and workstation he shared with his wife, Finn O'Connor chuckled as he aligned sliced grilled chicken atop a customer's Caesar salad. He was clean shaven, with strong nose and sharp cheekbones, nut brown hair, some graying on the sides

"She could be stubborn." Coffee-brown eyes glanced sideways at his wife. "Comes by it naturally."

"Remember that night she stormed in our bedroom at eleven o'clock?" Angelina positioned some shrimp, cucumber and curry cream cheese canapes on the plate. Angled a look at Levi. "She argued with us for a solid ten minutes. Couldn't understand why she and Susan shouldn't be allowed to go to a mall in Richmond by themselves. The more we said 'no', the faster she argued. Then," Angelina shrugged a shoulder, wiped her hands on a towel as she glanced toward Levi, "she just stopped talking. Said 'okay' turned around and marched back to her room." Angelina shook her head, smiled at her husband. "We just stared at one another. Exhausted."

"How old was she?" Levi asked eying the other cucumber hors d'oeuvres. Wondered what the red stuff was on top of each slice.

"Fourteen," Finn grumbled as he set the plated meal on the warming tray at the end of the counter, tapped the round silver bell.

"She more than made up for the boys," Angelina chuckled. "But I wouldn't want her any other way. She's independent, strong, has a big heart and has worked hard to make the B&B a success."

Angelina stepped over to Levi, offered him a canape. "Be patient. She has a lot riding on today."

"THEY ARE HERE!" Levi studied the text.

"Guess that's my cue," he said, eyeing the plates. "Would you like me to deliver those?"

Angelina wrapped the plates in cellophane, handed them to Levi. "Don't be stopping along the way to sample any more, mess up my arrangement." She warned with a smile.

"**Y**ou know I want to get married here," Piper Richardson's brandy-colored eyes sparkled at Brooke as she sipped her champagne. Her ash brown hair pulled back from her oval face, creamy skin, she flashed her wide smile. Long fingers with short, manicured nails raised her glass toward the lawn and magnolia trees beyond the arched opening. "In the garden, next to the gazebo."

"That's where I first observed you," Aaron Young leaned over, kissed Piper's cheek. "Sat right here, in fact, eavesdropping on every word of your conversation with Abby." Dressed in tailored dark gray slacks and lighter gray sweater, his jet-black hair combed back from his elongated face and angular cheekbones, Aaron winked a gray eye at Brooke as he stretched his long legs out in front of him.

Brooke froze, her eyes grew wide. She wasn't aware they had made so much progress on the wedding plans. "Wedding? Here?" She swallowed. "When? You realize we'll be starting the renovations soon."

"We're thinking of a spring wedding," Aaron stated.

"Spring, huh," Brooke looked at her *Fitbit*, checked the time, took a sneak peek at her heartrate. "Um, this contractor my family has hired moves like molasses sometimes. Seems to enjoy plucking my nerves. Always late for meetings. I worry he'll be finished in time." She looked at her *Fitbit* a second time. "He was supposed to be here fifteen minutes ago."

Cilla Graham chuckled to herself. She and Brooke had gotten close the past two months as they finalized the plans for the community garden and school project, and she had heard more than a few complaints from the innkeeper about the contractor.

Tall and slender with platinum shoulder length hair and emerald-green eyes, Cilla was almost hesitant to return to the B&B. After her brief stop at the Restaurant months ago, locking eyes with Chelsea Donovan's ghost in the third-floor windows, Chelsea had haunted her dreams during her trip home to visit her grandmother. Even after learning Chelsea was her grandmother's great, great aunt, the fact that she was now inside what was Chelsea Donovan's home was unsettling. She hadn't had any more dreams, but thoughts of Chelsea flickered through her mind from time to time.

Cilla looked at Jake, thankful that they had crossed paths here, been given a second chance at love. Wondered if maybe that was what Chelsea wanted all along. A second chance for them both.

She offered a wide smile to Brooke. "You've been so vocal about this guy, I'm anxious to meet him," she joked, then winked. "I'm hoping to leave something behind." Meaning her relative's ghost.

"It might be good for business if you did," Brooke joked. "We need Chelsea here. I've had a couple guests complain about not being scared by our resident ghost."

Piper shivered. "I certainly remember when she visited my bedroom. Scared the willies out of me."

Cilla saw movement near the gazebo and watched the tall man approach the porch. The closer he came, the more he looked familiar. He was about to step onto the porch when she got a good look at his long, oval face with deep set gray eyes. She stiffened.

"Cilla?" Jake Carmichael's chocolate brown eyes studied her. He squeezed her hand when she remained silent. "Are you okay?"

Cilla bobbed her head silently, turned to Piper, realized her friend's face was white as a sheet.

*L*evi studied the gazebo as his long strides carried him toward the side porch of the B&B, a plate of canapes in each hand. Made a mental note that the gazebo could use a fresh coat of white paint.

Brooke met him at the edge of the porch, the step putting her slitted eyes level with his. His raised eyebrow registered her anger, dared her to say anything.

"Angelina said she and Finn will be bringing dinner later." He handed her one of the plates.

Brooke set the plate on the coffee table, arranged the other beside it.

"Everyone," she linked nervous hands, "this is Levi Matthews, the contractor who will be working on the renovations. Levi, Aaron Young and his fiancé Piper Richardson, Jake Carmichael and his assistant Cilla Graham."

She waved a hand toward each one individually. Worry lines creased her forehead when she noted Cilla and Piper's pale faces.

Cilla and Piper both sprang to their feet.

"Can we help you in the kitchen?" Piper asked as she and Cilla each grabbed an arm, navigated Brooke inside the house to the butler's quarters.

"Don't you see it?" Piper whispered.

"See what?" Brooke wondered.

"Levi," Cilla answered. "He's the image of James Donovan."

Brooke blinked. "What? What are you talking about?"

Piper grabbed her cell phone, searched her pictures for the Confederate soldier that had haunted her laptop months earlier. When she found what she was looking for, she handed it to Brooke. "Notice a resemblance?"

Brooke's mouth fell open when she studied the long, oval, unshaven face with deep set pewter gray eyes that matched the color of his hat. There was most definitely a resemblance between Levi Matthews and James Donovan. Same long nose; same serious expression.

"But-"

"Do you know anything about him? Where he's from?" Piper asked.

"He's from Richmond. But-" Brooke couldn't stop looking at the picture of the soldier that went off to war within weeks of his marriage, never met the son, Richard, who was born almost nine months later.

Piper looked at Cilla. "I don't know much about the family except that George, James' brother, took Richard to Richmond after Chelsea died."

"What do you know about Levi?" Cilla asked.

"Only that he can be a pain in the ass sometimes. Cameron's the one that did all the research. Gave him glowing remarks. Talked my parents into hiring him."

"This is just too much of a coincidence," Piper looked from Brooke to Cilla. "And we need answers." She turned back to the porch.

Five minutes later, everyone sat around the porch, staring at Levi.

"My mother was a Donovan," he explained. "The great, great granddaughter of Richard Donovan, James and Chelsea Donovan's son. I don't know too much other than that James died in the war, Chelsea stayed in her rooms after the war, supposedly died of a broken heart and Richard, their son, moved to Richmond with his Uncle George. When he was of age, he sold the house to a church that turned it into an Orphanage, just to get rid of it. That's really all I know.

"When I saw the RFP, I thought I would come to the town where my ancestors started. I'd heard stories about James and Chelsea but wanted to see the house. The first time I came here, I felt an instant connection. Decided I wanted to study the house my ancestors had built."

"Well," Brooke hesitated, "everything's all legal. I mean your family no longer has any connection to the house. And after the murder at the Orphanage, the house was empty for a long time. My great, great grandparents might have gotten the house at a steal, but it was all fair and square."

"I've never doubted it," Levi assured Brooke. "My degree in historic preservation just fuels my interest in the house. The more I work here, the stronger I feel a connection."

"What got you started in historic preservation?" Jake asked.

"My first job was restoring an old Firehouse in Edmondsville, outside of Richmond. These three women wanted to revitalize an old Firehouse and surrounding buildings, attract businesses to the area. We had to shut down for a while when we unearthed a skeleton buried behind the building. Turned out to be a woman who'd been missing for ten years.

13

They quickly solved the mystery, caught the killer and I was back in business."

Aaron nodded his head. "I think I remember reading about that. Brina Hollingsworth was one of the women. She was a personal shopper for me for a couple years."

"You won't need a personal shopper from now on," Piper bumped shoulders with him. "I'll gladly take on that responsibility."

Levi's lips twitched. "They did a Christmas walking tour of all the old buildings after the job was completed which led to me helping with renovations of some of the other buildings. That led to the glass house project."

"Glass house project?" Brooke frowned. "Who would want to live in a glass house?"

"Not people. It's a way of restoring a structure without a lot of rebuilding. You replace missing walls, floors and roof with glass so that you don't damage the original character of the building. It's new. Innovative. They're working on a project in the Northern Neck area of the state. Should be finished in next couple years."

"Have you worked with grants?" Aaron asked, thinking about Brooke's renovation grant.

"Not directly but I assisted with restorations of a theater and train station in Richmond. I prefer to do the work, oversee the project, restore it to its original site. Let someone else worry about the money. I'm self-sufficient and understand how funds can be tight. Willing to work within budgets, long as it doesn't alter the purpose of the renovations."

"What about meeting deadlines?" Brooke tried to nudge her concern about the upcoming anniversary.

Levi cast her a look. "I'm well aware of the centennial anniversary."

"Will the house be finished in time for a wedding?" Aaron asked. "Next Spring?"

CHAPTER TWO

Kristina Powell reached into the cabinet next to the stove for the salt and pepper shakers, flinched when the gown beneath her robe brushed the angry red welts on her back. She was average height with an average heart shaped face, narrow eyes, thin nose and normally creamy skin that was pale at the moment. Wished she could just be the average housewife.

Gary had been so angry last night. Meaner than usual. At least he hadn't touched her face this time.

She checked the stove clock, anxious to get his breakfast fixed so he wouldn't be late for work. She wasn't sure of his mood this morning as she had awakened at dawn, came downstairs to get her restless thoughts in order. Realized after last night she couldn't continue living this way.

When she heard him descending the steps, she jumped into action. Her small hands cracked open the egg into the sizzling grease, pushed down the lever of the toaster and pressed the button on the Keurig. All would be done at the same time.

"Something smells good," Gary Powell set his briefcase and carry-on bag beside the door to the garage. A self-employed CPA, he often travelled around the state for his job. He was dressed in a sweater that hugged his barrel-chest, dress pants that accentuated his narrow hips; his brown hair buzzed, square face and jaw clean shaven.

"I decided not to take the suit after all," he answered her blank stare. Leaned over to kiss her cheek, ignored the way she shied away from him. Continued to crowd her at the stove.

"Sorry I got upset last night. I have so much riding on this meeting, I need to make a good impression."

Kristina stiffened, screamed silently when his beefy fingers grazed up and down her back, irritating the fiery welts.

"Sorry," he apologized again, "shouldn't have done that."

She gave him a quick sideways glance but registered no sorrow in his expression. Rather, there was a little gleam of sarcasm in his hard eyes.

She plated the eggs, arranged the toast beside the bacon and grabbed the just filled cup of coffee. Set them on the placemat as he settled at the table in the dinette area.

She held her breath, worried she had overlooked something when he frowned at her. "You're not eating?"

"No, I'm not hungry." She sat across from him, studied the table to be sure she hadn't forgotten anything. Hoped the food was seasoned to his specifications.

"I should be back late tomorrow evening. We'll do something. Go to a movie. Shopping. Something."

Kristina remained silent. Clasp her nervous hands in her lap beneath the table. Waited patiently while he ate. Tried not to look at the ticking clock. Silently prayed nothing would prevent him leaving on time.

Fifteen minutes later, she peeked around the living room sheers, watched him back out of the garage, drive down the street. She waited a full five minutes to be sure he wasn't returning.

Like he did one day last week.

When she felt safe, she reached for her cell phone and texted, *"I need to schedule my appointment."*

She received an immediate response. *"4:45 this afternoon. Come through the back."*

*B*rooke poured the chicken broth into the tenderized onion and garlic mixture, added the shredded cabbage, diced potatoes and strips of cooked ham steak. Stirred everything, put the cover on the pan, lowered the heat to let it simmer for the next hour.

The weather had cooled after Aaron, Piper, Jake and Cilla left the B&B; they were calling for a storm later in the day. Brooke decided a pot of Irish ham and cabbage soup would hit the spot for the guests that were expected early this afternoon.

While Connie prepared the rooms, Brooke oversaw the food preparation before heading over to the restaurant for the lunch shift.

She loved experimenting with her Irish recipes. The cranberry scones were always a hit; raisin oat scones were next on the list but today she was going to offer Irish shortbread cookies shaped like shamrocks to their guests.

She reached for the *Kerrygold* butter, shook her head at the loud slam of the back door.

"Don't suppose you considered that I might have guests sleeping in?" She scolded Levi as he stepped into the kitchen.

"And good morning to you," Levi's lips twitched as he made it a point to softly close the Dutch door that connected the kitchen to the enclosed back porch. "Didn't see any cars in the parking lot."

He strolled over to the stove, lifted the lid to the pot of soup and sniffed. "Wanted to let you and Connie know I was in the house."

He relaxed against the end of the counter, ankles crossed, arms folded across his chest. "What 'cha making?" He studied the deep yellow butter. "Why is that butter so dark? You sure it's good? Not dated?"

"It's Irish butter." Brooke stirred the vanilla and butter until it was smooth. "Eighty two percent butterfat, less water. The cows are grass fed which gives it a buttery flavor." She mixed in the sugar, added flour and cornstarch. "I'm making Irish shortbread cookies."

"My Mom always stuck to the basic chocolate chip cookies. Knew the recipe on the chocolate chip bag by heart."

Brooke dumped the batter onto the floured pastry sheet, kneaded it for thirty seconds, before reaching for the rolling pin.

Levi studied the rainbow of colors on the ends of the kitchen utensil. "Never seen a rolling pin like that. What's with all the colors?"

Brooke shook her head at the endless questions. He was like a big kid.

"Each color is a different thickness." She chose the red disc. "These cookies need to be one quarter inch in thickness."

"Humph. My Mom just had the old-fashioned wooden roller with wooden handles and eyeballed it. Aren't you going to sample it first? Be sure you didn't forget anything?"

"I've made them before; know they are good." She pressed the shamrock shape into the dough, rubbed the edges of the cutter between each cookie cutting.

"What's with dabbing the cutter with flour each time?"

"Makes for a drier, even cut," Brooke responded as she concentrated, tongue between teeth.

"Why not just dab some flour over the dough?"

Brooke gave him a frosty look. "Then I wouldn't have the nice golden color."

Levi's jaw dropped when she put the pan of shaped cookies into the refrigerator.

"Wait. I thought you cooked them."

Brooke let out an exasperated sigh. "You DO. I let them chill at least an hour so they will keep their shape." She rested fisted hands on her hips. "What's with all the questions? Don't you have better things to do than criticize my baking skills? Like work on the attic?"

She gathered the bowl, utensils, measuring cups, tossed them into the sink for cleaning. Turned to lean against the sink, mimicking his stance.

Levi's lips twitched. It fascinated him that her emerald, green eyes always turned a darker Sacramento color whenever he managed to aggravate her. Then she'll get a little flush to her cheeks and her back usually stiffens up.

He shook his head, chuckled to himself when she continued to stare at him in silence.

"That's why I'm here. I noticed you were nervous when Piper mentioned having her wedding here and Aaron asked if the renovations would be done by spring. Figured maybe we needed to sit down, discuss this honeymoon suite project. Prioritize some things."

His head jerked when he heard the baby cry. "Is someone staying here with a baby? I heard a baby crying yesterday but have yet to cross paths with any families here."

"It's one of our spiritual guests."

"Spiritual? As in ghosts? You have *two* ghosts?"

Brooke nodded her head. "Obviously, you haven't visited our website."

"I know about Chelsea Donovan, my multiple times great grandmother, that supposedly haunts the house. You're saying there's more?"

"In 1892, Richard Donovan, your multiple times great grandfather, sold the homeplace to a Church that turned it into an orphanage. Supposedly, the minister wasn't who everyone thought he was. He was abusive, sold some of the children to

19

slave labor camps, raped many of the young girls in the orphanage. He was murdered in 1915 and the orphanage was shut down. It's my understanding that the weaker female babies were killed and buried somewhere on the property. I can only assume one of those babies haunts the house. Cries every day at ten in the morning. Don't know whether that's the time the baby was born or died. Sometimes, it sounds like Chelsea, your multiple times great grandmother tries to sooth the baby as I've often heard her humming a lullaby."

"You've never had any paranormal investigators here to check it out?"

Brooke shook her head. "Too expensive." She turned to run water into the sink, added dish detergent. "Too much trouble. I've been working so hard to just get the B&B established, I don't have time for them."

"Understood. Which is why we need to look at the attic. See what you want to do as far as the honeymoon suite."

"I need to clean my mess first. Then help Connie with another suite of rooms. I can meet you around two. But I need to be at the restaurant by four to work the dinner shift, so don't be late."

Levi turned to leave, stopped at the Dutch door. "Will the cookies be baked by then?"

$\mathcal{A}$t two that afternoon, Brooke set a small vase of fresh flowers on the reception table in the lobby before heading up the front stairs, across the landing toward the five steps that led to the second floor.

She carried a Ziplock bag containing three shortbread cookies.

She paused a moment to check *Chelsea's Room*, the first bedroom on the right. Caught a whiff of baby powder, the scent of the yellow and orange coneflowers she'd put in there earlier that morning.

This was where Piper had stayed her first time at the B&B. Brooke smiled as she recalled Piper's comments about Chelsea visiting her room, nudging the curtains aside as if to investigate the courtyard below.

Another couple would be staying in the room this evening. She appreciated that Chelsea no longer haunted Cilla's dreams, hoped she might add a little excitement to the couple's stay.

Brooke opened the next door, flipped a switch that turned on the single bulb that suspended from the ceiling at the top of the narrow, wooden steps leading up to the attic.

She listened to the quiet as she climbed the stairs, irritated that Levi wasn't already there. Probably got involved with another project, still in town, or talking with her parents in the restaurant.

Maybe she'd eat his cookies just for spite.

She turned left onto the small landing at the top of the stairs, made her way past the open area on the right. Recalled when she would come up here as a child. Brushed her fingers across the old baby crib where she once played with her dolls.

She'd always stayed close to the door in case the man in chains, her parents enjoyed teasing her about, would come along. Even as a teenager, when she knew there was no such thing, she found herself looking over her shoulder.

Brooke stared across the long, open room with the wide, dusty floorboards, exposed rough wood beams that spanned the length of the ceiling. It was cool and dry with the smell of dust. Sunlight filtered into the cracks near the eaves, motes of dust danced in the shaft of light coming through the dormer windows covered with grime and dead flies.

Brooke acknowledged it would take a lot of elbow grease to whip the area into livable quarters. Hoped and prayed Levi Matthews was up to the job.

At one time, the attic had held Donovan furniture and trunks. Orphaned children may have slept up here. Now it stored an old rocking chair, faded boxes with contents written on the sides, Christmas decorations. Dusty sheets covered antique dressers that had been handed down through the generations of Comforts.

She looked beyond the contents, saw gleaming floors with area rugs, floor to ceiling drapes and a King size bed. Everything would be white with exception of the mahogany floors and bright navy rugs.

There were six dormers. Three on the right offered views of the front drive; three on the left, views of the parking lot and restaurant. The floor creaked as she stepped toward the middle front dormer, looked out to see the train depot in the distance on the edge of town.

Suddenly she felt light-headed. Sad. She hugged herself at the loneliness that overcame her, felt a thickness in her throat as if she wanted to cry.

Everything turned dark, and she imagined the glow of campfires on the front fields where the Union troops had camped so long ago. Her heart was heavy with longing, anxious for James' return home.

She needed to get back downstairs before the doctor realized she'd slipped away.

"You up there?" Levi called from the second floor.

Brooke jumped, rubbed her forehead. Wondered what had come over her as she listened to Levi's boots on the groaning stairs.

"You're late," she glared at him when he reached the top.

"Blame your mother," Levi defended himself. "She was telling me what she wanted to do in the kitchen, then made me eat a pastrami and rye sandwich." He smiled when his eyes zeroed in on the cookies in her hand. "Those for me?"

Brooke tossed him the bag. "Didn't have room for them on the plate."

Levi opened the bag, pitched a whole cookie into his mouth. Decided not to mention the one he had snuck off that plate on his way through the kitchen to the attic.

"Lot of stuff up here," he reached for a second cookie as he navigated around the furniture, leaned down to study an old trunk, jiggled the unusual lock then headed towards the far end of the room. "You want to make this entire floor a honeymoon suite?"

"With exception of one of the rooms at the far end." She followed him. "The one on the right, front side of the house has a hidden stairway down to the second floor – my loft area. I'd like to leave that room for storage but make the other room into a bathroom for the honeymoon suite. Then enclose a small section of my loft area which is below the proposed bathroom and extend the piping down to make a bathroom for my loft area. Does that make sense?"

"I guess," he nodded his head. "Don't want to mess the integrity of the building though." He tucked the empty bag into his back pocket as he strolled into the second room.

"Lot of stuff in here too," he walked around the table in the middle of the room with upended chairs covering the top, studied the old sofa that sat in front of the window, baker's rack with shelves filled with boxes and jars, tugged the lock on another trunk tucked away in the corner next to the sofa.

He brushed a hand down the tall, heavy oak wardrobe that took up one corner of the room. Decided it would be a bitch to move but refinished, would look good in one of the bedrooms downstairs. He strummed fingers against his chest as he debated mentioning the suggestion to Brooke.

He studied the walls, rapped them with his knuckles searching for studs. "Where is this hidden stairway?"

Brooke walked to the wall directly across from the door to the long room, pressed a button near the ceiling and a door opened. She led him down the steep stairs into the loft area of her living quarters.

"Cool," Levi turned at the base of the stairs, stared up into the attic.

"My great grandfather installed it when he enclosed the kitchen. Figured it would be easier to get to the attic rather than having to go all the way around to the other side of the house."

"Smart man." Levi strolled across the room, peeked into her bedroom. Turned to study the open space where she had her desk and a small loveseat. He took out his tape measure, noted the measurements on his spiral notepad.

"You want to put a bathroom here? Keep the door to the attic in your bathroom?"

"Well, it would be nice if the attic door opened into a closet but if that's not possible, it can be part of the bathroom. I just want my own private bathroom. Guess the only people to use it would be me anyway."

Levi headed back upstairs to the attic. Studied the proximity of the space above the proposed room below.

"Guess it's doable," he called down to her. "Even with the closet."

Brooke pumped her fists, did an imaginary happy dance. Her heart swelled as she raced up the stairs, ecstatic that for once he wasn't objecting to one of her suggestions.

She walked over to the door into the larger attic room.

"I'd also like to take this door out." She raised her arms to encompass the space. "If you enclose it, it will give me more wall for the honeymoon suite."

She turned to gauge his reaction, swayed when dizziness overcame her. Rested a hand on the forehead.

"Brooke?" Levi studied her face, watched the color drain away. "You, okay?"

24

Brooke heard Levi speak but found herself staring into deep-set gunmetal gray eyes. Saw a long oval, unshaven face with pointed chin beneath a gray hat. A deep longing overcame her, and she stepped up to him. Placed a hand behind his neck.

"I've missed you so," she leaned up to brush his lips. Wrapped her arms around his neck, held on tight as she deepened the kiss.

Levi's eyes widened with shock. His heart thumped and his body came to attention. Whatever came over the woman, he decided he liked it. His hands curled around her small waist hugged her closer as he angled his head to deepen the kiss, his tongue dipping in to enjoy the moment while it lasted.

Brooke leaned into the heat of his body, smelled the sawdust in his shirt, tasted traces of pastrami and cookies on his lips. She sighed, felt as if she was finally home. Finally found the love of her life.

Sensations of desire replaced confusion as Brooke registered Levi's caressing hands pressing her tighter against his chest. She stiffened in shock when she realized her breasts tingled, stomach churned, and hips were pressed against him as those caressing hands moved down toward her rear.

"What?" She jerked her head back. "What did you do?" She admonished him.

"*Me*?" Levi stared down at her. "You're the one that got a glazed look in your eyes. And by the way? *Your* hand pulled me into the kiss."

"That's ridiculous," Brooke sputtered, then realized her arms were still wrapped around his neck. She moved them to his shoulders, nervously brushed them down the side of her pants as she backed away. "I would never come on to a man like that." She turned to the door to her loft. "Certainly not you," she raced down the steps, slammed the door behind her.

"Hey," Levi called out to her. "Don't you want to discuss this project some more?"

25

He chuckled as he stepped toward the main room of the attic. Stopped in his tracks when he felt movement of air stroke his cheek, then the door to the main room suddenly slammed in his face.

*K*ristina Powell walked into the back entrance of *A Cut Above* Hair Salon at four forty-five that afternoon. She peeked around the door into the salon, exchanged looks with Becky her hairdresser, but stayed out of sight of the client in the chair.

She waited in the small utility room, turned to the drier when it buzzed, signaling the end of a cycle. Started folding the warm towels while listening to the murmurs of Becky's conversation with her customer.

She stacked the towels on the shelves, read the labels of beauty supplies arranged on the racks, found herself staring into the mirror of a station in corner. She watched the tears she felt welling in her eyes. Who was this woman? What had happened to the happy girl of her youth?

Becky walked in, tossed soiled towels into the hamper.

"My last customer and the front door's locked." Her hands resting on Kristina's upper arms, Becky studied her friend. "Are you okay?"

Kristina sighed. "Yeah, but it's time. I can't continue like this."

"Then let's get busy." Becky brushed fingers through Kristina's hair. "You have such beautiful coppery brown hair; I hate to color it."

"Color it and cut it," Kristina decided. "Anything to make me forget."

"Get settled while I turn the lights out up front. We can work back here."

"Do you want to talk about it?" Becky asked as she spread the black cape across Kristina, snapped it at the back of her neck, started sectioning her hair.

"It was awful," Kristina's tear-filled eyes locked with Becky's in the mirror. "Amy had stopped by, and we were talking about the baby shower. He came home early, caught me by surprise. He was rude as usual, so Amy left. As soon as she was gone, he immediately started in on what were we laughing about. Said it was probably about him. Or were we planning a big night out since he was going to be out of town. Then he asked if I had picked up his suit at the cleaners. I reminded him he said he was going to pick it up. He shouted about how he had to do everything. All I did was sit at home all day. I looked at the time, said I should be able to get the suit before they closed."

Becky continued to section and apply the color treatment to Kristina's hair, gave her the solitude to compose herself. She'd been doing Kristina's hair for five years, and like any other hairdresser, knew all her secrets and sorrows. Had tried more than once to convince her friend to leave.

Kristina took a deep breath. "I got home, and he'd found the shower gift I'd bought. An adorable little dress. He yelled about the price tag, didn't even give me a chance to say it had been seventy percent off," Kristina gulped. "Then," Kristina sobbed, "then he ripped the dress," she whispered.

"He ripped the dress?" Becky froze, stared at Kristina above the rim of her glasses, the color treatment brush suspended above Kristina's hair. "He ripped a baby's dress?" She repeated.

Kristina nodded her head quickly. "Then I got angry and shouted he shouldn't have done that. He just looked at me; said I didn't need to be wasting his hard-earned money on baby clothes. He grabbed my pocketbook, snatched all my credit cards out of my wallet before he yanked off his belt. I tried to run but he grabbed my hair and dragged me into the bedroom. It was awful. He straddled me, started whipping my back. I couldn't get up."

"Did you take a picture?" Becky demanded.

Kristina nodded.

"While I'm working on your hair, I want you to email all your pictures to me. Then we are going to erase everything off your cell phone and I'm giving you another which you will use from now on."

Becky studied Kristina's black backpack beside the back door. "Did you pack enough clothes?"

Kristina nodded.

"Money?"

"I have about five hundred. He watches me like a hawk and that's all I've been able to save. I guess I should have started stashing it away sooner."

"I can give you another hundred."

"What about my car?

"We're going to park it near the car dealership outside town, with your cell phone inside so they can't track you. Then I'm driving you to the bus station." Becky nodded her head toward an envelope leaning against the mirror. "That's your ticket to freedom. You leave at nine thirty this evening."

*B*rooke collapsed on her bed. Stared at the ceiling, brushed a hand across her lips. That kiss in the attic had haunted her all evening and she'd made herself run non-stop trying to forget it. Even Gran commented how restless she seemed.

What could have come over her to do that! She still didn't believe she initiated it, like Levi said. She didn't even like the jerk!

And they still hadn't finalized the plans for the honeymoon suite.

She heard the ping on her cell phone. ***Your package has shipped.***

CHAPTER THREE

Kristina jerked awake at the bus's sudden stop of motion and whoosh of the air brakes. She stiffened, peeked around the seat, down the long narrow aisle toward the front. Had Gary somehow tracked her down and stopped the bus?

She checked the time on her new cell phone. It had been a long nine hours. Except for the steady hum of the bus's engine, it was quiet. No one talked; they either slept, read or scrolled their cell phones.

She'd tried to relax, but worried that Gary would find her. Gradually, with each mile they travelled away from Oklahoma City, she felt the weight lift off her shoulders. Her racing heart had calmed, relaxed.

Now, it was almost seven in the morning, and she calculated she was over six hundred miles from home.

She reached for her backpack, glanced out the window to get her bearings. The bus stop was more a satellite, next to a train commuter station. The parking lot was half full of cars, commuters waiting to catch the train to their jobs in the city.

Before they left the hair salon, Becky had given her a red scarf. "Put this on when you get off the bus. Your contact will be looking for it." Kristina draped it around her neck, took a deep breath and stood. She let the other passengers exit the bus first, then made her way toward the front, stepped off the bus. Jumped when her new cellphone chimed.

Cab 752.

Kristina looked over and saw the man leaning against a bright yellow cab with the number seven, five, two on the door. He was tall, with long legs and slender frame dressed in worn jeans and white shirt. His dark hair showed some silver on the sides.

"Need a ride?" He smiled, opened the door for her and placed her backpack beside her. "I understand you've had a long night. And the adventure isn't over yet," he joked. "Hopefully you can get some shut eye shortly."

Kristina appreciated the scent of coffee as he settled behind the wheel.

"I have an extra coffee," he offered. "But you look like you need a nap more."

"I will gladly pay you for the coffee."

"My treat." His eyes gleamed at her in the rear-view mirror.

"I was too nervous to sleep," she confessed, taking a sip of the hot liquid. "Do you do this often? Pick up strange women at the bus stop? Offer them a free cup of coffee?"

He shrugged a shoulder. "Let's just say I've been needed more than I thought I'd be. I'm just a small part of a bigger network."

"Can I ask how you became involved?"

He turned the radio volume down. "Couple years ago, on a day a lot like today, I picked up a woman and a teenage girl. They'd come in on the bus, early in the morning. The girl was maybe fifteen. At first, I thought they were mother and daughter, but the woman was gruff, kept a firm grip in the girl's wrist. The girl got in first and when I settled behind the wheel, I looked down and there was a little piece of paper on the seat with 'Help Me' scribbled on it.

"I looked in the rear-view mirror and saw tears in that little girl's eyes. I happened to be wearing my headset and was able to discreetly dial nine-one-one, give them the location I was headed. When we got there, the police were waiting. Turned out, the woman was part of a sex trafficking organization. It made the news and within days, I got a call from a friend of a friend of a friend."

Kristina gave him a weary smile. "That was one lucky little girl. I never thought I would be in a situation such as this. Needing your help. You have no idea how isolated, desperate, and alone it feels. I can't thank you enough for all you and your friends do."

Despite the coffee and conversation, the purr of the motor during the slow drive through the city almost lulled an exhausted Kristina to sleep. She jerked when he turned at a *Shellback Suites*, drove past the lobby entrance, through a parking lot filled with cars, around to the back. Pulled up to the steps at the far end of the three-story building.

"What do I owe you?" Kristina reached for her purse as she stepped out of the cab.

"No charge," he waved a hand. "Part of the package." He handed her a key. "This is for room three fifteen. Sorry about the stairs but it's the best we can do. Draws less attention this way. More instructions are inside the room."

He set her backpack beside her, pat a hand on her shoulder. "Get some sleep and have a safe rest of your journey."

*L*evi bit into the apple as he took the final five steps to the second floor two at a time. Peeked into the first room on the right, the one named after his multiple times great grandmother, debated whether to check the tub then or on the way back downstairs. Connie had called him to say she thought the claw-foot tub was leaking.

He heard the roar of a vacuum from a room down the hall, decided he'd enjoy pestering Brooke more. Yesterday's kiss would be emblazoned on his brain for a long time to come.

The small area outside *Chelsea's Room* offered a window view of the landing and wall of windows that looked out on the back side of the B&B, to the restaurant beyond. A loveseat, small end table with an antique tiffany lamp and bookcase of books offered a secluded sitting area to for some quiet reading.

He continued past the door to the attic, sauntered down the long hall toward the noise of the vacuum. Glanced into the room of the first open door on the right. *Edwin & Wilma's Room* – named after Brooke's great-great grandparents who had bought the B&B. It was considered the master bedroom of the B&B, as it offered a view of the long, white-fenced front drive.

Across the hall, on his left was *William and Elsie's Room* – named after Brooke's great grandparents. It looked like a tornado had struck. Big enough for two full size beds, there were sheets on the floor, blankets and bedspreads piled on the beds, towels outside the bathroom.

He continued down the hall to the corner room, paused to appreciate Brooke's tight bottom in snug jeans as she bent down to vacuum beneath the bed.

He shook his head when the room suddenly changed. Saw a high four poster bed centered on the long wall, nightstand on one side, chest of drawers on the other. The furniture faced open windows decorated with a dark navy-blue valence across the top, half curtains that moved in the cool breeze. An oak rocking chair and candlestick table were stationed at the far corner of the room in front of the windows that looked over the magnolia trees, front fields, road in the distance.

In his mind, he heard a woman's laugh, felt the brush of soft lips against his.

Sweat trickled down his spine and he shivered. If Brooke hadn't been across the room, vacuuming, he would have sworn she'd laid another one on him. Like yesterday.

Levi leaned against the door, giving Brooke time to finish the room. He decided to remain in place as she backed up to him, obviously trying to keep the tracks of the vacuum symmetrical on the rug.

Brooke squeaked when she collided with Levi's hard body. "Don't scare me like that," she fussed. "Why aren't you upstairs working?"

She squinted her eyes at the apple. "Did you mess with my arrangement of fruit?"

"Why have a bowl of fruit if you're not going to eat it?"

"It's for the guests," she reminded him.

He took another bite. "Needed your opinion on something. Connie said you were up here."

"You could have at least let me know you were here. Instead of scaring me."

"Worried it might be your ghost?"

"Chelsea doesn't scare me, and she wouldn't have been so rock solid."

He continued to lean against the door while she unplugged the vacuum, wound the cord around the side hooks.

"You need to put a rocker and candlestick table over there next to the windows," Levi suggested. "And the bed should be centered on the wall. Not tucked in the corner."

"Then I wouldn't have enough room for the little conversation area with the loveseat and chair."

"Take them out. Too much furniture in here anyway."

Brooke cut her eyes at him as she rolled the vacuum ahead of her, deliberately across his boots. "I'll arrange the rooms like I want."

"But if you want to make it like it was, they didn't have as much furniture." He followed her up the hall to the tornado room.

"That was probably his room," he continued when she ignored him.

"Whose room?"

"James Donovan's."

"It's *Asher's Room*. James Donovan's room is down the hall, other side of *Edwin and Wilma's*. It was part of the original house."

"Who's Asher?"

"My uncle. He was killed in Desert Storm. My mother said that was his room when he was growing up. I wanted to honor his memory."

"Well, I'm saying it was James Donovan's room."

"Couldn't have been," Brooke argued. "This portion was added eighty years after James Donovan died."

"Well, I had a vision just as I approached that room. Saw the bed, dresser, rocker, candlestick table. I also heard her laugh." He stepped into the volcano room as Brooke began to gather the sheets. "Felt her lips," he murmured into her ear. "Like I felt yours yesterday."

Brooke jumped upright; her head hit his pointed chin before her elbow connected with his stomach.

"Would you just go somewhere else?" She tried to ignore her racing heart as she stuffed the sheets into the pillowcase, threw it into the hall. "Don't you have something else to do?" She tossed both bedspreads onto the second bed. "What do you need to talk to me about anyway?"

"Connie said the clawfoot bathtub in *Chelsea's Room* was leaking. Said you needed to replace the tub." She didn't but Levi knew the comment would get Brooke riled up.

His lips twitched when she paused in the middle of stuffing the sheets from the second bed into the pillowcase.

"I am *not* replacing that clawfoot tub. Not after it took three hours for Cameron, Jeremy, Dad and me to move it down from the attic. I reeked of vinegar for days after I cleaned the grim from that tub. All the elbow grease I put into sanding, priming and painting it? It stays."

"You did all that?"

"Yes. Cameron wouldn't have any part of it once we got it moved. Said I was crazy for wanting to use it anyway."

"Those things weigh up to four hundred pounds," Levi rationalized. "Maybe I need to check the foundation walls below, make sure everything is structurally sound."

"Everything is fine," Brooke snapped as she grabbed both pillowcases, marched past him out of the room.

Levi followed her down the hall through *Harry and Rita's Room* to the second door that exited to the back porch.

Brooke dropped both pillowcases into the open space of the porch below, turned and walked into his chest.

"My grandfather made sure of that when he did his renovations," she side-stepped him, headed back to finish the volcano room. Hoped she'd lose him along the way. "That's why we have the columns downstairs in the parlor below."

"I'll still give it a check," Levi decided. "And I'm putting my foot down about a clawfoot in the honeymoon suite or your bathroom." He followed her, appreciating the sway of her hips. "Not happening."

"You don't need to be second-guessing my grandfather's work. And I have no desire to put a clawfoot tub in the honeymoon suite. Or my bathroom. Only reason I wanted to use the one we have is because it was available."

She turned outside *William and Elsie's Room*, glared up at him. "Why do you keep following me? Getting in my way? You need to be working upstairs in the attic. I don't have time to be arguing with you. I still have *Harry and Rita's Room* to clean before I head over to the restaurant."

"Tell me something," Levi leaned against the door frame while Brooke gathered the towels. "Why do you have Connie? Seems to me you're the one doing all the work."

"Connie is prepping for tonight's dinner. We have a group of seven arriving this afternoon at two."

"Then maybe you need to hire more help." Levi suggested. "I'll talk to Cameron about it."

"I can't afford to pay more staff right now. And you don't need to be talking to Cameron about anything," she nudged him out of her way as she tossed the towels on the floor in the hall. "I'm the one who makes all the decisions about the B&B."

Levi threw his hands up in the air. "So, you're the lady of the house now?" He snapped. "I thought this was a family business. Now, everything needs to be your way or no way?"

Brooke did an abrupt about-face, her eyes bored into him.

"It *is* a family business, and this house was an extension of the restaurant. I've lived here, played here, worked here. When my parents built their own house, I asked my family if I could open it as a B&B. I spent countless hours cleaning up that courtyard. Pulling weeds, killing poison ivy. Bullying Cameron and Jeremy to help me with the pavers. Cleaning and arranging each room to be accommodating.

"I started small, developed my website, built up my clientele, recruited Connie to help."

Tears shimmered in her eyes.

"So yes, maybe I think I'm the lady of the house but it's because I love it. I want to preserve its integrity; see it shine."

Suddenly the door to *William and Elsie's Room* slammed shut beside them. Brooke and Levi both jumped when *Edwin and Wilma's* door slammed shut behind them, followed by *Asher's* and the remainder of doors on the hall.

Brooke tried the doorknob to *William and Elsie's Room*, found it locked.

Then the baby started crying.

"Now look what you've done," she barked. "It's noon and you've got the baby crying."

"What *I've* done?" Levi stared at her in disbelief.

"You've upset both Chelsea and the baby with your arguing."

"It takes two to argue," Levi stepped to where Brooke was staring at his chest. She looked up to see anger flaring in his eyes. "And they're your ghosts. Not my problem." He turned and walked away.

$\mathcal{K}$ristina parked the car on the outer edge of the parking lot outside the Barnes & Noble Bookstore. Reread the note that had been left in the room with the car keys.

Get some rest. These keys are to the white Prius parked outside. When you are ready to travel, text this number, take Interstate 40 to Little Rock, Exit A to the Barnes and Noble Bookstore. It should take two hours. Be sure to wear the red scarf. Someone will contact you in the store.

After a hot shower and long nap, she had awakened refreshed. Still nervous but ready to continue her journey to freedom. She texted the number, drove the two hours, now stared at the brick building with the white columns on either side of the entrance.

New territory and new sights made it a quick two hours. She checked the clock on the dash. Gary should be getting home soon. She wondered if he had tried to contact her. If he knew she wasn't home.

Had he even thought of her?

Had she been too rash? Should she have thought this out more? What was going to happen next? So many questions, doubts, flickered through her mind. Would her life ever settle down again? Or was she on an endless adventure?

She studied the almost full parking lot, observed people going in and out of the store. Looked for anyone familiar. It occurred to her that Gary never told her where he was going. She hoped she hadn't been travelling toward him.

After five minutes, she adjusted the scarf, ventured toward the bookstore.

She opened the doors, inhaled the dry scent paper and coffee, and sighed. The smell of books always appealed to her. Soft, easy listening music piped through the speakers while people mulled about the area. To her left, ringing cash registers, ruffling bags being filled and lines of people indicated business was booming.

The chain store always overwhelmed her as she stared down aisle after aisle of shoulder-high bookshelves of books – fiction, biography, travel, business – so many subjects to choose from.

People were everywhere. Browsing the shelves, paging through books, juggling stacks they wanted to buy. Seated in chairs or at café tables perusing possibilities.

A table was centered and front of the entrance with current best sellers. Kristina brushed a finger along the cover of Nora Roberts' newest release, sorry she had to conserve her cash and couldn't buy a copy. Didn't resist the opportunity to read the summary of the book on the end flaps of the colorful jacket.

Children's excited voices hailed from the back of the store where a group of toddlers dashed among displays oohing over their favorite Dr. Seuss titles.

Much as the scent of coffee, cinnamon and nutmeg tempted her, she strolled past endless shelves being restocked by employees, the sound of keys clicking on keyboards at the information center as managers or staff researched customer requests and found herself in the *Self-Help* section. Began perusing the display of books.

Her life was a mess and there were so many topics – self-love, forgiving, relationships, emotional healing, marriage – where should she start.

Make Your Bed caught her eye. The author talked about how making your bed accomplished the first task of the day. Was her bed of life too tumultuous to make a difference or did Gary change?

Book of Calm, 250 Ways to a Calmer You sounded interesting, but she doubted she would truly relax until she knew Gary was out of her life for good.

Jane Goodall's *Book of Hope, A Survival Guide to Trying Times* might offer some tips to get through the coming months. She just couldn't afford the thirty dollars right now.

She was reaching for *Happy Days. The Guided path from Trauma to Profound Freedom and Inner Peace* when she felt a presence beside her and stiffened. Worried she would turn and see Gary frowning at her.

"That is a beautiful scarf," a cheerful voice exclaimed. "Was it a gift?"

Kristina almost dropped the book; she was barely able to breath. She studied the woman a little taller than her maybe mid-fifties, gray hair, bright smile.

Could this be her next contact? She was in a strange town, by herself.

"It- it was a gift," she murmured.

"It's okay," the woman patted her hand. "I know you're a little apprehensive but I'm here to help. Offer you a place to stay the night on your journey to freedom."

She smiled, offered her calloused hand. "I'm Charlotte. Excuse my tough hands but I own a cleaning business. Just spent the day spiffing up a mansion in preparation for a retirement party this evening. Now, I'm ready for a glass of wine and a hot meal. How about you?"

"Well, a relaxing evening after hours of travel sounds tempting."

"Fortunately for us, my husband, Chuck, probably has dinner almost done and the wine chilling. How about joining us."

"That sounds wonderful." Kristina followed Charlotte out of the store.

"By the way, my Chuck is also a lawyer. I know you're probably not ready for it yet, but he will be glad to discuss options in a case like yours."

"I appreciate it," Kristina stopped next to the Prius. "Everything's so new for me. I don't know where to start. What I want to do?"

"You don't need to do anything yet. Just look at the options. Now," Charlotte pat Kristina's cheek, "you just follow me, and we'll see what we can do about getting this all straight. You're not the first to be in this kind of situation and unfortunately, you won't be the last."

"I had to go downstairs to the lobby to get the key to the *William and Elsie's Room* so I could finish cleaning it," Brooke complained to her grandmother, Rita Comfort.

Rita chuckled. "You two sure like to argue. If I didn't know better, I'd think you had a liking for one another."

Brooke was headed to clean a table but stopped in her tracks. "Gran," she scoffed. "Liking? Levi Matthews is like a fly that just won't go away. No matter how hard I try to swat him down, he keeps coming back. I don't know how I let Cameron and Mom and Dad talk me into agreeing to let him do this project. He's always under my feet, complaining about this or suggesting something ridiculous. This job can't be done soon enough for me."

"He just wants to do things right, honey," Angelina spoke as she nudged her way through the groaning, resistant swinging door from the kitchen. "And a lot of his ideas for the kitchen are spot on. Will save us lots of room."

"Mom, am I unreasonable?" Levi's accusations had been nagging her all day.

"Unreasonable? Of course not. Why?"

"Levi accused me of thinking I was the lady of the house. You know I just want the B&B to look nice. Cameron and Jeremy don't really care. They have their own interests. And you and Dad are talking about retiring. You've never really said anything one way or the other about the B&B. He thinks things should be the way they used to be but that's not always the best. People today want modern conveniences."

"True, but there also must be compromise. The two of you need to learn to listen to one another."

"But he's the contractor. He signed on for this job. Shouldn't he do what is proposed?"

"That may be, but it doesn't hurt to consider his suggestions. Now," Angelina handed Brooke a basket of cleaned linen-wrapped cutlery. "Your Dad and I are off for the evening. Jeremy says he can handle the evening crowd. Maybe you and Levi need to give it a rest. I'd be willing to bet he's already regretting saying anything and will apologize tomorrow."

*B*rooke collapsed on the bed, considered what her mother had said. If Levi was going to help her get that extra rating point, maybe she needed to listen to him as well.

Her phone pinged a new Facebook post - *So happy to have run into a college friend who was passing through, talked about old times.*

CHAPTER FOUR

Brooke sat upright in her bed. Someone was outside her room. That footstep was too heavy for a ghost. She studied the glowing six zero five on her digital clock. The sun isn't even up she groaned as she fell back on the bed.

It had been a restless night full of conflicting thoughts of her argument with Levi. And their loud guests.

The party of seven had arrived late yesterday and enjoyed the Jameson's in the library until the wee hours of the morning. They weren't rowdy, just loud. She was going to have to rethink offering free access to the stocked bar.

And maybe a noise warning. She guessed they figured since they were the only guests in the house, they didn't need to worry about being quiet.

She heard another step. Jumped out of bed, grabbed the baseball bat, quietly opened the door. Her mouth fell open when she found Levi kneeling beside the wall, scribbling notes into his spiral notepad.

"What are you doing," she almost shrieked, bat raised ready to strike.

Levi jumped at the sudden shout. His heart lodged in his throat he managed a respectable stand as he turned to face her. And blinked. That same heart galloped as he studied what had to be the shortest PJ's he'd ever seen. His eyes traveled down

Brooke's slender legs to the bare feet with pink toes. Back up to the tiny patch of yellow material covering narrow hips. Appreciated the small breasts, two peaked nipples plainly evident in the yellow tee.

He rested a hand on his heart. It would be a long time before this memory faded.

That whopping kiss the other day, fiery argument yesterday – which he'd quickly regretted – now this? This job was getting more and more interesting by the day.

He cleared his throat, tried to regain his senses. "You want the bathroom done, don't you?"

"Yes." Brooke lowered the bat and sighed. What was wrong with him, she wondered. Then drew in a sharp breath when she looked down at her PJ's. She rested the bat against the door frame, reached for her robe.

She wasn't a prude. She'd grown up with two brothers. But this was Levi. She certainly didn't need to be encouraging anything.

"Have to start sometime," Levi continued, sorry to see the end of the fashion show. "You don't want me waking the paying guests and you always get up with the roosters, I thought I'd start here."

"This is my morning off." She tied the belt.

"How was I to know?"

Brooke shook her head in resignation. He had a point, she realized, but damn, she'd finally managed to get to sleep.

Levi opened his mouth to apologize about yesterday's argument, but she closed the door in his face.

Three hours later, Brooke settled at her desk in the loft. Since she couldn't go back to sleep, she'd decided to get a head start on the breakfast preparations. Freshly baked Blueberry and Irish muffins were arranged on the tiered dish. Chopped fruit was chilling in the fridge.

Levi's wake-up call nagged her thoughts no matter how busy she tried to be. Once again, she squirmed mentally, felt her cheeks grow warm. She probably should have put her robe on before accosting him, but it was an instantaneous reaction. She frowned when she recalled the way his eyes had focused on her tank top. Remembered the butterflies that fluttered in her stomach, sudden hardening of her nipples, the heat in her midsection.

Just when she had been thinking about apologizing for the argument yesterday.

Mortified, embarrassed and frustrated, she had slammed the bedroom door, changed into jeans and sweatshirt, and charged downstairs to the kitchen to start the preparations for the guests' breakfast. The same guests that kept her awake until the wee hours of morning and were still dead to the world.

Now, there were emails to answer, future guests to schedule, updates to the website, *Free Spirits* Facebook posts to review.

She welcomed the silence, until it occurred to her that since he ruined her attempt to sleep in, Levi was nowhere to be seen. Or heard. Even though she'd noticed a blueberry muffin missing from her tiered arrangement, there had be no other sign of him all morning. For someone so anxious to get started, he had suddenly disappeared.

She wasn't about to go looking for him though. She was still undecided on how to apologize.

She studied her inbox, realized there were several new emails that needed to be answered.

Anna Marshall wrote about her granddaughter, Molly, who had just gotten engaged and wanted to get married next summer. Anna went on to explain that she had heard so much about *Victory Hill* from Piper Richardson when she and her friend, Stuart Hankins had travelled with Piper in Alaska.

"My sweet Stuart passed away three weeks ago, and my daughter and granddaughter want to take me away for a girls' weekend. I wondered if we could come to *Victory Hill* to check it out as a possible wedding venue."

Oh my, Brooke thought to herself. Another wedding possibility. Levi really needed to get moving on the project.

Brooke sent a quick email to Piper informing her about Anna's inquiry and possible visit.

"**Saw your email. Keep me posted**," Piper texted within minutes. "**So sorry to hear about Stuart's passing. He was a sweet man**."

Brooke's eyebrows shot up when she read, then reread another email. James and Chelsea Monroe wanted to book *Chelsea's Room* to celebrate their tenth anniversary.

What were the odds that they would share the names of one of their resident ghosts?

Brooke leaned back in her chair, closed her eyes, rubbed for forehead with her fingers. Tried to ignore the dull headache that had been brewing all morning. Decided she'd have to take a quick nap before her shift in the restaurant this afternoon.

She thought about Chelsea Monroe who was about to celebrate ten years of marriage. Then thought about Chelsea Donovan who hadn't had the chance. What was it like to get married so young, then lose your husband to war? Have him leave home within weeks of your marriage and never see him again. Then to find out you're pregnant; realize you must face it alone. Worry that your child might never know his father.

Suddenly she felt lightheaded. Like she was floating in a pool of water. She gripped the sides of the desk to gain her balance, slowly opened her eyes. Stared at the stairs on the far side of the room. Heard footsteps on the attic stairs behind her and turned in time to watch the door open.

A man stood in the doorway. Her eyes recognized Levi but in her mind, she saw James Donovan, the lean soldier with an unshaven face, thin lips, long narrow nose, deep-set eyes.

Her heart rejoiced.

"It's been so long," whispered through her thoughts. "I've missed you so much."

Brooke stood, felt an urgent need to run into his arms but quickly realized Chelsea had once again taken control of her thoughts. She jerked awake.

"Brooke?" Levi studied the wide glazed eyes full of longing. "You, okay?" He watched the glazed look disappear as Brooke shook her head right and left as if to orient herself.

It occurred to him he had seen that same look two days ago; wondered what she would do.

Brooke pushed the chair back, covered her mouth with her fingers. What was wrong with her? Her cheeks felt flushed, her heart was racing on the verge of bursting with joy. She needed to get away or there would be a repeat of the other day's kiss.

"I need to get over to the restaurant," she mumbled, desperate to escape.

"In your jeans and sweatshirt?"

Brooke grabbed her cell phone, tucked it in her back pocket. "My mother just texted. She needs help in the kitchen."

She dashed down the two steps to the landing, past the door to *Harry and Rita's Room*, to the steps on the other side that led to the porch below.

"Hey," Levi called out as she jogged down the steps. "You were going to kiss me, weren't you?" He took off after her. "Maybe I'd like to be kissed." His long legs took the stairs two at a time.

Brooke heard his heavy boots on the wooden planks, almost giggled to herself when she realized she was running from him like a flirting teenager. But she had no intention of giving in to Chelsea's desires. If she was going to kiss a man, it would be because *she* wanted to. Not some ghost pining for her dead husband.

Brooke grabbed for the hamper at the bottom of the steps, tossed it in his path as she yanked the back door open, raced down the three steps toward the gardens.

She heard the thud of his boots on the grass behind her.

"Go away, you idiot," she laughed out loud as she turned running backwards. Shrieked when she realized he was gaining on her. Felt his arms around the small of her back as he tackled her.

Levi cushioned her head against his shoulder and shifted so he took the brunt of the fall. Rolled a couple times before landing on top of her.

His weight held her captive as she laughed, swung her arms to punch him. He dodged her punches, zeroed in on her lips, his tongue parting her lips, to explore hers.

"Hm," she murmured in frustration, bucked beneath him as she tried to break his hold, nudge him off her.

"Hm," Levi responded in appreciation of her breasts against his chest.

"Hm," they both say in unison as the kiss deepened. Her hands made their way across his shoulders, caressing rather than nudging him away.

Levi raised his head, stared down at her lips.

"That was for the fashion show this morning. Won't forget that for a *long* time." He brushed her nose with his. "This is for Chelsea."

He swooped down for another kiss.

Brooke sighed when his tongue dueled with hers, deepened the kiss. Rather than punch or push him away, her hands wove through his short hair, pulling him closer.

"This," he nibbled at her chin, on his way back to her mouth, "is to say I'm sorry."

"I'm sorry too," she murmured. "And for the record, I had no intention of kissing you," she contradicted when he finally raised his head.

"Not how I saw it," he studied her lips, swooped down for another.

"My mother needs me in the kitchen."

"Don't believe that for a minute." His lips moved to the side of her neck. "She says you're a disaster in their kitchen."

"There are guests in the house."

"Well now," he paused, looked over his shoulder at the second story windows, "I guess we'll give them a show."

Angelina and Finn O'Connor sat in the staff patio outside the kitchen of the restaurant, taking a break after the breakfast shift. Watched their daughter be tackled from the shade of the hundred-year-old tree that also shaded part of the side yard of the B&B.

"What the hell," Finn jumped up, prepared to race across the yard.

"Wait," Angelina grabbed his arm, smiled. "I don't see her trying to stop him." Figured her daughter and Levi had made up after their argument yesterday. Now, maybe things would settle down for a while.

Kristina smiled as she packed her cleaned clothes in her backpack. Nothing like a solid ten hours of sleep to make you feel refreshed, ready for another day. She had stripped the sheets, remade the bed with cleaned sheets she discovered in the bathroom closet.

She had spent the night with Charlotte and discussed options with Chuck the night before.

"I will be glad to help you," Chuck had offered when they relaxed in the den after the meal, "but you need to decide what you want to do."

"I'm so confused," Kristina had worried. "These past two days have been a blur. Suddenly I'm hundreds of miles away from home. I have no job. No place to live," she confessed. "What was I thinking?"

"Understandable," Charlotte had patted her hand. "You took a big step and now you need to decide on your next one." She had seen the pictures, heard about the abuse. "Do you still love your husband?" Charlotte asked. "Want to continue to live like that?"

"Honestly?" Kristina's eyes filled with tears. "No. He's not the smiling, fun loving man I married. At first, I thought it was me. He was always yelling at me. Criticizing me. I used to have lots of friends. Now...I don't have any. He complained about them, was rude to them until eventually, they stopped visiting. I became numb. Ashamed."

Kristina shook her head. "How could I have let that happen?"

"You are not the first woman to find herself trapped in such a situation. Do you see your husband admitting what he did is wrong?" Chuck asked. "Getting help?"

Kristina bowed her head and shook it. "He's very vain. Always talks about the image he needs to project. Says he needs to keep me straight. The least little thing will set him off. And afterwards," she raised a hand to her mouth, "afterwards, he's apologetic, promising not to do it again. Then something will happen, and it starts all over again. I just can't live like that."

Charlotte squeezed Kristina's hand. "Honey, that's not a marriage and you shouldn't have to live in fear every day of your life. Chuck and I watched our niece go through the same thing. She wasn't so lucky. She went back one last time and two months later, he beat her so severely, she was comatose for a week before she died."

Kristina covered her mouth with her hand. "I'm so sorry," she sobbed.

"Chuck was the driving force in having charges brought against the husband who is now in prison. That's how we got involved with *Free Spirits*. We are a small part of a larger network that is here to help you."

"And I really appreciate it. I do."

"How about this?" Chuck had offered. "I'll start working on the paperwork, but we'll wait until you get settled. I've made copies of your photos; when you're ready, I'll send it to your husband. Unless he wants to be arrested for spousal abuse, face the publicity, he should agree to the divorce and in a matter of time, you will be free of him."

Kristina straightened the wrinkles from the freshly made bed. She was certain that by now, Gary knew she was gone; wondered if he had alerted the police. Or did he even care. She had awakened refreshed; knew she had come to a decision.

She reached for the pillowcase containing her used sheets, grabbed her backpack before heading downstairs where she found Chuck seated at the kitchen table enjoying a second cup of coffee, Charlotte loading the dishwasher.

Kristina set her backpack beside the door. "I've decided what I want to do."

Chuck lowered the newspaper, gazed at her over the rim of his glasses.

"If the offer still stands, I'd like for you to email Gary. Tell him I'm okay but will be filing for a divorce. He should know by now that I'm not just missing. I'm not ready to see him though."

"I can do that. It will give us a chance to gauge his reaction, prepare for any repercussions."

"Thank you. I don't know what I would have done without the help of ALL of you in the *Free Spirits* network. I had no idea Becky was involved. You, Charlotte, the cab driver, all of you have been so understanding. I hope someday I will be able to repay everyone for giving me my life back."

Charlotte wrapped her arms around Kristina. "You are so welcome, honey. You still have a long journey ahead of you, but at least now, you're headed in the direction of solutions, not more hurt. Your turn to give back will come.

"Now," Charlotte led Kristina to the table, "you're going to give Chuck the information he needs while I fix you a big breakfast and pack you a lunch to go. The car is full of gas and ready to take you to your next stop."

*F*ive hours later, Kristina pulled into the parking lot at the Amtrack station in Nashville. As instructed by Charlotte, she tucked the key beneath the floor mat.

Almost immediately, her phone signaled a text. ***"Inside Wendy's. Seated near the back. Wearing a purple top."***

Kristina spotted the logo of the freckled red head with pigtails on the fast-food building across the street. She stepped inside, returned a wave to the woman seated in a booth in the far corner of the room. She had short salt and pepper hair and a broad smile.

"Perfect timing. I just finished a brief, impromptu meeting with the parent of one of my rowdy students. Myra Cooper," her small hand offered a firm grip of introduction to Kristina.

"I didn't know they held parent teacher meetings in fast food restaurants."

Myra chuckled. "Normally, no, but this student's mother works here. He got in a spot of trouble today at school today, so I decided to check in. I hope you had a good trip here. The train ride will be a long one."

Myra looked up when a woman in the khaki pants and red top with the Wendy's logo approached.

"I'm sorry to interrupt, Ms. Cooper, but do you see that young girl across the way?"

Myra and Kristina studied an obviously pregnant teenager seated at a corner booth on the opposite side of the room.

"She's been sitting there since two this afternoon. Watching the traffic outside. Every time the door jingles and someone comes in, she slouches down. I feel like she is trying to hide from someone. I just went over, asked if she was okay, but she shrugged me off."

"That looks like Faith Henderson," Myra recognized one of her students. "Quiet, not mousy, but a loner. I've noticed a little bullying recently, said something to the kids but it still happens. She's been absent from school this past week." Myra slid out of the booth. "Excuse me a minute."

Kristina watched Myra approach the girl she guessed to be sixteen. She had long brown hair that hid much of her thin face. She appeared to be on the short side as her feet barely touched the floor under the table.

Myra calmed the girl when she jumped. Seconds later, Myra motioned for Kristina to come join them.

"This is Kristina Powell," Myra settled beside the teenager. "Kristina, this is Faith Henderson, one of my students." Myra formally introduced them. "Faith, maybe we could join you for something to eat?"

"I really don't have any money. I was getting ready to leave," Faith shifted in her seat, realized Myra had her boxed in.

"Faith," Myra rested her hand on Faith's arm. "I don't want to scare you, but one of the ladies that works here is concerned. She thinks you might be trying to hide from someone. Does your mother know you are here?"

"No," Faith looked down at her swollen stomach. "She kicked me out of the house."

"Hmm," Myra shook her head. "How about this? Let's order something to eat, then go out to my car. I'm helping Kristina with a problem, maybe we can help you too."

Tears filled Faith's eyes. "You would do that?" She whispered. "After I left your class; quit school."

"Honey, if you are in trouble, I want to help you." Myra offered her credit card to Kristina. "Would you mind getting us a couple burgers, fries, drinks. A chocolate Frosty, Faith?"

Faith nodded, looked up nervously when the door opened.

It was obvious to Myra that Faith was trying to hide from someone. She touched Kristina's arm as she started toward the counter.

"On second thought, why don't Faith and I wait for you in my car," Myra decided. "It's the gray RAV-4 straight across from the doors. I'll turn my parking lights on so you can find us." She reached for Kristina's backpack and escorted Faith outside.

"She gave you a discount," Kristina settled in the front passenger seat, handed Myra her card and the receipt. "Said she hoped everything was okay."

"We will certainly see what we can do," Myra asserted with a smile, handing Faith her milkshake. "Faith, I don't live too far from here. Would you be more comfortable eating at my place?"

Ten minutes later, the three women sat around Myra's dining room table.

"Are you sure your mother wanted you to leave?" Myra asked.

"That's what she said."

"What about your father?"

"He died two years ago. Then my mom met this guy. She's been spending all her time with him. I don't like the way he watches me, always seems to be touching me. I just want to get away from here. I'm worried my boyfriend will hurt me and the baby. Take my baby."

"Why would your boyfriend take your baby?" Kristina exclaimed. She'd remained quiet while Myra tried to access

Faith's situation but the thought that someone would try to take the girl's baby was unsettling.

Faith pushed her burger away. "I overheard him talking to someone yesterday. Said I had another month but once the baby was born, he'd bring it to them." She rubbed circles on her stomach. "I didn't tell him, but I've been having these pains. I'm worried the baby will come sooner."

Myra and Kristina exchanged looks.

"Are you up to a fellow passenger?" Myra asked. "Your next journey was supposed to be later this evening, by train, but I don't think Faith can handle it in her condition. I'm not even sure I could get another ticket at this point."

"Ms. Cooper, I don't have any money," Faith pleaded. "I can't afford to repay you."

"You don't worry about that," Myra reassured Faith. "I can help you get away but at some point, you're going to have to tell your mother." She balled up her burger wrapper, tossed in into the bag. Stood as she grabbed her cell phone from her purse.

"I need to make a couple calls, but we'll work this out." Myra wandered into her bedroom.

Kristina and Faith studied the TV in the living room when a missing person report flashed across the screen.

"The Oklahoma City Police Department is looking for any information on a missing woman, Kristina Powell who has been reported missing from her home. She is twenty-nine years old, auburn hair, five feet ten inches in height and weighs one hundred fifteen pounds. She was last seen by her husband on Wednesday morning when he left for an overnight trip. Her car was discovered at the *OK Car Sales*, her cell phone inside. No foul play is suspected but anyone with information is asked to call our anonymous tip line at 405-555-9911."

Faith studied the picture on the screen, then stared at Kristina. "Is that you?"

*B*rooke was working the dinner shift at the restaurant when her phone signaled a text. **"Change in plans. Will email you the details."**

She caught the tail end of the news report, stared up at the TV screen in the restaurant in time to see Kristina's picture before she nudged the swinging door to the kitchen aside to check on an order.

"That poor girl," Rita remarked as she sat at the small worktable near the drink station. She watched the TV in the kitchen while she tucked and wrapped silver eating utensils inside linen napkins. "I hope they find her."

"Yeah," Brooke sighed, "let's hope nothing has happened to her. Makes you wonder, though, why some people just suddenly disappear. I mean, look at Connie. Her stepdad was hassling her at home. Tried to rape her. She could have run away, disappeared, been snatched up by one of those cartels.

"Instead, she texted me, asked if she could spend a few days with me. Begged me not to tell anyone where she was. Not even Mom and Dad. Thank goodness they were understanding when they discovered her in my closet. Willing to take her in."

"You were a good friend," Rita smiled at her granddaughter. "And she shows her appreciation by helping you in the B&B. Don't know what we'd do without her sometimes."

"Did you know Alaska has the most missing person cases," Jeremy O'Toole commented from the grill. Two years younger than Brooke, he had taken up his parents' affection for the culinary arts. He'd inherited his height and sharp cheekbones from his father, auburn hair and gray eyes from his mother. He also preferred to take the evening shifts at the restaurant and had a hand in maintaining their five-star rating with his ever-evolving French cuisine.

Trivia was also a hobby, and he was always reading up on not so mundane subjects.

"And look at Roanoke Island, where one hundred fifteen people just disappeared in the fifteen hundreds. John White sets up the colony, returns to England for more supplies, gets caught up in another war, comes back two years later to find not a person in sight."

"They think the settlers intermingled with the natives," Brooke contradicted.

"Still missing," Jeremy smirked at his sister from across the warming tray.

"I was just reading about a guy in Texas – can't remember his name – who had a fight with his girlfriend. Called his father to say he was coming to visit. Little later, he called his brother to say some guys had chased him out of town and he'd run out of gas. Then he called nine-one-one, said he was in the middle of a field being chased. The nine-one-one operator heard gunshots in the background. His brother and a deputy arrived at the same time, found his truck but not him. Suddenly, the brother's cell phone rang, and the guy said he could see them. Everyone looked but he was never found. Weird. Anyway, they think they found his remains earlier this year. Not far from where everything happened." Jeremy put another plate on the warming tray. "Guess they didn't look hard enough."

"Well, let's hope nothing has happened to this poor girl," Rita commented.

CHAPTER FIVE

Brooke hurried with the biscuits. It was early Saturday morning, but she had a full day ahead of her. Mums to plant, lunch and dinner shifts in the restaurant, delivery tonight.

Fortunately, *Harry and Rita's Room* would be available for the delivery, but things would change on Tuesday.

"Are you sure you can handle breakfast this morning?" Brooke asked Connie.

"I've got this," Connie laughed, her full wide mouth grinning, sienna brown eyes gleaming. Tall and coltish – she'd run track in school – her sandy blonde hair was pulled back from her oval face in a ponytail. Strong hands emptied the dishwasher. "Get outta here. I know you're itching to get those mums in the ground by the gazebo."

"Thanks. I wanted to get it done yesterday but Levi decided he needed to put those wagon wheel wood brackets all around the top of the gazebo. I will admit the brackets adds some pop, but I wish he'd get started on the attic. We're on a time crunch, you know."

"Have fun," Connie called out as Brooke raced out the back door.

A large smokehouse stood between the B&B and the restaurant which the family now used as a storage shed. Brooke dashed inside the shed, grabbed her gloves, rolled the cart already loaded with the gold and burgundy mums outside. She made her way around the corner of the B&B past the back door. Stopped abruptly, frowned when she spied Levi and Cameron on ladders on each side of the entrance to the gazebo.

"What are you doing?" She charged up to Levi's ladder, hands on her hips. "I thought I told you yesterday I wanted to get these plants in the ground today."

Levi glanced over his shoulder, returned to brushing white paint on the wood frame. "You want me to finish the project, don't you?"

Brooke squinted up at them.

"We should be finished by noon," Cameron called out, tried to appease his sister's obvious frustration. Two years older, he was used aware of her short temper.

Solid body with muscular arms and strong hands like his grandfather, Cameron was a veterinarian with an office in town. After a broken engagement six months ago, he'd buried himself in the business.

He'd also offered to let Levi stay with him in his house while working on the B&B – said it was no sense in him renting a room in town when he lived through the woods – and couldn't believe he'd let Levi talk him into spending the first free morning he'd had in two weeks painting the gazebo.

"And I'll be busy with the lunch shift," Brooke snapped.

She pushed the cart over to the side porch twenty yards away. She'd start with the planters here, maybe they'd move along, and she could still get the gazebo done in time.

Levi peeked over his shoulder, knew Brooke was within earshot. Painting wasn't his favorite pastime even though the new brackets looked good. He decided he'd enjoy stirring Brooke up while he was at it.

"Hey Cameron," he called out, "Brooke and I were discussing the attic the other day."

"Yeah?" Cameron looked over, a frown creasing his forehead. Something about Levi's tone alerted him his friend was up to something. Usually any time Levi mentioned Brooke, it was to complain.

"You know she wants to put a fancy honeymoon suite up there, but I've been doing some research. What do you think about a game room? Or a home theater?"

Cameron almost dropped his brush, then shook his head. Decided the man liked to live dangerously. "Game room, huh?"

"Yeah," Levi's mouth twitched when he peeked around, saw Brooke hesitate a moment; she'd obviously heard him. "We could sand and polish the floors, put a big pool table in the center. Add some neon signs for effect, dart board on the walls. Install a big seventy-eight-inch TV against the walls to the back side of the attic, put four or five recliners facing it. Would be another draw for people to come. Women are always having their girls' time away. Why not offer a men's weekend in the man cave."

Cameron looked over to where Brooke was jabbing plants into the planters. Thought he could hear her mumbling to herself, something she always did when she was irritated. It had become obvious to him that Levi enjoyed riling his sister any time he could.

"Something to think about," he decided to add fuel to the fire.

Both men chuckled when Brooke tossed her small shovel into the cart and marched towards the shed.

"Man cave, my eye," Brooke grumbled as she rounded the corner of the B&B, approached the small shed. Might as well forget about planting, she fumed to herself. Realized she was a little too rough with the plants in the planter. Levi had obviously destroyed any plans she had for fun morning with her beautiful mums.

Why did he and Cameron have to decide to paint the gazebo today of all days? Why not tomorrow? Next week?

"Why couldn't he just get started on the damn attic," she grumbled to herself as she stepped around the cart, yanked the door to the shed open.

Brooke turned to wheel the cart inside, looked over and saw a little girl standing between the side entrance to the laundry room and root cellar. The child looked to be about four years old, dressed in a loose smock dress that ended above the ankles of her bare feet.

That's odd, she thought as she wheeled the cart inside. She didn't recall any children checking in yesterday or scheduled for today. Seconds later, when she stepped outside the shed to shut the door, she noticed the child was gone. She looked in both directions – from the gardens on her left to the restaurant parking lot on her right – but saw no one.

*B*rooke put more effort than usual into nudging the right swinging door between the dining room and kitchen aside. It had been sticking and grumbling for weeks now. Thank goodness it wasn't the left one she thought. Difficult enough balancing plated food on her arms without having to put the effort into getting through the door.

She stepped into the small drink station to refill some drinks, frowned when she heard Levi's voice. Looked over to see him and Cameron leaning against a supply cabinet munching sandwiches.

Paint was spattered in Levi's hair, on his cheek, the front of his work jeans. They were talking with her parents, obviously finished with the gazebo. Why wasn't he in the attic?

Levi caught her piercing look, appreciated the ginger red braid down her narrow stiff back, punched Cameron with his elbow.

"Angelina," he winked at Brooke's mother when she looked up, "I was talking with Cameron earlier about the attic area. Brooke wants to make it a honeymoon suite, but you already have enough bedrooms in the place. What you really need is an event room. Or a large dining room, big enough for family reunions. If you're going to have weddings here, you could use the event room for the reception area in inclement weather. I mean, it's big enough you could even have a dance floor."

"Even I know that wouldn't be handicapped accessible," Brooke barked, setting the filled glasses on her tray.

"We could put in an elevator," Levi ignored Brooke.

"I was also talking to Connie about making it a play area for kids. Brooke could offer babysitting services so parents could go sight-seeing. Could even section part of it off for a small apartment for Connie. What do you think?"

Angelina exchanged a questioning gaze with her son who rolled his eyes. She studied Levi, noted he was talking to her, but his eyes were on Brooke's stiff back, a silly grin on his face.

Angelina almost jumped when she heard glass against the sink.

Levi chuckled softly when Brooke stormed back into the restaurant.

"You obviously like to live dangerously," Angelina warned. "I can just hear the wheels churning in her head. You better watch your back."

Finn chuckled, remembered his observations in the back yard the day before.

"Been meaning to ask you, Levi, about some action I observed in the back yard yesterday."

Levi stood up straight, cleared his throat. "You saw that, huh?"

"What action? What happened?" Cameron asked noting Levi's uncomfortable stance.

Finn raised an eyebrow, tilted his head to the side as he studied Levi. "Had me a little concerned when I saw you tackle my little girl."

"Tackle? Brooke?" Cameron turned to glare at Levi.

Levi looked from one man to the other. "It was all in fun," he shrugged a shoulder, defended himself. "You know, I would never deliberately hurt any woman. And your *little girl* is plenty capable of defending herself. I just like to keep her on her toes, that's all. Nothing like a riled little red head."

Levi tossed his napkin in the big trash can at the end of the drink counter. Paused when Brooke stepped through the doors, a glass of water in her hand. She stared up at him.

"You have paint in your hair and on your face." She dumped the water over his head. "You need to wash up." She set the glass on the counter, reached for the plate on the warming tray. "And mop the floor before you leave," she called over her shoulder as she returned to the dining room.

Cameron chuckled as he tossed his napkin in the trash, handed Levi a rag. "You asked for it, man."

While Brooke struggled to get through the day – which improved greatly after soaking Levi – Kristina and Faith worked their way out of Tennessee, across southwest Virginia.

With the change in plans, Myra had dropped them off at the *Wendy's* to get Kristina's car. But before leaving town, they visited the local thrift store. Since Faith had left spur of the moment, she had nothing but the clothes on her back and her pocketbook. She didn't want to risk going to her boyfriend's place, so they spent thirty minutes searching the crowded racks and stuffed shelves for some outfits and other necessities.

Kristina even found a few tops and another pair of jeans.

"Don't worry about the cost. Just tell them I sent you," Myra had told them. "We have a special account there which we keep funded for emergencies such as this."

Faith had cried.

"Honey, you just get yourself settled somewhere safe, have your baby, then we'll work on repairing your relationship with your mother," Myra consoled her. "You and Kristina deserve a better life and you have to be patient, let us help."

Finally, Kristina and Faith were on the road for their six-plus hour trek toward Roanoke, Virginia. Myra had explained that their next stop would be the last for a brief period until further accommodations could be arranged.

"So that was really you on the TV last night?" Faith asked once they were on the interstate.

Kristina nodded. "I had hoped the haircut and color would give me some anonymity."

"It does," Faith assured her. "It's just that I saw your reaction, then the little scar on your chin. Did he give you that scar? Did you run away too?"

"Yes," Kristina rubbed a finger along the slight ridge on her chin. "This was the first time he hit me. I fell, hit it on a broken glass. I should have left him then."

"Do you love him?"

Kristina stared at the road ahead of her for a moment. "I did. Then he changed. He hit me and like I said, I should have left then; a long time ago."

"My boyfriend hit me. That's another reason I wanted to get away. Besides the baby."

"He hit you?"

"Yes," Faith's fingertips brushed tiny circles on her swollen stomach, as if protecting her baby, "when I told him I wanted to keep the baby. Then when I heard him talking to that person on the phone later, I knew I needed to get away."

Kristina reached over to squeeze Faith's hand. "You did the right thing and I'm proud of you for being so smart. Something I should have done a long time ago myself."

"Who are these *Free Spirits*, Ms. Cooper was talking about?"

"I don't know the specifics. All I know is when I texted my friend, Becky, that I needed to get away, she put the wheels in motion. Before I knew it, my hair was shorter, a different color and I was on a bus out of Oklahoma City. Then this cab driver met me at the bus station, took me to a hotel so I could get some rest. There was a note in the hotel room with the keys to this car telling me to drive to Memphis, Tennessee where I stayed with an older couple. Her husband is a lawyer and he's working on the divorce while I travel. I left their house yesterday to meet Myra where we ran into you.

"When we arrive in Roanoke, these *Free Spirits* will have helped me put over one thousand miles between me and my husband. I have no idea what my next stop will be, but I figure the further away I get, the more I have time to think things through and decide what I want to do. I hope that somehow, I can return the favor one day."

"Do you think we'll ever be free? The entire time we were in that thrift store, I kept looking over my shoulder. I swear it felt like someone was watching me. That's why I didn't argue when you told me to just stay in the changing room."

"I know what you mean. That first night I was on the bus? I kept worrying my husband would come on board and take me off. Then when I was driving to Memphis, I realized I had no idea where he had gone for his out of town meeting. I worried I might be driving *toward* him, not away." She looked over at Faith. "And I have to say the hairs were up on the back of my neck as well when we were in the thrift store. Hopefully, one day, we will feel free."

Faith sighed, leaned her head against the head rest, stared into the distance. "I miss my dad so much. We were so happy. But after he died, my mother withdrew. First, she was always crying, then she was always working. Then she met this guy and all she wanted to do was be with him. It was like I no longer existed to her. I guess she figured I was old enough to take care of myself.

"Then her boyfriend kept staring at me, watched everything I did, made me feel so uncomfortable. One night, he cornered me in the kitchen. Squeezed my breast. Rubbed my butt. When I slapped him, my mom came in, but when I told her what he did, she didn't believe me."

Faith looked at Kristina, tears in her eyes. "He said I came on to him and she believed him."

"I'm sorry," Kristina said.

"I started staying away and that's when I met Bobby, my boyfriend. He was so nice to me. Gave me things, made me feel good about myself. Then he started telling me what to do, what to wear. Told me my friends were whispering behind my back. I got scared when I realized I was pregnant. Worried he would want me to get an abortion; knew I couldn't afford it. But he said it was okay. I thought maybe we'd get married; never thought he would want to take my baby away from me."

"Honey, you did the right thing – leaving him. There are people out there that can't have children. Would give anything to have a baby, but not through the black market which is what your boyfriend seems to be part of." She looked over at Faith. "You have a decision to make, whether you want to keep your baby or not. But it will be *your* decision. Not his. He obviously has no attachment to the baby."

"I love my baby and want what's best for him or her. I just don't know whether I can do it by myself. My mother got so mad at me when I told her. Said it was my problem. That's why I let Bobby tell me what to do. Figured he'd take care of me and our baby."

"I have a friend that couldn't have children," Kristina commented. "She became a foster mother but always wanted a child of her own. One day, a teenager about your age was in a similar situation as you. She didn't have a boyfriend that wanted to sell her baby, but her parents had kicked her out of the house. She'd been taken in by social services and stayed with my friend until after she had the baby. She knew my friend would take care of her baby, so she offered to let my friend and her husband adopt the baby."

Kristina smiled over at Faith, tears brimming her eyes. "That was five years ago. She had a little boy, and they are still friends. The biological mother went on to college and will be graduating next spring. The little boy will be starting kindergarten this fall. They plan to tell him when he gets older."

Faith smiled. "I'm happy for your friend. I still don't know what I want to do. Let's hope I have a happy ending as well."

*U*nbeknownst to Kristina, a black sedan followed her on the interstate. It had been luck that he happened to see them going into the thrift store. Almost lost her when she went out another entrance to the Wendy's but sat outside the house all night.

He reached for his cell phone, decided it was past time to check in with the boss.

"Found her."

"Where?" A deep voice demanded.

"I-81. Been driving for a couple hours now. No idea where this is leading."

"Stay with her but keep me posted."

CHAPTER SIX

Brooke helped Jeremy arrange the food in the back of the van. Every evening they boxed up leftover foods and carried it to a homeless compound on the outskirts of town.

Unlike the homeless in the big cities who slept on the sidewalks, park benches, streets, or abandoned buildings, the Williamtown homeless had settled in a clump of trees just off the interstate. She knew some veterans and other transients who had fallen on hard times lived there; had seen them in town.

She thought of Jake Carmichael and his *Jacob's Foundation* that supported programs to rehabilitate veterans who often became homeless. *PC Warriors* were veterans who designed apps and repaired computers; *Old Pro* vets were CPAs for corporations and small businesses.

War Horse Coffee was maintained and staffed by veterans at coffee farms that had expanded to small coffee shops across the country. The *Shellback Suites* hired veterans to work in their chain of hotels and restaurants, offered handicapped accessible accommodations to veterans on the entire first floors of all facilities.

Cilla's grandmother had recuperated from hip surgery at the *Old Salt Nursing Home* in Greenville, Texas where veterans stayed for free.

Brooke thought about the Foundation's recent awards banquet she had been unable to attend. Sal Diaz had been awarded funds to expand his soup kitchen and mini homeless shelter where Jake and Cilla had worked briefly during their trip home to see Cilla's grandmother.

Once her grant for the community garden and school nutrition project was established, Brooke hoped to convince Jake to consider a project to revitalize the homeless compound. She appreciated that they wanted their privacy but wanted to spruce up the property, add a shelter to the site.

But that was for the future. Right now, she needed to drop off tonight's contribution – fried chicken, grilled vegetables, cinnamon rolls, bags of sliced bread, pastries, bagels. It was almost eight thirty and she still needed to pick up the muffins, fruit and sandwiches Connie had boxed up from the B&B.

"I'll take care of the delivery tonight," Brooke stated. She reached for the plastic tub of coleslaw.

"You sure?" Jeremy paused, "Mom told me to do it. Said you'd done your share today. Started earlier than usual this morning."

"You did the early run to the Food Bank of the canned goods Granny collected this week." She settled the container of soup next to the box of fresh fruit on the verge of over-ripeness. "I'll take the evening delivery."

Brooke turned, rested a fist on her hip. "And did she by any chance tell you why I started earlier this morning?"

Jeremy's lips twitched as he cut his eyes at his sister. "Did it have anything to do with why you poured a glass of water over a certain person's head?"

"Ha, ha. I think that man looks for any way possible to make my life miserable. He knew I wanted to plant those mums this morning."

Jeremy raised both hands. "Not taking up for the guy, but did you think that maybe he wanted to get it painted first so they wouldn't be in his way? So, he wouldn't get any paint on them?"

Brooke frowned at her brother. Whose side was he on, anyway? She hadn't thought of that.

She'd found a window of time between the lunch and dinner crowds to get the blooms in the ground. Had to admit they did look perkier beside the bright, freshly painted pavilion. She'd even taken a picture on her phone to add to the website.

And searched once more for the little girl she'd seen earlier that morning outside the shed. She recalled the loose dress. Now that she thought about it, her hair had been disheveled; there might have been smudges of dirt on her cheek. She looked more like an orphan. A turn of the century orphan. Brooke shivered. Did they have a third ghost?

"Hey, you didn't by any chance notice a little girl hanging around the shed, today, did you?"

"As busy as we were, no." He shut the doors to the van. "Why? Do we have another missing person?"

"No, I just saw her earlier today. She was there one minute," she snapped a finger, "then gone when I looked again."

Jeremy studied his sister. "Are you trying to say we have another ghost?"

He shook his head when she shrugged a shoulder. His sister was always talking about the ghosts in the house. He'd never been so glad to get away from it all when ten years ago, his parents decided to build their own house up the hill from the property.

He put a hand on Brooke's forehead as if checking her temperature. "Maybe you should go up to your room and lay down, let me take this delivery."

Brooke laughed, swat his hand away from her. "I'm fine." She grabbed the keys from him, jumped behind the wheel to start the vehicle. "I have another appointment in town anyway.

And I *did* see that little girl," she called through the open window as she drove the van the short distance to the B&B.

Brooke parked between the shed and the side door to the laundry room, checked the clock – eight forty-five – decided to leave the van running as she raced around to the back door.

For safety reasons and because Connie lived there, they kept the laundry room door locked.

Brooke gave Levi a suspicious look when she spied him coming down the steps from her loft. Wondered why he was up there this time of night. Noted his hair and clothes were cleaner.

"What're you doing here?" She muttered as she dashed into the kitchen.

"Measuring your bathroom space, honeymoon suite, working on an order for supplies."

Didn't mention he'd timed it, so he'd be here when she got off work. Figured they needed to set things straight about this morning.

"I see you got the flowers in the ground," he called out. "They look good." He waited for her to complement their joint effort.

Brooke grabbed the box, waved to Connie who was loading the dishwasher, closed and locked the Dutch door to the kitchen. "Figured you'd be home sleeping."

"Where are you off to in such a hurry?"

"Doing the delivery to the homeless camp." She raced down the steps. Didn't have time for conversation. Was still mad at him anyway. "And I'm running late."

"Who's going with you?" Levi's long legs followed her down the back steps.

"Nobody. I don't need anybody. All I do is unload the food, then come back."

"Connie's still here. She could go with you."

"Connie's still cleaning the kitchen." Brooke rested the box on her hip while she opened the back door to the van.

"I'll go with you," Levi reached for the box. "Help you. It's late, you shouldn't go by yourself."

"No," she shifted the box out of his reach. Everything was all planned. She had places to go that didn't include him. She was on a tight schedule, and she was already late.

"I'm not coming right back. I need to pick up a couple things at the Walmart."

"I'll still go with you. I probably need a few things myself."

"No," she jumped into the driver's seat. "Levi, I *need* to go. I'm already late." She put the van in gear and drove off.

"But" Levi watched the taillights get dimmer as she sped between the restaurant parking lot and brick enclosed courtyard on the back of the B&B around to the front drive into town.

*B*rooke pulled up to the clearing on the side of the road, smelled smoke from the campfires on the other side of the trees. Streetlights at the far ends of the clearing cast a dim light on the two picnic tables with long benches on each side. There was a large wood box on the edge of the woods everyone used for deliveries in bad weather.

It was still dark and if she didn't have to pick up her delivery, she might have taken up Levi's offer to ride with her.

Thankfully she wasn't alone, she thought as she waved to the driver with the local pizza advertisement atop his car. They also supported the cause with pizzas ordered in error, left over bread sticks and pasta.

She didn't feel so bad when she sniffed the lingering aroma of pizzas on the tables. She hated to be late for anything. Deliveries, meetings, appointments.

It was quiet except for the echoes of cars on the interstate. The people never came out of the shadows, but she could always feel their presence. She started unloading the food. Imagined the sound of rumbling stomachs, mouths watering.

Had to appreciate Levi's concern about her safety but hoped and believed no one would hurt the hands that fed them.

Depositing the last box on the table, she jumped into the van, sent a text.

"Running late. Sorry. Be there in twenty."

Within seconds, as she raced onto the interstate ramp, she received a thumbs up emoji.

Nineteen minutes later, Brooke pulled onto the black pavement of the parking lot at the Roanoke train station. Considering it was a Saturday night, there were rows of empty parking spaces but still a fair number of cars in the lot.

Tall pole lights and the evening mist cast eerie shadows above the vehicles. Although she was sure most of the cars were empty, she knew two people sat in one. And if her inner instinct was correct, there were others whether they were getting ready to leave, security guards on duty, police officers on break, or teenagers making out.

She had the distinct feeling she was being watched and decided to scope the area, drove up one row, then around to another. Flashed her lights when she recognized the white Prius parked amidst five on the outer edge. Noted two heads inside.

Her purpose here wasn't dangerous but she needed to be careful, so she drove around a second time before pulling up close to the front of the Prius. She jumped out, raced around to the back to open the doors while Kristina and Faith leaped out, their bags in hand.

No one spoke as Brooke and Kristina helped Faith into the back of the van, then Kristina jumped in behind her.

Brooke shivered. She still felt the watchful glare from somewhere nearby as she slammed the doors, ran around to the driver's seat.

"Everybody okay?" Brooke whispered as she drove around the lot one last time, before heading back to Williamtown.

*H*e ducked in his seat just as the van's bright headlights spotlighted his car when it came around the row of cars. He remained lowered on the seat, listened to the puttering engine drive past. Peeked over the steering wheel to watch it drive away.

He'd already made a mental note of the *Victory Hill* name on the side of the van when it drove through the lot the second time.

He waited ten seconds, pulled out of the lot and followed. He'd have to call the boss later.

*L*evi sat in the cushioned seat of the gazebo. Appreciated the fresh smell of paint.

Brooke had no business making that delivery by herself. Look how many women went missing every year. He recalled the television alert about the Oklahoma City woman that was missing. There was still no report on her.

He knew Brooke was tough but what if someone should come up behind her. Could she defend herself?

He checked his watch – nine forty-five. She'd said she needed to go to the Walmart. He leaned back, crossed an ankle over his knee. He'd just wait a little longer; be sure she got back okay.

He turned his head toward the front entrance when he heard the engine, then saw the headlights crawling toward the B&B. Why was she driving so slowly? He wondered. She walked faster than that. After following the curve, he imagined it making its way around the courtyard, past the restaurant where he expected her to park near the kitchen. Instead, she pulled up close to the back door.

The porch lights were out but the headlights reflected off Connie as she stepped out the back door. He decided maybe they needed help unloading her supplies from Walmart.

Brooke silently helped Kristina and Faith jump out of the van and into the B&B where Connie rushed them upstairs to *Harry and Rita's Room* at the top of the back stairs.

Brooke jolted, her heart lodged in her throat when she rounded the van to take it back to the restaurant and bumped into Levi.

"What are you *doing* here?" she roared. "You scared the life out of me."

"What took you so long? Where are your Walmart bags?"

"I didn't go," she answered without thinking.

"Then what took you so long? I was worried."

"Levi, I don't have time for this. It was nice of you to worry but I need to move the van." She jumped into the driver's seat, shifted the van into reverse. "I'll see you tomorrow."

"But"

What was wrong with the guy? Brooke fumed as she parked the van in the staff parking lot next to the kitchen. Checked the side mirrors, watched his dark figure making its way towards the kitchen.

She didn't have time for him tonight. She ran inside, waved to Jeremy who was finishing up cleaning the grill before depositing the keys on the board next to the door. She heard Levi's voice as she charged through the swinging doors towards the main room and out the front doors of the restaurant.

"Hey, did Brooke just come through here?"

"Yeah, she went that way," Jeremy nodded toward the front room.

By the time Levi backtracked to the B&B, the back door was locked, and all lights were out.

Brooke sat on the top step, breathless and grinning as he tried the door then kicked it.

*A*n hour later, Brooke, Connie, Kristina and Faith sat huddled on the two full size beds in *Harry and Rita's Room*, the room Brooke had specifically left vacant for her delivery. It was close to her loft and convenient to the kitchen and back door.

They'd enjoyed Connie's light snacks while Kristina and Faith shared their experiences.

Brooke shook her head when Faith finished her story. She reached over and squeezed Faith's hand.

"First, let me say how proud I am that you had enough foresight to get you and your baby out of a bad situation. From what you've told me about your boyfriend, it sounds like he is part of a black-market adoption ring.

"I've done a little research since talking to Myra last night. There are so many couples out there that are desperate to adopt infants, mainly because they can't have one themselves. Babies are scarce and the emotions of the adoptive parents are off the chart – ripe for the black market.

"The foster care system is too slow and unfortunately, these," she made quotation marks with her fingers, "private adoption agencies are all over the Internet. I think they even have a Craig's List. They have websites that are full of testimonials advertising their services. They claim they want to help these families, but it boils down to the almighty dollar. There are hidden fees, commissions, some totaling up to tens of thousands of dollars. Unless they've aroused suspicion, no one tracks them or their sales.

"More than likely, your boyfriend, or the agency he works with, has already collected an initial fee from the adoptive parents. That's why he's become so possessive. He may have also received another deposit for matching you with this couple.

"Or he may be the actual middleman providing the babies and needs to maintain his quota. Even though you haven't received any money, he has invested in your care and won't willingly let you just walk away."

"But I never agreed to give my baby away," Faith sighed. "I thought he was taking care of me, and we'd eventually get married."

"You never signed anything?" Connie asked. "He never hinted about it?"

Faith shook her head. "No. Like I said, I happened to overhear him talking and decided to run away."

"That's why we need to keep you in seclusion. Until we know for sure he's not coming here looking for you. So, for your safety I must ask that you please not go outside this room without one of us with you or nearby. This is a business to these people, and he apparently has an investment in the baby. He may come looking for you. Let's hope no one saw you leave.

"But at some point, you're going to have to contact your mother to let her know you're okay. Maybe not right away," Brooke put a hand up when Faith started to argue, "but you need to let her know. She's your mother and you two might have had a difference of opinion but I'm sure she's having second thoughts by now. Especially if your boyfriend should ask about you."

Brooke turned to Kristina.

"I want to help," Kristina spoke first. "You and your friends have done so much for me. And Faith. I need to repay you. I don't mind cleaning rooms, cooking, doing the wash. I'll do anything. I just want to help any way I can."

Brooke smiled. "We still need to be careful. Your friend did a great job with the haircut and color, but you've been in the news and until your husband owns up to his behavior or retracts the missing persons report, you need to be careful. Protect your reputation and decide where you want to go from here."

"Chuck is working on that. I have no desire to return to that hell and appreciate all everyone has done to help me."

Connie exchanged looks with Brooke. "We can always use the extra help, just need to decide how to explain Kristina's being here."

"For now, she's a visiting friend who is helping out," Brooke decided.

CHAPTER SEVEN

Brooke's eyes popped open when she heard the hammer outside her bedroom door. She studied the digital clock – seven ten – then plopped the extra pillow over her head. It's Sunday, she moaned to herself. The restaurant didn't open until one and the guests said they wanted a late breakfast. Ten would be good. After the late night with Kristina and Faith, she'd hoped to sleep until eight thirty.

Did the man ever take a break?

It occurred to her that she'd neglected to warn Kristina and Faith about Levi. They needed to catch up on their sleep as well and had probably been frightened awake by the noise.

When the hammering continued, Brooke bolted out of the bed, made a point to grab her robe. She was *not* going to give him another floor show.

She yanked the door open and stared at Levi. "Seriously?"

Levi looked up from the studs he'd set in place to mark her bathroom. Glared at her through narrowed eyes. Too bad, he thought, he wasn't in the best of moods either. He was tired of not being appreciated and hadn't slept well after being shrugged off last night. Decided he'd pound his frustration out on the framing.

She'd never said a word about how good the gazebo looked. His squared shoulders turned back to the board, he set a nail in place, whacked it with a firm grip on his hammer. Gave it several more whacks for measure.

Always complained about how things inconvenienced her, he mumbled as he shifted, reached for another nail.

Everything was about what *SHE* wanted. Like she was the queen of the house. He pelted the nail then flinched when he recalled that argument.

Maybe the gazebo wasn't part of the project, but it needed to be done. And it looked good, dammit. He gave the nail one more clobber.

He'd been trying to get started on the bathrooms, but she was never available to discuss it. How was he supposed to get anything done if she wouldn't talk to him? If she wasn't cleaning rooms, she was cooking or working in the restaurant. Running here and yonder, *by herself*.

They could have discussed the bathroom while delivering the food to the homeless shelter last night. But no, Queen Independence had to do the delivery all by herself.

"Ahem," Brooke interrupted his thoughts.

His jaw tightened as he turned to glare up at her through narrowed eyes, experienced a feeling of the *Groundhog Day* movie when he is once again outside her bedroom saying, "You want this bathroom, don't you?"

"It's Sunday," Brooke gave him a frosty look, stuck her nose in the air. "My one morning to sleep late."

"Well, excuse me, your majesty. I'll try to remember that next Sunday." He plowed another nail into the stud then tossed the hammer aside, jumped up to tower over her, his hands fisted at his side.

"I tried to tell you last night that I planned to get an early start, but you were so bent on getting rid of me. What was the rush with the delivery anyway? It's not like the people don't live there. Like they're going to turn their backs on you and your free food if you're five minutes late."

Brooke's eyes went round as she stepped back. She'd never seen him so angry.

"I wasn't in the mood for company," she lied, sorry she couldn't be more forthcoming. Knew he had been trying to be considerate of her safety and didn't deserve the cold shoulder she'd given him. "I was tired. I'd had a busy day yesterday and just wanted to go to bed," she continued to defend herself.

She thought of Kristina and Faith. "We also have guests that wanted to sleep a little later so could you just keep the noise down?"

Unwilling to give him a chance to continue his complaints, Brooke turned abruptly and shut the bedroom door in his face.

*L*evi tried to be considerate of the guests and realized he probably should have waited to start working but the framework for Brooke's bathroom was in place and he felt much better. Tired but better.

He had ignored her when minutes after shutting the door in his face, she'd marched past him on her way to the kitchen downstairs.

Working on his supply list for Brooke's bathroom, he remembered he needed to look at the clawfoot tub in *Chelsea's Room*. Since most of his work was in the attic and Brooke's loft, he'd gotten used to using the long hall between *Harry and Rita's* room and the attic door at the other end. Walking through the house was a lot shorter than going down and out of the porch, around the side of the house, through the courtyard, in and out the lobby doors, then up and down the main stairs. Sometimes it felt like ten thousand steps.

He left the loft, stepped toward *Harry and Rita's Room*, walked into the locked door.

"What the hell?" He'd checked the register, knew there were no reservations for the room yesterday. He turned to stomp down the stairs into the kitchen.

"I didn't know you had guests in *Harry and Rita's Room*."

Stirring pancake batter, Brooke exchanged looks with Connie who was loading the dishwasher.

"You need to go out the back door and around," Brooke ordered when Levi stepped toward the dining room. She knew he was headed for the front stairs. "Guests are eating in the dining room."

His good mood quickly dissipating, Levi expelled a frustrated breath, did an about face and stomped across the porch. Decided he'd just count those steps. Start charging a nickel for every step of aggravation.

"Why do men have this thing about not closing a door?" Connie wondered as she shut the Dutch door.

Minutes later, Kristina knocked lightly on the glass pane, peeked around the kitchen door.

"Someone just tried to come into our room."

"Yeah," Brooke sighed. "That's Levi. I forgot to warn you about him. We're going to have to be extra careful about him. He's doing renovations in the attic and my loft area. He's also famous for showing up at the oddest times. Hope he didn't scare you earlier. You and Faith will need to be sure to keep the doors locked."

Worry lines creased Brooke's forehead as she poured pancake batter on the hot skillet. No one, not even her family knew about her *Free Spirits* network. Or that Kristina and Faith would be staying in the house. She hoped to keep it that way long as possible. At least until it was safe for the two to come out of hiding.

"How's Faith?" Connie offered Kristina some coffee.

"Still sleeping," Kristina shook her head. "She slept right through Levi's pounding earlier this morning. Does he normally start that early? Work on Sundays?"

"We're on a time crunch but I don't know what his problem is today. What about Faith's contractions?" Brooke asked, a worried look on her face.

"I think they've eased up. She didn't complain too much when we settled down last night."

"Maybe they're those Braxton Hicks contractions," Connie speculated. "But we might want to keep a close eye on her. Be prepared."

Brooke was still worried. "Has she ever said how far along she is? Mentioned a due date?"

Kristina shook her head, settled at the dinette table tucked in the corner of the kitchen. "No. I've only known her such a short while. I'll see if she'll share with me what the doctor has told her." She stared into her coffee. "I just had a call from Chuck."

Connie and Brooke exchanged looks. "Is everything okay?" Connie settled across from Kristina at the table.

Kristina shrugged a shoulder. "Chuck said he emailed Gary. He included his cell number and of course Gary called him. Chuck said Gary was angry, wanted to talk to me. When Chuck said that wasn't possible, Gary threatened to send the police to his house. His typical hot air response. Which he really couldn't do since he has no idea where Chuck lives.

"Anyway, Chuck said that would be okay. Said he had pictures he would be glad to share with the police." Kristina smiled, took a sip of her coffee. "Gary hung up on him."

"Don't worry about your husband," Brooke assured Kristina minutes later when they headed back up the stairs. The restaurant would be opening soon, and she needed to change, get ready for her shift.

Kristina carried a tray with pancakes, eggs, sausage, fruit, and milk for Faith.

"Let him stew for now; I'm sure he will come to his senses." Brooke opened the door to *Harry and Rita's* room for Kristina. "I've never met Chuck, but he's done good things for us." She waved to Faith who was sitting on the bed. "Remember," she whispered, put a finger to her lips, "keep your doors locked."

Kristina nodded and Brooke continued toward her bedroom.

She inhaled deeply when Levi stepped down from the door to the attic. Wondered how much he had heard but continued past him to shut her bedroom door.

Levi stared from Brooke's bedroom door to the stairs and back to her bedroom door. He could have sworn he'd heard voices. And two sets of footsteps coming up the stairs from the kitchen.

He'd forgotten about the hidden stairway to the attic from Brooke's loft – wouldn't do that again. More convenient.

He stiffened when he felt a brush of air against his cheek, knew there were no open windows or doors to cause the breeze. I'm *not* imagining it he thought as he recalled the same thing happening yesterday.

He returned to the attic, studied the small room that would eventually be the honeymoon suite bathroom. Not a large room but big enough to accommodate a walk-in shower, pedestal sink, commode, maybe a drying rack. Another reason he'd wanted to talk to Brooke last night. See how elaborate her plans were.

Unless Brooke got it into her head she wanted another claw-foot bathtub which he planned to nix. Or some big jacuzzi. He doubted the floor could hold the weight.

He looked up from his notepad and a sudden lightheadedness overcame him. The room darkened as if the sun was swallowed by clouds. There was no conception of walls, rather a foggy, blurry haziness.

He blinked, jerked as he watched a young man dressed in brown pants and white cotton shirt with billowy sleeves, kneel on one knee to the floor. Suddenly he felt propelled forward as if he'd stepped into a time warp and had become the man. Felt the hard surface of the floor against his knee.

Levi stared down in awe as his hands pried a board loose from the floor and set it aside.

His thumb and forefinger stroked the smooth material of the small velvet bag as they opened it and ten shiny gold coins fell into the palm of his hand. The metal was cool as he studied one. Despite the fog, the gold glowed brightly. *CSA* and *20 Dollars* was centered on the front with the initials of eleven southern states in connecting links around it. He turned a coin over to see *Lady Liberty* seated in a field with sugar cane, cotton, and tobacco plants around her. Metal clinked on metal as he returned the coins to the pouch.

Next. he saw a thin, ivory colored book. *Legend of Sleepy Hollow* was written in plain script across the front of the cover. He felt himself take a deep breath as his fingers brushed lovingly across the parchment paper before placing the book between the joists of the floor, setting the pouch of coins on top of it.

Before replacing the board, those same hands sawed off the sharp points of the nails so it would rest evenly with the other boards. A small niche was chipped off a corner to distinguish the board from the others in the floor.

A fingernail lifted the board to be sure it would be accessible in the future.

Levi blinked, found himself leaning against the door frame again. He stared at the hundreds of dingy, dusty dark boards that formed the floor. It would take a lot of light and possibly a magnifying glass to find that single board with a chipped corner.

Those coins and that early publication of the Washington Irving book might be worth something today, he decided. He and Brooke needed to start cleaning this attic with a fine-tooth comb. Who knew what else they might find up here?

*F*aith paced the room. Walked from the window to the door to the side porch, to the door to the long hall, back to the window. She hadn't been here twenty-four hours and already she was getting stir crazy.

Her stomach stiffened and she rubbed it hoping to sooth the baby. It had started doing that from time to time and she worried something might be wrong with the baby. She began to wonder if she'd made the right decision to leave. The stress and travelling might not be good for the baby.

If only she had her cell phone or her laptop, she could google it, see what to expect. But Ms. Cooper had said to leave everything behind. They couldn't risk going back to Bobby's place to get anything. The only thing she had brought with her was her purse and the clothes on her back.

And the new clothes from the thrift shop. Which she should wash before wearing. Brooke had said she could add them to her daily wash.

If only she had something to read – a baby book, love story, anything. Brooke had given her some magazines, but she'd read them all. She envied Kristina being able to get out of the room. Worried that the contractor guy would find her. They had told her to keep the doors locked, but it was always so unsettling, and she jumped every time he bumped into the closed door. Someone had just tried the door to the long hall.

Suddenly she heard their secret knock – two taps, followed by a second, then three taps – at the door to the side porch.

Brooke smiled at her when Faith unlocked the door, peeked around it.

"How's it going?" Brooke carried a basket into the room. Bored yet?"

Faith shrugged a shoulder, "Maybe a little," she admitted sheepishly.

"I'm sorry," Brooke rubbed a hand up and down Faith's upper arm. "I'm headed over to the restaurant but thought you might like to fold these for me. You can just leave them outside the door, Connie said she'd come up and get them in a bit. And I have some books in my room if you want to venture over there after Levi leaves."

"Oh, thank you. Much as I appreciate you letting me stay here, these four walls feel like they're closing in on me."

Brooke hugged her. "I understand. Faith, I hate that we must keep you secluded, but we need to be careful too. We need to be sure your mother hasn't reported you missing."

Or that your boyfriend isn't looking for you, Brooke thought to herself.

"Maybe in a couple days when things have settled down, you'll be able to venture out some."

Faith wrapped her arms around Brooke, hugged her tightly. "Please don't think I don't appreciate all you're doing for me. I do. I'll get these sheets folded. And might take you up on the offer of a book later."

*H*e studied the comings and goings at the house through binoculars. Earlier that morning, before daybreak, he'd hiked in from the road, almost got caught by some tall dude who drove down from the woods at the crack of dawn.

After studying the property to get the lay of the land, he figured he was going to have to camp in the woods if he was going to keep up his surveillance. He frowned. He'd been told to follow her but didn't consider camping in her backyard part of his job description.

Between the restaurant and house, the place was a hive of activity – people were everywhere. He couldn't simply park in the parking lot, hide behind a tree, even stay in the barn without attracting somebody's attention.

He'd circled around, finally found a section of woods across the back field that offered him a decent view of the property.

He'd watched the redhead leave from the back door of the house, walk toward the rear of the restaurant. Twenty minutes later, a blonde greeted a couple in the courtyard, assisted them with their luggage. Decided they were having work done inside as tall guy was in and out, hauling supplies into various doors of the house.

He smiled later in the morning when he saw a brunette sweeping off the courtyard. Glanced up when he saw movement at one of the second story windows.

Figured it was time to check in with the boss.

"Fuck," he snapped when he checked his cell phone, saw he had only two bars and the battery was almost dead. At least that would keep the conversation short. Boss wasn't in the best of moods since learning she'd gotten away from him.

A deep voice answered almost immediately.

"Got her," his voice faded in and out.

"Where?' the deep voice barked. "You're breaking up."

"Place called *Victory Hill*. I'm in the woods, service is sketchy here. Looks like it's a B&B or some sort of hotel; people are coming and going with luggage. There's also a restaurant there."

"But you've seen her."

"Yeah."

"Text me the address. And keep me posted."

CHAPTER EIGHT

By three that afternoon, Brooke had a full-blown headache. For a Sunday, the restaurant was hopping with several families celebrating special events, mothers deciding to take the day off from cooking, weary travelers taking a break from the crowded interstate. The noise level was up, seating was at capacity and the lasagna special was flying out of the swinging doors of the kitchen.

There had already been several instances of spilt chocolate milk. Since the B&B maintained the restaurant's tablecloths, she, Connie, and Kristina would be busy soaking and washing an extra load of linens tomorrow. Brooke decided if Faith was up to ironing them, it would give her a break from the boredom.

Brooke groaned silently when the jingling front door announced another arrival. She clenched her jaw, looked heavenward when she glanced over and watched Peggy Adams flounced into the restaurant, hips swaying, nose in the air, perky pout on her lips. Peggy was followed by two of her mean-girl friends.

My day is now complete, Brooke grumbled to herself. She hoped her grandmother would seat them in Wanda's section. Unfortunately, the only table vacant was in her section.

She, Connie and Peggy were in school together. Brooke had never cared much for Peggy even in grade school but after rescuing Connie from Peggy and her bullying friends, the dislike had turned to loathing.

As if her day couldn't get any worse, Levi strolled into the restaurant moments later. He searched the crowded tables, accepted Peggy's invitation to join her at her table.

Brooke frowned. When did Levi meet Peggy? She gnarled as she grabbed her pad, headed toward their table.

"Oh, hello, Brooke," Peggy smirked, "you're still bussing tables?" She winked at Levi. "I would have thought cleaning houses would be enough."

"What can I get you," Brooke decided not to exchange snarls.

"Well, since my handsome friend here decided to join us, I thought maybe we could share the special."

"Sold out," Brooke announced. "If you'll give me your drink orders, you can read over the menu, decide what you'd like."

While filling their drink order, Brooke watched Peggy bump shoulders with Levi, brush a hand along his arm and laugh out loud as if sharing a joke.

Rita ambled over, tucked an arm around Brooke's waist. "You're going to bore a hole in the poor boy's head, you keep staring at him like that."

"Maybe I should go over and pour a little common sense inside."

"He seems to be enjoying sitting with Peggy and her friends."

"He should be working."

"It's Sunday, honey."

"That's what I told him when he started pounding nails into the floor outside my bedroom at seven ten this morning. If he's so determined to get started with the bathrooms, what's he doing here?"

"Guess he needed a break? Some lunch?"

Brooke gnashed her teeth when Peggy laughed out loud, leaned in to rest her head on Levi's shoulder. "That does it." Brooke grabbed the tray of drinks.

"Now, Brooke," Rita recognized her granddaughter's determined look, "behave yourself." Her eyes widened when Brooke marched across the room, deposited their drinks in front of them. Then she tucked the tray under her arm, grabbed Levi's hair, tilted his head back and locked lips with him.

"Angelina, come quick," Rita whispered loudly over the swinging doors.

Angelina stepped up in time to see Brooke lift her head, do an about-face, and walk away, a satisfied smile on her face.

Levi stared straight ahead. Much as he appreciated Brooke's assault on his mouth, she was the complete reversal of the woman that had traded barbs with him that morning. He didn't know the details but had immediately picked up on the bad vibes between her and the women at his table.

His lips twitched. Much as he enjoyed the kiss, he was certain Brooke was marking her territory. It was her order to get back to work that grated on him.

"Excuse me," he spoke to Peggy as he stood and stepped toward the kitchen.

Rita and Angelina quickly jumped back when he moved past them. His hands circled Brooke's waist from behind and he propelled her through the kitchen, past her puzzled father out the back door.

Rita and Angelina scurried behind him, peeked from the back door.

Levi turned Brooke, backed her against the side of the building. Both hands on either side of her head, he leaned to within inches of her mouth.

"Get back to work? Seems like we have a few things we need to get straight, *boss*. I'll pick you up at six thirty this evening. Be ready." He turned and tramped across the yard to his truck.

"I have to work," Brooke barked to his retreating back. Her heart raced as she stomped her foot, her hands fisted at her waist in anger.

"Be ready," he shouted over his shoulder.

"She'll be ready," Angelina called out. She exchanged looks with her shocked daughter. "You know we close at six on Sundays."

"I have a splitting headache," Brooke complained, "I don't feel like arguing with him tonight."

"You two have been at each other's throats for days now," Angelina retorted.

"But "

"No buts. No arguments. If your head hurts, go take a nap."

Angelina turned to Rita. "Give Sandy a call, will you? See if she can cover for a few hours. The second lasagna dish should be ready by now. I have a few other things I need to take care of."

Brooke brushed her freshly shampooed hair, smiled at her reflection, grateful that her mood was much improved. She'd taken an Advil, had a quick nap and a long soothing shower.

Much as she hated to admit it, maybe her mother was right. It seemed like all she and Levi did lately was argue. And it must be bad if other people were noticing their constant tiffs. When she'd stormed into the B&B, complained to Connie about what had happened, Connie seconded her mother's suggestion about the nap. Said she and Kristina could handle the guests that evening.

Even Kristina had encouraged her to take the evening off.

Brooke sighed as she gave her hair one last stroke having decided to wear it down this evening.

She had so much on her plate right now. The B&B was getting busier. Levi had started the renovations and decisions needed to be made. Now she had Kristina and Faith to take care of; there was so much secrecy with them.

It felt good to be able to help people, but she worried how she would handle it too. Their safety depended so much on concealing their presence here. Not that the *Free Spirits* were doing anything illegal, she didn't want to involve her family any more than necessary. They would only worry.

She had dressed in black jeans and a dark sapphire cashmere sweater. She didn't know where Levi planned to go but the evenings were starting to get cooler.

She touched up her makeup, added some apricot color to her lips.

Maybe she'd been aloof toward Levi, needed to do better. After all, he was working to make those dreams come true. She stepped out of her bedroom, studied the framework in the corner. Smiled that she was finally getting her own private bathroom.

And he'd taken care of the gazebo. There were already positive comments from the pictures she'd posted on the website.

She recalled his parting words that afternoon. Yes, they had more than a few things to get straight.

Levi set the basket and blanket in the back seat of his truck. His mood was greatly improved. He'd vented with Cameron who had offered him a beer and listened quietly.

Angelina had called to apologize for her daughter's behavior. She'd asked what he had planned and when he said he hadn't made any, just acted on reflex, she said she would take care of it and fix a picnic dinner.

He remained by the truck when Brooke stepped away from the back door at six twenty-nine. Sized her up as her slim black-clad legs walked toward him, the blue top hugging her hips.

92

Something was different, he thought, then realized her hair was loose – almost to her waist – when she nervously brushed it over her shoulder.

"I had no idea your hair was so long," he turned her, threaded a hand through her mane. "Beautiful," he murmured as he wrapped a lock around a finger, lowered his head to sniff the fresh floral scent.

"Thank you," Brooke whispered, tried to hide the shiver that thrilled throughout her body.

"You're welcome," he crooned softly, the corners of his eyes crinkling. Oh, this was going to be an interesting evening he thought as he closed her door, rounded the truck to the driver's side. He'd watched, almost felt, the slight jiggle of her body. He'd never seen her so nervous.

"I understand now why your mom suggested the meadow," Levi stated ten minutes later as he stared out over the pasture that sloped down to a man-made pond. The sky glowed pink and orange as the sun inched its way behind the trees.

Cradled pillar candles glowed at the corners of the blanket they spread across the grass at the top of the hill. A full moon peeked above the trees behind them.

Brooke sat Indian style as she studied the contents of the basket. Handed Levi the Sauvignon Blanc wine and wine glasses.

"We used to come here all the time as kids." She arranged the two oversized croissant rolls filled with her mom's chicken salad on the plates, added the individually wrapped strips of dill pickles, alongside a scoop of macaroni salad.

"There's a shooting stand over there," she nodded to the long rectangular shed at the top of the hill. "Probably can't see it now, but the target board is down the hill, on the edge of the woods."

Brooke smiled when she discovered the insulated cups in the bottom of the basket. She closed the basket, set the plate of fruit atop the lid and unscrewed the top off the insulated cannister. "Mom's cucumber soup is to die for," she rolled her eyes as she scooped a spoonful into her mouth.

Levi had to admit he agreed.

Brooke pointed her spoon toward the patch of trees behind them. The moon was almost crested and would soon be glowing across the water.

"I always thought that spot over there would be a good place to build a house. You've got the sunsets, the water and the moon all in one spot. I was surprised when my parents decided to build on the other side of the B&B."

Levi studied the area she had pointed out, once again had to admit he agreed with her.

"Your family has pretty much made this a compound. Cameron's house is closer to the edge of town, your parents in the woods. Where does Rita live?"

"She and Grandaddy built a small bungalow in the woods between my parents and Cameron. Grandaddy lived in the big house for so many years, he wanted something smaller when he decided to retire." She frowned as she reached for the pickle. "He only lived there five years though."

"You miss him? Your grandfather?"

"I do. More than I thought I would. He was the glue that kept us all together."

"Cameron seems settled in his house. What about Jeremy? Does he want to build on the property? If you like this spot, maybe you should do something before he gets any ideas."

Brooke smiled. "Jeremy's happy where he is. Cooking in the restaurant, no other responsibilities. My parents seem okay with it. For now."

She sipped her wine, stared out across the meadow. "Much as I'd like a house here, that's for the future. Right now, I want my own bathroom, the honeymoon suite in the attic and that half-point needed for a five-star rating." She set her glass on the lid of the basket, reached for her sandwich. "And maybe a small-scale greenhouse."

"Greenhouse? As if you don't have enough to do, you want to grow plants too?"

"Small-scale," Brooke reiterated. "Big enough that I can grow my own herbs for the B&B and the restaurant. And maybe a few other plants."

"Hmm," Levi murmured. The woman never ceased to amaze him. She had big ambitions.

Brooke took another bite of her sandwich, studied him while she chewed. "You know, you once accused me of thinking I was the queen of the house. I'm not. That would have been Granny."

"Rita?" Levi asked for clarification.

Brooke nodded. "I've always felt like the princess. I loved playing in the attic, thought of it as my castle. I'd look over the half-wall of the stairs to the door to the second floor, pretend I was Rapunzel in my castle. Granddaddy even braided three ropes, painted it red to match my hair, attached a bell on the end of it. He nailed it at the top of the half-wall, and I would fling it over whenever I played up there. Mom would ring the bell whenever it was time for me to come downstairs."

Levi smiled. "I get it. I have a sister. I was always the dragon that destroyed her pretend castle of boxes."

"Cameron and Jeremy would sometimes sneak up there and try to scare me. Pretend to be the man in chains my granddaddy always joked about. I never believed it was real but caught myself looking over my shoulder from time to time.

"Sometimes, I felt as if Chelsea was nearby." She waved a hand past her face. "Like a brush across my cheek. I felt so sorry for her. She must have been so lonely. And then to have lost her husband so soon after marrying him."

"Did you ever see her?"

Brooke shook her head. "No. But Piper and Cilla can tell you a few stories. James haunted Piper's laptop. Seriously," she responded to Levi's frown. "His face would appear out of the blue, so she decided to research him. That's how we discovered he died in the war at the battle of Petersburg.

"And Chelsea haunted Cilla's dreams. Cilla dreamed about the wedding, their wedding night, when James left for war. Having their baby – your multiple times great grandfather. Chelsea hid in the root cellar when the soldiers came. Then when she was discovered, the doctor made her nurse the wounded soldiers. Cilla dreamed of her hiding some things in a special place in the attic before the soldiers came."

"Funny you should mention that. I had a vision today."

"A vision?" Brooke paused as she put her empty plate in the basket.

"Yeah, you know, like the one I had in *Asher's* room?"

"What did you see?" She added his plate, set the basket aside, lay back to stare up at the stars.

"Maybe it was this special place you just mentioned. I saw him kneeling on the floor with a bag of Confederate coins and a book."

"Cilla said Chelsea hid a pistol with her dress and some cash. Come to think of it, she mentioned a book. What was the title?" Brooke paused to think.

"*Legend of Sleepy Hollow*," Levi stated.

"Um, yes," Brooke exclaimed. "*Legend of Sleepy Hollow*. For some reason Cilla thought that was James' favorite book because of the fact he hid it. You saw coins?"

"Yeah. Twenty-dollar gold coins. Might be worth searching for. They have no monetary value but might be of interest to collectors."

"It *would* be nice if we could find them," Brooke pondered. "I could put them on display. Add to the mystery of the B&B."

She turned her head toward him. "Wouldn't you want to find something that belonged to your ancestors? And if we did, would you allow me to display them here?"

Levi shifted on his side. His elbow bent, head resting in the palm of his hand, he toyed with a lock of her hair. "We need to find them first." He brushed his finger along her chin. "We also need to talk about the honeymoon suite."

"So, you're not trying to sell Cameron, Connie or my mother on your ideas?"

Levi's mouth curved into a smile as he studied her lips. "You know I was teasing. Although they aren't bad ideas." He grunted when she elbowed him in the stomach.

"I'm trying to decide about that kiss this afternoon. Considering it was outside the big house, I figure Chelsea didn't have anything to do with it." His raised eyebrows challenged her to dispute him.

Brooke nibbled on her bottom lip.

"And I definitely picked up on some bad vibes between you and the ladies at the table," he spread her splendid mane of hair across the blanket. "Makes me wonder if jealousy might have something to do with that kiss."

"Jealousy?" Brooke smacked at his hand. "Why would I care who you eat with? I haven't even slept with you."

"Not yet," Levi lowered his head, brushed his lips against hers. "Soon though," he raised his head to gauge her reaction.

Brooke studied him. He sounded pretty sure of himself she thought as she pulled him down for another kiss.

CHAPTER NINE

Cameron stepped into the main hall that served as the entrance and lobby area for the B&B. The front door to the original foundation was on the side of the house but when his great-grandparents and grandparents had added onto the house, everyone took to using the side entrance from the courtyard.

The original wide solid oak front doors were now part of the small parlor between the library on the left that faced the front lawns and smaller sitting room on the right that was often used for meeting space when needed. Two steps up separated the parlor from the main hall.

Brooke often opened the wide doors in the spring and fall for the view and air the house.

An antique spinet mahogany writing desk with straight legs, drawer along the front, storage cubbies in the back served as Brooke's registration desk. Her ledger logged past, present and future reservations as well as comments from guests.

Cameron preferred his animal patients, but he also enjoyed perusing the ledger from time to time, curious about where Brooke's guests hailed from and comments they had about their stay at the B&B.

He skidded to a halt when he spied the unfamiliar woman dusting the banister to the stairs. She was tall and slim, her dark brunette hair tucked into a short ponytail. She also hummed as she worked. His heart did a slight flip when she turned, and he stared into chocolate brown eyes, watched her full lips form a smile.

"Hello. Can I help you?" His stomach did a somersault at the sound of her husky voice. "Do you have a reservation?"

"Uh, no," Cameron tapped a hand over his heart. "No, I'm looking for- Who are you?" he couldn't resist asking.

"Me? Oh, I'm," Kristina hesitated. Should she tell him her name? With all their careful planning, she and Brooke had never considered a name for her to use. Would someone this far from Oklahoma City be looking for Kristina Powell?

She decided to go with her middle name.

"I'm Marie. A friend of Brooke's. I'm, ah, just helping for a few days."

"Hmm," Cameron pondered, his narrowed eyes studied her. "I thought I knew all of Brooke's friends, but you've somehow slipped my radar."

Kristina hadn't experienced it in a long, long time, but she knew when she was being hit upon. She didn't mind a nice-looking man taking notice, she had enough problems and wasn't interested in men.

"Brooke's working in the library. The UPS guy delivered some new books this morning. I'll be glad to show you the way." Kristina turned toward the parlor steps.

"That's okay," Cameron stopped her. "I know where the library is. I used to live here." He smiled, offered a hand when Kristina gave him a puzzled look. "I'm Brooke's brother, Cameron."

"Oh," Kristina chuckled, then blinked at the light spark that bolted from their joined hands up her arm.

"Where have you been hiding her?" Cameron was still shaking his hand when he joined Brooke in the library.

Brooke looked up, confused about the 'her' he was talking about.

"The brunette you have dusting the banister. She said she was a friend of yours."

Brooke's eyes went round, hoped Kristina hadn't used her real name; fretted that they hadn't decided what name to use.

"Marie?" Cameron continued to study her.

"Who? Oh, Marie," Brooke quickly corrected herself. "I met her in town. She's going to be helping for a few days."

"Yeah," Cameron was skeptical. "That's what she said. Where's she going after a few days?"

"How would I know?" Brooke complained. "I didn't think it was any of my business," she snapped. "Did you have a reason for disrupting my morning?"

"Yeah, ah- "Cameron tapped his chest again as he looked back toward the front hall, his mind going blank. Decided he needed to check this Marie a little more closely.

"Cameron?"

"Hmm? Oh, yeah, we need to set up a Zoom call with Aaron. Levi asked about the procedure for ordering supplies for the project. He's also paid for some of the recent repairs out of pocket – like the paint for the gazebo."

"Why didn't he say anything to me?"

"Apparently, you two haven't been communicating these last couple days?" Cameron gave her a questioning look. "Haven't talked to him since your date last night, though."

"It wasn't a date," Brooke retorted.

*B*rooke yawned as she shook the flat top sheet across the bed in *Chelsea's Room*. Shook it again to center it. Levi's kisses had competed with her dreams last night. She smiled at his ridiculous suggestion that she might be jealous. She just didn't like Peggy Adams, she thought as she tucked the sheet between the mattress and box spring. Decided to let Peggy know he was off limits.

It felt good to have their differences ironed out.

Now all she had to worry about was keeping Faith entertained. A teenager, a *pregnant* teenager wasn't going to want to spend but so much time in one room. She had already read one of her books and when she asked about another, Brooke had given her Nora Roberts' newest suspense. The one she herself was half-way through reading.

She thought about the linen tablecloths that were being washed. Hoped Faith wouldn't mind ironing them before folding them.

That should keep her busy this afternoon while Levi was working.

Brooke stiffened when she heard the sniffling. Looked across the room to see a woman seated at the desk next to the window that looked down on the courtyard. She was slender, wore a long blue dress; her long blonde hair pulled back from her face, flowing down her back. There was a sheet of parchment paper on the desk, quill in her hand.

Brooke was scared to move, make any noise.

Was this Chelsea?

Whoever she was, she was obviously upset, stopping every few seconds to brush a handkerchief against her nose, cheeks. Was she writing to James? She wondered.

What should she do? How long would Chelsea be there? Should she just ignore her?

Brooke jumped; her heart flew to her throat when the lobby door slammed downstairs. So much for giving Chelsea time to finish her letter, Brooke thought when she looked over and saw the vacant desk.

Brooke recognized Levi's boots on the steps, figured he was looking for her. And from the sound of the stomps, he wasn't in a good mood. She decided to keep quiet. He would find her soon enough.

"What's with all of the locked doors all of a sudden?" Levi barked from the door.

Brooke patted her shirt, pants, wondered if she had a tracker on her, he'd found her so quickly.

She spread the comforter over the bed, fluffed the pillows.

"It's a B&B. Of course, there are locked doors."

She gave the room one last glance-over before gathering the bed linens and heading down the long hall to add them to the growing pile of bed linens outside *Harry and Rita's* room where Faith was in hiding. When she knew the coast was clear, she planned to knock the secret knock, dump all the linens into the large basket on the porch.

"Not when no one's staying in them," Levi complained to her back. "There's no one signed up for *Harry and Rita's* room but suddenly, the doors are locked. *All* the time."

Brooke stopped in the middle of the hall, turned to study him through slit eyes.

"Have you been snooping in my guest book?"

"No. Yes," he amended with a frustrated breath when she continued to glare silently. "When I keep finding closed, *locked* doors and no activity, I wanted to check it out."

"Our daily business is none of your business," she marched past *William and Elsie's* Room.

"If there's something wrong with the room," Levi persisted, "tell me and I'll fix it. What's with the locked doors."

"Again, it's just some precautions we're taking. None of your business."

"Are you hiding someone in there?"

"Of course not," Brooke turned toward the back hall. He was getting too close to the truth, she worried. "Connie and I just decided to close them off. Conserve energy."

"Conserve energy my eye," Levi reached for her elbow, turned her toward him. "You've got to come up with a better story than that."

"I don't have to tell you anything," she snapped.

Brooke hated being so secretive, but they couldn't afford to tell him about Kristina, especially Faith. Not yet.

"Why did you talk to Cameron about scheduling a zoom call with Aaron and not me?" She decided to distract him. "You could have mentioned it last night."

"I had other things on my mind last night," he towered over her.

"Well, I don't have time to argue with you right now. Why don't you just mosey on back to your work."

"Just tell me what's with the locked doors," he barked.

"No," Brooke looked heavenward, turned to stomp toward *William Donovan's* room.

"Then unlock the damn doors so I can at least navigate through the house. Do you know it's almost one thousand steps from your loft all the way around the house? I'm thinking of charging per footstep. I promise I'll keep them closed if that's what you want."

"No, I'm sorry, I can't," she continued past the open door to *William Donovan's* room. Briefly understood Levi's frustration when she saw the mound of linens outside the closed, locked door to *Harry and Rita's* room.

Levi ignored the brush of air against his cheek, covered his head in frustration. "For god's sake..."

Suddenly a window in *William Donovan's* room slammed shut. Glass shattered on the candlestick table, across the floor.

"Now look what you've done," Brooke raced inside to inspect the damage. Turned quickly when there was another loud noise followed by a scream from *Harry and Rita's* room.

"Chelsea might have caused the windows to slam shut but that's the first time I've heard her scream," Levi headed for *Harry and Rita's* door. Gave the locked knob a twist.

"Open that damn door," he demanded. "I know I heard someone scream from inside that room."

"Oh, shut up," Brooke reached for her keys, resigned that her secret was about to be exposed.

She took her time nudging the bed linens aside, breathed a sigh of relief when she opened the door to an empty room. The beds were made, everything was in place and Faith was nowhere in sight.

Levi walked around the beds to the window, his boots crunching broken glass.

"Are you happy now?" Brooke rested her hands on her waist, did her best to hide her pleasure that her secret was safe a little while longer. Wondered where Faith had hidden.

Levi stared in silence when he felt the brush of air against his cheek. It dawned on him that his multiple times great grandmother Chelsea just might have a temper as fiery as Brooke's.

*B*rooke, Levi and Cameron sat in the library for their Zoom meeting with Aaron. Brooke was at a square marble top table, Levi in a rocker, Cameron on the loveseat, their laptops in their laps.

Cameron started the meeting. "We appreciate that Levi not only worked a Saturday when he could have been off but took on a job not related to the project. And Brooke, you must agree the gazebo does look better."

"Of course," Brooke nodded her head. "My mums add some pop as well," she couldn't resist adding.

Aaron smiled. "Piper showed me the pictures on your website. I'll have to check it out next time we visit. You know," he shifted in his seat, "that's where I eavesdropped on Piper. Levi, I look forward to seeing it."

"We also seem to have had another incident with damaged windows caused by our ghostly inhabitant," Cameron added. "Again, Levi has said he will take care of it."

"Least I can do, since I'm partially to blame," Levi defended himself, a raised eyebrow aimed at Brooke.

"I hope no one was hurt," Aaron inquired.

"Old houses," Brooke shrugged a shoulder, "accidents happen."

Aaron studied the three blank faces, saw no further explanations forthcoming.

"I guess we need to address an easier way to fund this project," he officially started his agenda. "I realize all of you are busy but maybe we need to establish a project management procedure. Cameron, I'm hoping you could start giving me weekly updates.

"Levi, my assistant has overnighted you a charge card you can use for supplies. Any expenses you've had so far, you can discuss with Cameron and send a detailed invoice. I'll see that it is taken care of.

"Brooke, I know you are busy as well with the B&B and restaurant, but I take it you and Levi have been discussing the renovation plans."

Brooke felt color blush her cheeks, hoped Aaron wouldn't notice.

Before she could answer, Levi spoke up. "We had a good discussion last night. I think we're all on the same page now."

"As long as the project is done by April. Piper and I are still discussing the actual date."

"It will be done," Levi assured Aaron.

"That's five months from now," Brooke exclaimed when the call ended. Cameron had headed toward the kitchen, on his way to the restaurant for a quick lunch before heading to his office in town.

She and Levi stood in the small parlor. "Are you sure you can do it?"

"I've already discussed it with the county inspector. Got the necessary permits this morning."

"If you say so. There's just so much that needs to be done between now and then." She checked her *Fitbit*, turned to leave. "I need to get ready for my shift tonight."

"Brooke," Levi reached for her elbow, "I'm sorry about the windows. Maybe I got a little too vocal, but it just seems strange things have been happening. Chelsea's getting more active, I keep thinking I hear voices and open doors are suddenly closed and locked. All I'm asking for is a little cooperation."

Brooke shifted from one foot to the other as she stared into Levi's tired eyes. She remembered their kisses from last night, felt terrible that she couldn't share any of her secrets. Not yet. She sighed deeply.

"Levi, it's not just you. The two of us seem to set something off at times. Everything's okay. There's just so much on my plate right now."

She stepped up, kissed his cheek. "Just know I appreciate everything you've been trying to do."

Levi watched her slow, tired walk as she made her way toward the dining room and kitchen.

Yeah, he thought, something always seemed to be exploding whenever they were around one another. Not a bad thing, he defended but maybe he needed to be more patient. Make her more comfortable around him.

Maybe then she'd share some of what was crowding her plate.

Maybe he just needed to try another tactic. Put more effort into courting her.

Cameron stopped in his tracks when he spotted Kristina loading the dishwasher in the kitchen. Once again, his heart rate perked up.

"Hey, they've got you busy here." He returned Kristina's smile as he ambled over to the end of the bar, leaned against it while he watched her.

"I know I said I knew all Brooke's friends, but you do look familiar. Have we met before?"

Kristina's heart raced. Did he recognize her from the alert? "No. I don't think so."

"Where are you staying?"

"I have a room in town." She reached for the dishrag, started cleaning the stovetop. She wasn't good at lying; it always made her nervous. "Brooke and I hooked up in town, struck up a conversation. Since she was so busy, I told her I'd take a few days to help her out."

Cameron studied her in silence. He knew there wasn't a motel in town. And come to think of it, he hadn't noticed any strange cars parked in the parking lot.

Kristina wrung out the dishrag, draped it along the edge of the big sink to dry. He might be a nice guy, but she didn't need any questions right now. Realized she needed to get away before he asked any more.

She spied the bowl of fruit next to the fridge and reached for it.

"I'm sorry, I just realized I need to get these upstairs to one of Brooke's guests."

She moved to brush past him and once again, sparks thrilled through her as she felt the heat from his body.

Cameron jumped back when she slipped past him. He didn't see the frantic look Kristina shared with Brooke when Brooke appeared at the door.

*H*e'd been watching the house for almost two days now. Tall guy just left in his truck, apparently done for the day. Red had gone to the restaurant. There'd been no sign of the blonde or brunette, he figured now might be a good time to check things out.

He circled around the front of the mansion, less action that way. Checked the back door at the porch. It was locked, but an easy pick. He stepped inside and waited. Listened to the silence. Knew all the activity was usually at the back door so if no one was here….

He studied the open porch. Stairs to the left, cabinet next to the Dutch door to what looked like a kitchen. There was another door on the right with an ironing board leaning against it.

Everything was locked.

He turned to the open stairs, studied the door and window that faced the landing, loft to the right with railing that looked down on the porch.

He cursed the steps when they creaked under his weight, watched for movement from the window and loft.

He tried to peek into the window but found the curtains pulled. Picked the locked door to the bedroom, found it empty. Moved past the door toward the open area that was a mess of bare walls, open studs, drop cloth covering a desk and another locked door.

*F*aith stirred in her sleep. With Levi installing temporary tarps over the damaged windows in *William Donovan's* and *Harry and Rita's* rooms, Brooke had suggested that Faith bunk in her bedroom.

With all the excitement, the contractions had become uncomfortable, so she tried to relax on the bed with the book and drifted off to sleep.

She stirred once again when she thought she felt a nudge on her shoulder.

Wake up suddenly interrupted her fuzzy world.

She sat upright, heard the noise on the steps. Was it Levi? She wondered. Was he finished with the windows? Heading home for the day?

She looked over to the door, glad she had thought to lock it before laying down. But when she saw the knob turn, heard the lock being picked, she scrambled from the bed to hide in the closet.

Surely Levi wouldn't be picking Brooke's lock. Or was it Levi, she worried as she backed further into the closet, arranged some clothes in front of her, peeked over one of the hangers.

She took in a deep breath; her eyes went round with terror when the bulky stranger walked into Brooke's bedroom.

CHAPTER TEN

"We have a problem." Brooke, Connie, Kristina and Faith huddled in *Harry and Rita's* room. "Actually, we have two," Brooke looked at Faith. They had discussed the intruder in her room last night, but it was late, everyone was tired, and no one had a solution other than to worry.

Looking at the circles beneath Faith's eyes, she realized the poor child was probably frightened and had hardly slept a wink.

"Are you sure you didn't recognize the guy?" Brooke asked Faith.

Faith exchanged looks with Kristina. "I have no idea who he is, but I remember feeling like someone was watching us when we were at the thrift store. That's why Kristina told me to stay in the dressing room."

"I don't recall feeling like we were being followed when we got on the interstate," Kristina added. "Of course, I had a lot on my mind. And Faith and I talked so I wasn't really paying attention. Then, it was dark and there were so many cars at the train station, when we arrived, I wouldn't have been able to tell."

Brooke reflected on the night she picked them up at the train station.

"Now that I think about it, I remember feeling like someone was watching us. That's why I drove around the lot twice."

"What are we going to do?" Connie wondered. "Change the locks?"

Brooke didn't relish the idea of asking another favor from Levi. Locked doors were already a sore subject between them right now. He would also be full of questions.

"We're just going to have to be more careful. I'll talk with one of my deputy friends. But we can't afford to have Levi, or my family, questioning why we're having the locks changed."

She looked at Faith. "Maybe since he didn't find anything, he won't come back, but we're just going to have to be more careful from now on."

"You said we had two problems?" Connie continued.

"Yeah," Brooke sighed. "Remember, I told you I got this email from an Anna Marshall? She said her granddaughter was getting married next summer?"

Connie nodded her head.

"Well, Ms. Marshall emailed me this morning. Asked if we had any rooms available this weekend. It seems Ms. Marshall's daughter wanted to have a girls' weekend and thought *Victory Hill* might be the place to go since they were considering the B&B as a wedding venue."

Connie flipped through her calendar. "We should be okay. We have James and Chelsea Monroe down for *Chelsea's Room,* another couple for *William Donovan's Room.*"

"Wait," Brooke lifted a hand, "it gets crazier. While I was reading Ms. Marshall's email, another popped up. It seems this guy has visited the website and wants to reserve *Edwin and Wilma's Room* on Sunday. Said it would have to be a late check-in but would like it ready by seven in the evening. Wants candles around the room, fresh flowers, dinner prepared and waiting, few rose petals on the bed."

"Sounds like a proposal or anniversary," Connie stated.

"He did say it's a special occasion, so he wants it as a surprise for his friend."

"Wonder if the friend is male or female," Kristina chuckled.

Brooke laughed. "Before I could finish reading this guy's email, Piper Richardson called. Said she and Cilla had this weekend free, hoped they could come back for a visit."

"Weren't they just here?" Connie wondered.

"Yeah, but they said they'd be back to start planning Piper's wedding. Turns out this Ms. Marshall was on the Alaskan cruise with Piper and when I mentioned she would be here this weekend, Piper got all excited. Said it would be great to see her again. Now, Piper wants to stay in *James' Room* since he's the one that possessed her laptop. And Cilla wants to stay in *Chelsea's Room* since Chelsea is a distant relative of hers."

"Hmm," Connie frowned. "Do you think the Monroe's will be okay with *Edwin and Wilma's* Room? It's bigger. We could give them a tour of all the other rooms if they get here in time."

"I guess," Brooke commented as she considered the arrangements. "Piper and Cilla will be at one end of the hall. The Monroe's will have their own master bathroom. We still have Ms. Marshall and her daughter and granddaughter which is the problem. The rooms that are most convenient for them are *William and Elsie's* and," Brooke looked at Kristina and Faith, "*Harry and Rita's.*"

Seated next to one another on the other bed, Kristina squeezed Faith's hand. "No problem. Faith and I can find a room in town. But I'll be glad to continue working here, since you'll have a house full."

"No," Brooke vetoed Kristina's suggestion. "We still have *Asher's Room,* but it's smaller. Only one bed. I was thinking Kristina, you can stay in my bedroom. You're out and about and can use Connie's and my bathroom when needed. Faith, you can stay in *Asher's Room*. I just hate to make you move."

"Well, I don't much like taking your room," Kristina stated.

"I have a cot. That's no problem."

"But what about Levi?" Faith asked. "I know it will be the weekend, but the guy seems to work all the time. He almost caught me yesterday when I was looking through your books."

"Yeah, he can be nosy. Doesn't seem to miss much either. He noticed that my books had been shuffled around yesterday. We're just going to have to be more careful."

"What about that room in the attic?" Faith asked. "The one you use for storage. I don't mind using the cot in there."

"No. It will be cold and too isolated. I don't mind using the cot for a couple days."

Kristina studied the picture of the couple. She'd offered to dust the library, figured she'd be out of the way, no one would see her there. She studied the background in the picture, wandered over to the window to look at the semi-circular porch on the side of the house. Realized the couple was standing on the same porch.

"That's my great-great grandparents, Edwin and Wilma Comfort. They're standing on what was the front porch then." Cameron spoke behind her.

Kristina jumped, almost dropped the picture at the sound of his voice.

"Sorry," Cameron apologized. "I came in here to get my laptop; didn't realize you were here until you moved."

He reached for the picture. "Edwin and Wilma bought *Victory Hill*. It was vacant at the time. They'd always been interested in the old house and when Wilma supposedly saw Chelsea's ghost, she decided it was a sign they should have it.

"Wilma made it into a restaurant of sorts, opened the bedrooms to boarders."

He set the picture on the shelf, picked up the picture of another couple. "This is their son, William, and his wife Elsie. My great grandparents. William was two when his parents bought the house, so he grew up with people coming and going, either to eat or stay. Elsie also enjoyed cooking and after he and Elsie were married, William talked his father into upgrading the kitchen. *Victory Hill* became a popular spot for homecooked meals, Sunday dinners.

"These are my grandparents, Harry and Rita Comfort. Grandaddy decided to separate the restaurant from the house and built the new facility across the parking lot. They also had four children, so they needed the bedrooms.

"My Mom is the only one of the four kids who showed any desire in continuing the business. Uncle Andrew moved away as soon as he turned eighteen, lives in California. My aunt Abigail lives in Richmond; she's unmarried, enjoying the museums and heading a foundation. Uncle Asher was killed in Desert Storm."

"One of the rooms upstairs is named after him?"

"Yes. It was a big blow to my grandparents and when Brooke decided to make the house a B&B, she named the room for him."

"I haven't met your mother, but it's lucky she married someone interested in cooking as well."

"Yeah. And it looks like my brother Jeremy might be carrying on after them."

"You never developed an interest?"

Cameron shook his head. "I prefer animals. I'm a vet, have a practice in town."

Kristina smiled. "That sounds so interesting."

"What about you? Do you have family? I know you said you hooked up with Brooke in town, are you passing through?"

"Oh," Kristina gulped, why did he always have so many questions? Questions she wasn't sure how to answer. "I used to manage a shop in Richmond. When it was bought out, they didn't include me in the restructuring, so I was on my way to Roanoke when I ran into Brooke. She said she needed some help, so here I am. For now." She waved the dust cloth. "I guess

I should get back to work," she murmured and made a quick exit.

Cameron frowned as he watched her leave the room. Watched her skip down the two steps from the little parlor head toward the dining room.

Much as she interested him, he appreciated the mystery of her more.

*L*evi smiled as he navigated his truck onto the interstate, headed toward the B&B. It had been a good, productive morning.

He'd made a special trip to Richmond for the window replacements and hit pay dirt. *Relics of the Past, Inc.* was a vintage glass supply shop that specialized in authentic and classic glass and window hardware, aged and weathered wood.

He had worked with Steve Johnson on several historic preservation projects in Richmond. A retired carpenter, Steve had trained under his dad and continued the business when his father died. Steve's father had hated seeing people throw out old windows and had bought many at estate sales or found them in alleys even the dump.

Levi called Steve that morning and was pleasantly informed Steve thought he had two windows the size Levi needed on hand. Not only was Levi able to find the two windows but the bed of his truck was loaded with other windows for another project that occurred to him as he toured the inventory. Only problem would be getting permission from Finn and Angelina, not Brooke, to do this project.

He needed to replace the B&B windows before asking. It wouldn't do to have guests staying in rooms with the windows covered with bright blue tarp.

He looked over at the box containing the clawfoot wall mount Steve assured him would work in *Chelsea's* bathroom.

*F*aith stared at the blue tarp covering the window. She was tired and fidgety, scared to sleep. After seeing the man in Brooke's room, she'd had a nightmare. Dreamed she had a baby boy, then Bobby came into the room and took the baby away from her.

Feeling restless, she cracked the door to the porch, listened to the quiet then scurried up the steps towards Brooke's bedroom. Closed the door, settled in the chair appreciated being in a different room for a change. Brooke was working at the restaurant, Connie and Kristina in the kitchen downstairs and Levi had gone to Richmond. She still couldn't do anything but at least she had a window with a view.

She absently twirled soft circles along her swollen stomach The baby hadn't been moving as much the last few days and she worried there might be something wrong. She'd been reading up on the pregnancy and figured they were the Braxton Hicks contractions getting the baby in place before delivery.

At least we're away from Bobby, she murmured to herself as she stared out over the long gardens on the back of the house, longed to go outside but knew she needed to stay out of sight. Huge magnolia trees lined the edge toward the front fields, reminded her of a picnic lunch she and her parents had shared in the park many years ago. How could things have changed so drastically? She missed her parents, especially her father. Couldn't understand how her mother could just turn away from her.

She'd rifled through Brooke's books again. Looked for another Nora Roberts mystery suspense that sounded interesting. Thought about writing a letter to her mother but didn't feel it was time.

It occurred to her that she hadn't locked Brooke's bedroom door when she heard the handle of the attic door rattle. She recognized Levi's muttered complaints about locked doors and smiled as she listened to his boots stomp up the steps back to the attic. Poor guy, she thought, feeling sorry for him.

He was obviously back from Richmond, and she worried that maybe he was coming down to work on Brooke's bathroom or replace the window in *Harry and Rita's Room*. She tiptoed over to unlock the attic door; listened for any movement from upstairs. Debated going up the stairs.

When she heard the back door open downstairs, she dashed back into Brooke's bedroom, hid in the closet.

Levi stomped up the stairs to Brooke's loft, intending to unlock the attic door, groaned in frustration when he found it open and unlocked.

"You might be my multiple times great-grandmother," he complained to his ancestor, "but could you just go a little easy on me? I know damn well that door was locked five minutes ago."

His eagle eyes looked toward Brooke's bedroom, saw that her books had been moved. Had Brooke been in here? Was she trying to play tricks on him? He stepped toward her bedroom, looked inside but found it empty. Noticed the Nora Roberts book on the chair.

Levi grabbed his tool belt which was what he'd needed in the first place and headed upstairs to the attic.

Faith stepped out of the closet, made a beeline for the attic door and locked it. She had no idea how long he intended to work up there or when he would be working on the windows in *Harry and Rita's* and *William Donovan's* rooms. At least this way, she'd have some forewarning should he come back downstairs.

An hour later, Faith heard Levi come back down the attic steps, curse loudly when he discovered the door was locked.

Faith panicked, grabbed the book, unlocked the door, ambled up the steps as quietly as possible. She listened from the top of the stairs. Heard him enter from the back door, make his way to *Harry and Rita's* room, figured he was installing the window there. She decided maybe she'd stay up here. She didn't want to risk him finding her in Brooke's room.

She walked around the attic, checked his progress, hoped no one was downstairs to hear the creaking floor as she moved about the room. She returned to the small storage room. Studied the wardrobe in the corner of the room, an old trunk had obviously been pushed in front of it recently as she studied the fresh scrape marks on the wood floor. A short sofa covered with a sheet sat next to one of the dormer windows that offered a view of the front drive. She settled on the sofa, became engrossed in the book.

Ninety minutes later, she heard Levi's footsteps on the steps, looked over and saw she left the storage room door ajar. It didn't have a lock and she worried he might come in. She climbed over the trunk, hid in the corner beside the wardrobe, opened the wide door to hid herself better.

Levi immediately noticed the opened door and decided to investigate, nudging the door open. A quick scan found the room empty, but his forehead creased, eyes narrowed when the bright cover of the Nora Roberts book on the sofa practically glowed on the pale, dusty sheet. Was that the same one from downstairs?

Cameron heard Kristina's voice as soon as he stepped into the lobby of the B&B later that evening. He followed the sound into the dining room, glanced over to observe her talking with one of the guests, holding the tray in front of her.

The exchanged looks were brief, but Cameron continued past the tables toward the butler's quarters and kitchen. Figured he'd strike up a conversation when she returned there.

Kristina, on the other hand, remembered his questions in the kitchen the day before, this morning in the library and decided maybe she needed to be scarce. He made her nervous. She could tell he was interested but now, her life was a mess.

She quietly excused herself, tucked the tray between the buffet and the wall, headed for the stairs in the front lobby. Figured she would make herself scarce either cleaning one of the rooms or take the long way around to *Harry and Rita's Room*.

Her phone signaled as she started up the stairs. She checked the ID and saw it was Chuck.

"I heard from your husband." Chuck said after inquiring about how she was doing. "He wants to meet you."

Kristina collapsed on the love seat in the little sitting room at the top of the stairs outside *Chelsea's Room*.

"I can't. I've come so far. I don't want to return to that life."

"And you don't have to. I'm just telling you what he demanded. But first, I want to be sure you want to proceed with the divorce."

"Yes. I can't live like that anymore. All I did was live in fear."

"I told him that. He said he would do better."

"He has said that before. It never worked."

"I understand. And after talking to him several times, I doubt it ever will. I've put together a proposal. Would like to email it to you. Let you look it over."

"Could you email it to Brooke? He knows my email address; I'm sure he has hacked it by now."

"I will email it this evening. You look it over, *DocuSign* it and email it back to me."

"Thank you. Thank you so much for all you and Charlotte have done for me."

119

Cameron stood at the bottom of the steps. Felt guilty that he had eavesdropped, but glad he had. Sounded like she was running from trouble. Had she gone missing? Was that why she looked so familiar?

He pulled his cell phone out of his shirt pocket, reviewed recent alerts he had received. Found Kristina's. Except for the darkened and shortened hair, it was her. Her eyes called to him, both in person and in the picture.

But why is she here? Brooke would obviously have some answers. Especially if she would be getting an email later this evening from this person Marie – or Kristina, he corrected himself – was talking to.

*B*rooke unwrapped the Hersey's kiss, popped it into her mouth, enjoyed the melting milk chocolate as she stepped out of the back door of the kitchen, meandered toward the B&B. Someone had left it on the counter at the drink station.

It had been a slow night. Granny said they had enough help, ordered her to take the evening off. "Go to bed. Get rid of those circles that are under your eyes," Rita told her granddaughter.

Circles, Brooke chuckled. If only Granny knew.

Her problems seemed to be escalating. First Faith, Kristina and their situations, someone had broken into the B&B, and she couldn't tell anyone. They were going to have a full house over the weekend and needed to start preparations for the weekend.

As she stepped past the shed, she glanced over to the laundry room door, once again, saw the little girl in the corner, near the doors to the root cellar. Was it a coincidence? Or a sign she was supposed to go there?

It had been a long time since she had been inside the root cellar. Not since she was a teenager she decided.

She looked around, to see if there were any other adults in the area that might be the parents. When she looked back, the girl was gone.

She lifted the heavy latch type doors that lay at an angle on the ground and was immediately hit with the cool, damp air, before she descended the three steps into the cellar. Reached for the lightbulb that hung from the ceiling.

Instead of stacks of lumber and tools, discarded equipment, Brooke saw baskets of vegetables on the floor next to shelves of canned pickles and peaches. There were also wooden crates of wine.

Brooke remembered Cilla telling her about the dream she had of Chelsea hiding in the cellar with her baby and two women servants when the Union soldiers first occupied the house. Chelsea, Mamie, Violet and the baby hid in the cellar for two days living off bread and water. They slept on the cold ground before Chelsea was discovered and almost raped by one of the soldiers. She had been saved by the doctor who forced her to help him tend the wounded soldiers.

Brooke brushed a·hand across her forehead, shook her head to clear it. What had just happened? She turned to leave. Didn't need to be fainting down here.

Cameron cornered Brooke as she came out of the root cellar.

"Are you okay?" He worried when he saw her pale complexion.

"Yeah." She snapped the padlock on the root cellar door. He wouldn't understand her vision. Who would? She wondered.

Cameron opened his phone, showed Brooke Kristina's missing person alert.

"If I didn't know better, I'd say this is the Marie you said was a long-lost friend of yours. Working for you in the B&B."

Brooke studied the picture in silence. "Maybe there's a resemblance. Why do you care?"

"Is it Marie?"

"Before I answer any questions, I want to know just how interested you are? She's told me how you've been pestering her."

Cameron's mouth dropped open in surprise. "I haven't been pestering her," he defended himself.

"You didn't box her in the kitchen? In the library? She texted me how you trapped her in the library. Started talking about the family. Tried to ask her questions about hers."

"I didn't trap her. I was just trying to make a little conversation." Cameron threw his hands up. "Okay, maybe I'm a little interested. I mean, she looks good, I happened to overhear her just now. I wasn't eavesdropping on purpose. Couldn't hear the whole conversation, but I got the feeling she's on the run. Said something about not wanting to return to that life. It got me concerned, that's all. Then I wondered why she looked familiar. Pulled up this alert. See now that her middle name is Marie."

"That's not what she goes by," Brooke sighed heavily. There were too many suspicious men in her life. First Levi asking about all the locked doors. Now Cameron.

"She goes by Kristina. And yes, she's on the run. I'm helping her out for a few days. But if you want to know more, you're going to have to ask her yourself. She's had a rough time and I don't want you snooping. Hurting her."

"Will she talk to me?" Cameron pleaded. "Since I met her the other day, I can't get her out of my head." He raised his hands, took a step back. "I'll back off if it makes her uncomfortable but honest Brooke, she's been in my thoughts since we met."

Brooke smiled. She'd seen her older brother weather more than a few failed romances. Maybe he was finally rebounding from the broken engagement.

She smiled, cupped his face between her hands and gave him a soft, brief peck on the mouth.

"I'll see what I can do."

CHAPTER ELEVEN

Levi cornered Brooke in the kitchen the next morning. He munched on a raisin oat scone while watching her small hands knead bread dough.

"The windows are done in *Harry and Rita's* and *William Donovan's* rooms. If we're going to meet the deadline for Aaron and Piper's wedding, we really need to get started on the attic renovations."

Funny, Brooke thought with a smirk, she'd been trying to make him realize that for days now.

Levi saw the smirk. "I can read your mind, you know." The corner of his mouth curved up when she looked up, bat her eyes at him. "I wondered if you had any free time this morning to discuss plans."

"Connie's cleaning *Asher's Room*, Kristina's keeping an eye on the lobby for our next guests, I've got an hour before I need to check in at the restaurant." Brooke dropped the dough in the large bowl, mounded it, covered the dish with a clean dishtowel. "Let me just set this aside, tell Kristina where we are."

Levi followed Brooke up the front stairs, opened the door to the attic stairs. Waited for her reaction when she saw his addition.

"Oh," she studied the big knot at the end of the red braided rope, "where did this come from? I haven't seen it in years."

"Found it in the barn when I unloaded the supplies I picked up in Richmond yesterday. Cleaned it up. Thought maybe we could have a mural resembling a castle wall painted in the stairwell. Give the honeymoon suite a fairy tale entrance."

Brooke turned on the step to face him, her eyes level with his. "Levi, that's so thoughtful. And not a bad idea." She smiled, brushed a hand across the bare wall. Thought of Deborah, one of her *Free Spirits* that freelanced as an artist. "I just might know somebody that could do the job."

At the top of the steps, they turned, studied the long room with sloping roof lines.

"Did you have to get any special permits?"

"Because it's in the attic, yes. Like I mentioned yesterday, I've already discussed it with the county inspector; he's on board. New concept for him so he's interested in seeing what we do."

"This guy's new. And I've heard he's tough, hope he doesn't give you any problems."

"Another reason why I included him in the overall scope of things. Now," he stepped further into the room, "how elaborate do you plan to get? Rustic? Simple? Classy?"

"I'd like to keep it simple. And light," she followed him. "Lots of white. Add color with the accessories."

Levi pulled his little notebook from his back pocket, made notes. He looked up, studied the ceiling, exposed beams. "The room will look bigger if we don't enclose it. Use what we have. Clean it. Lightly sand the rough edges. Paint it white."

Since she'd be marketing it the honeymoon suite, Brooke visualized the room a glowing, virginal white color. Pale blue pillows on the bed, navy rugs on gleaming polished floors. She wandered the room, studied the wall between the two dormers on the front side of the house.

"This seems the logical place for the bed." She stopped a couple feet away from the sloped ceiling. "Have to situate it out from the wall to allow for head room."

Levi stood next to her. "Yeah, right about here. Still plenty of height for a tall guy. Space is going to be a premium up here. Could maybe put a half wall here, between the windows, use the other side of the opening for storage. I'll see what I can come up with."

Levi made more notes, strolled toward the wall on the far end, with the doors to the two smaller rooms.

"Maybe we could make this the accent wall. Add some wallpaper, paint it a different color for effect."

He stepped toward the dormers on the back side of the house. Ignored the brush of air against his cheek, figured Chelsea was also present at this meeting. Recalled Cilla stating that she saw Chelsea standing at this very window.

He studied the views. One dormer offered a view of the courtyard, the fishpond directly below. The other the small shed with the restaurant in the background. He paced back to the window overlooking the courtyard.

"You still interested in the fairy tale theme?"

Brooke shrugged her shoulder. "Hadn't really thought about it until you mentioned it."

"I might be able to replace this window with a permanent door. Add a small semi-circular balcony – for looks only, not to use – that overlooks the courtyard. It's the center window so it will balance with the roof line. Add a little pop to the back appearance of the house."

Brooke moved to stand beside him, saw Connie greeting the guests that had just arrived. Stared at the fishpond, looked over the brick walls that enclosed the courtyard to the fields and barns in the distance.

"Oh, Levi," she covered her mouth in surprise and wonder. "That would be so amazing."

"Maybe we could suspend the red rope from the balcony, just for effect." He leaned close, whispered in her ear.

Brooke's heart skipped; her skin tingled when she felt the heat of his body behind her.

Brooke turned her head to stare into his gunmetal gray eyes, caught a whiff of his aftershave that always had a touch of sawdust blended in. "Let's hope it works out."

Levi was half-way joking with the suggestion, but her warm reaction shook him. His heart leaped in his chest when he gazed into aquamarine eyes that had a shimmer of tears, then moved to her lips. His head lowered slightly when he realized he wanted to kiss her. He hesitated, cleared his throat, stepped back instead.

If he started kissing her, things might escalate and when he made love to Brooke O'Connor, he intended to do so in the comfort of a bed when he had the entire night to enjoy her.

Levi wandered toward the intended bathroom. "It's fortunate that you have those two smaller rooms. You still want to keep the storage room free and the other for the bathroom?"

Brooke nodded her head in silence. Realized she had wanted him to kiss her.

Levi leaned against the doorframe, his back to her. "Makes it easier to tie this bathroom in to your new one below. Still need to work with the slope of the roof but like the bed, we could situate the tub away from the wall to accommodate enough head room. Build a cabinet between the tub and the wall, install the plumbing fixtures there, put shelves on either side for towels and linens. This way, we can go for a more elaborate, larger tub."

He sauntered toward the dormer in the corner of the room. "If you really want a shower, I could tint the windowpanes, suspend the shower plumbing in front of the window. Put up a glass panel on this side to make it a walk-in shower."

Brooke's mouth dropped open as she watched him think out loud. Where did he come up with these ideas?

"Still want to go with white. Or tile for the walls?" Levi called over his shoulder, making notes in his notebook.

"Oh, eggshell tile sounds interesting. Floor and walls? Won't it be too heavy?"

Levi shook his head as he scribbled. "Will give it more depth."

Brooke squat down to study the floor. "Do you think this might be the room where James Donovan hid the treasure?"

"Considering that the other room is full of furniture," Levi looked up, "let's hope so."

"Maybe we should give it a good search before covering it up with ceramic tile."

Levi tucked his notebook in the back pocket of his jeans. "No time like the present." He crouched down, began to study the dusty floor.

Brooke joined him, lightly brushed her fingers over the long wide planks, feeling for any indentions.

"You know, I had a vision in the root cellar last night."

"Yeah, Cameron told me. What possessed you to go in there?"

"I saw a little girl standing between the laundry room and cellar doors. One minute she was there, the next she was gone."

Levi gave her a guarded look. "You're working too hard. You need to rest more."

Brooke chuckled. "Maybe. But I'm serious. I had just left the restaurant when I saw her. Looked around to see if her parents were nearby and when I turned back, she was gone. But it was the strangest feeling. Something made me *want* to look there.

"So, I lifted the doors, expecting to see Grandaddy's old construction supplies. Instead, I saw baskets of vegetables on the floor, shelves of canned pickles and peaches, wooden crates of wine. Made me wonder if there's anything down there. I mean," she paused to look over at Levi, "why would I have a vision of what it used to be like? And that's not the first time I've seen the little girl. In the same spot."

"Levi," she gasped when she looked back at the floor, "I think I found something. I think this is it."

Levi crawled toward her. Studied the board. Slipped a finger into the indention at the corner, smiled when it lifted.

Their mouths dropped as they stared at one another; eyes wide with wonder. Each sat Indian style as Levi removed the board and gaped at the blue dress.

"Is this Chelsea's dress?" Brooke reached for the material. "The one Cilla dreamed she hid here." Brooke picked it up, quickly set it back down when she felt the weight. Unfolded the dress to find the revolver nestled in the folds of the material.

Levi examined the revolver, studied the walnut grip, noted the dings in the recoil shield, pulled back the hammer safety, twirled the barrel.

Brooke stood to hold the dress up in front of her.

"She was so small," Brooke exclaimed, one hand holding the top against her shoulder, the other pressed the waist against her stomach.

"Same as you," Levi studied her. The material was faded but matched the blue in her eyes.

They both shook their heads in confusion.

When Levi looked at Brooke, he saw Chelsea; when Brooke looked at Levi, she saw James.

"I cried buckets when you left," Brooke's lower lip trembled as tears shimmered in her eyes.

Levi blinked, felt his throat tighten as an emptiness overwhelmed him but he was determined to be strong.

"Those tears shall be the last you shed for me." He responded as he set the pistol aside, stood, stepped toward her.

He wrapped his arms around Brooke, crushing the dress between them as his mouth pressed against hers, swallowed her sob as he took hungry possession of her lips.

Strong hands brushed up and down Brooke's back, pressing her tightly against Levi's chest, then cupped her bottom grinding her center to his aching loins.

Her own hands trapped between their bodies; Brooke could only surrender to the joyful lust that coursed through her body. She felt the slight stubble of his beard as his mouth curled around her chin, rained kisses along her jaw, back to her lips once more.

Brooke's breathless sobs shattered the overwhelming lust that controlled him. Levi jerked his head away, gasping for breath as he rested his forehead against hers.

"Levi," Brooke managed to free her hands, wrapped them around his neck, tucked her head into the curve of his neck and held on tight. "Levi," she repeated, "what just happened to us?"

"I don't know, but it's going to stop," he snarled as he lifted her in his arms, carried her toward the steps to the second floor. He didn't appreciate having some lovesick soldier take control of his body, his emotions. Their bodies, he amended as he thought of Brooke's initial reaction.

When he made love to Brooke, it would be on his terms.

Cameron parked his truck behind the restaurant, intending to go inside to mooch some dinner off his parents. He looked toward the B&B, saw Kristina sitting in the gazebo. Once again, his heart skipped. Didn't know what it was about the woman that caused his heart to react like that every time he saw her.

She looked so lonely. Decided now might be a good time to encourage her to talk to him.

He snipped a rose from the garden, offered it to her when he approached the steps into the gazebo. "I feel like you've been trying to avoid me."

Kristina smiled, brushed the soft petals against her cheek, appreciated the sweet scent. "It's not you. I'm just off men for a while."

"Bad situation?" He stepped up, sat beside her.

Kristina smiled, cut her eyes toward him. 'You don't give up, do you."

Cameron sighed. Reached for his cell phone. "Look, I'm not sure what your circumstances are but I showed my sister this picture. She said your name is Kristina. Not Marie. And that was all she'd tell me. Said if I wanted to know anything else, I'd have to ask you myself."

"I just can't imagine why you would even be interested in anything about me."

Cameron grinned, shrugged a shoulder. "When a guy sees a pretty woman, curiosity gets the best of him."

Kristina smiled.

"Are you in trouble?" Cameron persisted.

"No," she sighed heavily. "No, just trying to get out of a bad situation, that's all."

"How bad?"

Kristina frowned. "Again, I can't imagine why you're interested."

"Look," he turned on the seat to face her, "I've got to be honest. Normally, I don't force myself where I think I'm not wanted but ever since I met you the other day, you're all I think about. And based on some vibes I get whenever I'm around you, I think you share the same feelings."

Kristina studied him. Recognized his honesty and concern. He was Brooke's brother, so he had to be okay. "Okay. Yes, my name is Kristina. Kristina Powell. I was missing from Oklahoma City because I'm running away from an abusive situation."

"So, you're married."

"For now, but I'm in the process of filing for a divorce."

Cameron expelled a sigh of relief. "Good, I don't believe in moving on another man's wife. And for the record, I don't believe in hitting women either."

"I didn't think that of Gary. Then, one day, he did hit me, and I discovered he had a mean temper. It got to the point I never knew what to expect. I felt like I was living with a time bomb."

"How long were you married?"

"Three years."

Cameron reached for Kristina's hand. "I don't know how you hooked up with my sister, but I have to say I'm glad you did." He gently squeezed her hand. "No man should be allowed to get away with what he did. And if you decide to stay around here, I hope you know you can come to me for help."

Kristina pressed her hands to her cheeks, stared off into the distance before turning back to him. "How did I get so lucky? A week ago, I wasn't sure what I was going to do. Just knew I couldn't continue down the same path I was on. I decided to do something about it and that led me here. Your sister and her friends have been so good to me. They're giving me the opportunity to do something better with my life. I have no idea what my future holds or how I'll ever repay everyone."

Cameron's lips twitched. "My sister can be a handful at times, but deep down she has a big heart. And too many ideas sometimes, as Levi is finding out."

Kristina chuckled. "Those two do like to argue. I sometimes think Levi does it on purpose."

"Speak of the devil," Cameron shook his head as he watched Levi juggle a metal baker's rack into the back door of the porch.

Kay Brooks

"What do you suppose he's up to now," Kristina wondered.

"Not sure, but before he sees us, I suggest we escape." He stood, pulled her behind him. "I was going to beg a meal off my parents but what do you say we ride into town? I know another little diner, not five stars, but they make good burgers. Also have good gelato."

"If they have chocolate gelato, I'm game."

"Got you covered." He pulled her into a run past the back door.

*B*rooke cast a cautions peek around the shed before making her way toward the back door of the B&B. Was thankful to not see the little girl outside the root cellar. Today had already been a full one with the find in the attic followed by Levi's surreal and possessive kisses.

He had carried her down the attic steps, cradled her in his lap as they sat on the loveseat in the little parlor outside *Chelsea's Room*. Took the time to let their bodies calm. Vowed they would not allow it to happen again.

She whirled the chocolate kiss in her mouth. She'd found this one in the basket of linen-wrapped utensils, wondered who was leaving them.

Certainly not her mother She knew she was watching her figure and resisted sweets whenever she could.

Jeremy wasn't a fan of chocolate, certainly wouldn't think to give her any.

Gran? Maybe for Halloween but that wasn't for another couple weeks.

She decided somebody must have found a good sale and decided to share them with her.

She hugged the bag containing Chelsea's dress to her chest. Smiled when she recalled her mother's and grandmother's reaction to the treasure she and Levi found in the attic.

"I can't decide whether to have it professionally cleaned," she'd said. "It's not dirty. Maybe a little faded, but for the most part it's clean. And I'd like to display it somewhere in the house. Maybe the front parlor? Or Chelsea's room?"

She told them about the book, pistol, Confederate money and gold coins.

"What about the Library?" Gran had suggested.

Brooke bounced up the porch steps, surprised to see a light in the window. She closed the door quietly. She was sure Connie was already in bed, Kristina and Faith resting in their room. She didn't feel like conversation. Just wanted to relax, examine the dress closer. Decide what to do with it.

It occurred to her that the porch was brighter than usual. They had a small night light at the foot of the steps, but she turned to see a small lamp resting on the top shelf of an antique baker's rack that smelled like it was freshly painted.

Where did that come from? She wondered.

Three clay pots rested on the middle shelf. She brushed fingers over the light green oval leaves, brought her fingers to her nose, appreciated the clove smell of basil. Next to it was woolly gray leaves with the of musky smell of sage. Next to that, the prickly needle like leaves and woody rosemary. There was a large split-oak basket on the bottom shelf, waiting to be put to good use.

She smiled at the thought of having herbs so convenient to the kitchen. Would have to shop for a few more – thyme, oregano, parsley, even cilantro – to fill the other pots.

Wondered who would think to do something so nice for her? She'd have to be a little more observant.

*H*e swatted at the bug that landed on his nose, irritated that he hadn't signed on for all this camping shit. This assignment was getting old, fast. He decided it was time to check in with the boss, get reassigned.

"I don't see her going anywhere soon. Nobody has moved much the last two days."

"Come on home them. I'll be making my visit soon anyway."

CHAPTER TWELVE

"Connie, where did you find that spice rack? It's adorable. And I love having the herbs so handy to the kitchen."

"Wish I could take the credit but it's all Levi's doing."

"Levi?"

"Yeah. I heard this racket on the porch when I was cleaning the kitchen last night. Went out to find him setting it up. Said he found it in the attic storage room, so he cleaned it up. Knew you wanted an herb garden?"

Brooke recalled her conversation with him in the meadow.

"I told him I thought it was so sweet of him," Connie continued. "Especially after he'd already put the bird feeder in the courtyard."

"Bird feeder? In the courtyard?" Brooke stepped over to the window that overlooked the courtyard. Watched two birds settle on what looked like a miniature porch swing hanging from a shepherd's hook. Another bird landed on the back of the white seat as if waiting its turn. "That's a birdfeeder?"

Connie chuckled. "Yep, isn't it cute? It has a mesh seat. He filled it with sunflower seeds."

Brooke's eyes travelled to the base of the hook. "Is that a turtle?"

"What?" Connie joined her at the window.

They both studied a concrete turtle poised on the edge of the fishpond. His head was pointed in the direction of the kitchen with what looked like a smile on his face, his front paw raised as if getting ready to step into the fishpond.

"That wasn't out there when I refilled the feeder yesterday afternoon," Connie exclaimed in surprise. She cut her eyes at Brooke. "If I didn't know better, I'd say somebody was smitten."

"Smitten," Brooke blurted out, "Levi? With whom?"

Connie rolled her eyes, turned back to the kitchen. "You know who."

"That's ridiculous, Levi and I can't be civil with each other for more than five minutes." She ignored the flickering memory of the kisses they had shared in the attic yesterday.

"That's just ridiculous," Brooke repeated, a frown creasing her forehead. She was going to have to talk to him about all these little incidentals. He needed to focus on the attic renovations.

Brooke raised a brow when she glimpsed the Hersey's kiss tucked into the curve of the base of the bowl of fruit on the bar. Cast a quick look at Connie who seemed oblivious of the chocolate. Thought more seriously about the herb rack, bird feeder and turtle; began to wonder if Levi was the one leaving the Hersey's kisses.

And if so, what was he up to?

*F*aith gazed out of Brooke's bedroom window. It is almost dusk; the sun was beginning to settle behind the trees.

It had been another long day. There were no guests, and everyone was out of the house. Brooke was at the restaurant for her evening shift. Connie decided to visit with her mother in town since she had the evening off.

Even Levi was done for the day and had headed toward the barn.

Kristina was enjoying the quiet time in the gazebo. Probably hoping for another visit from Cameron. Faith recalled being envious of Kristina's flushed cheeks and happy smile when she returned from her evening of burgers and gelato with Cameron last night.

Faith didn't need burgers or gelato, but she would certainly appreciate an opportunity to sit outside. In the gazebo, on the side porch, anywhere for a breath of fresh air. It had been five days since she'd been outside the house.

The baby hadn't been moving much the last two days which continued to worry her. Should she be getting more exercise? She dreamed of taking a walk in the beautiful pastures in the distance. Or the colorful garden outside the window.

Brooke's bedroom window was on the side of the house that faced the shed and restaurant beyond. She saw a couple sitting on a bench under the tree behind the restaurant, wondered if that was Brooke's parents.

Movement and the bright glare of the sun's reflection to her left drew Faith's attention to the front of the restaurant. A line etched between her brows as she watched a familiar car pull into the parking lot, park close to the courtyard of the B&B.

Faith gasped when she recognized the man step out of the vehicle. He leaned forward, rested his arms on the roof of the car, studied the area. She jumped back when his gaze swept the side of the B&B. She knew she was too far away for him to see her but paranoid enough to worry that he did.

She grabbed her cell phone and texted Brooke.

Bobby Turner sneered at the old brick building. Who would want to stay in a dump like this?

He heard voices, turned cold eyes to watch a young couple step outside of the restaurant. His mood darkened when he saw the baby carrier in the man's hand.

Won't be long now, bitch, he thought to himself. She should've known he'd find her.

Hands in his pockets, Bobby wandered toward the courtyard. Shook his head at the corny bird feeder, spit into the fishpond. Why have a fishpond with no fish, he mocked. He balanced a boot on the turtle's head, tried to kick it over but the concrete proved too heavy and stable on its paws.

He turned to the arched porch with the *Welcome* mat at the foot of three steps, *Enter Here* sign hanging on the door. His jaw tightened when he tried the screen door, found it locked.

He'd be back, he decided. Once he'd scoped the property, determined where everyone was. Time was running out. Her disappearing act couldn't have come at a worse time.

He headed back to the entry into the courtyard, stared left to see a barn down the hill, pastures in the distance. Turned right to check for a more isolated entrance into the house. He looked up, thought he saw movement of the curtains in one of the windows.

Yeah, he snarled up at the window, I'm coming for you bitch.

He had just stepped past the doors to the root cellar, headed for the laundry room door when he saw a red headed woman walking toward him. She looked as happy to see him as he did her.

"Can I help you?" Brooke studied the man she guessed to be a few years younger than herself. Average height, a little stocky, she figured he could be classified handsome if he smiled. Then he did smile but it didn't resonate in his dark, cold eyes.

Bobby sized her up, decided he could take her down easily if necessary. All he wanted was to get his property and head back to the city. They were beginning to hound him about her obligation.

He recognized distrust in Brooke's stiff stance, narrowed eyes. That didn't bother him either, he was used to the look. "I saw the sign at the end of the road, thought I'd stop by, check it out."

"The restaurant is over that way," she gestured with her thumb. "If you go in now, you should be able to avoid the dinner rush."

"Sure," he gave her a bright smile. "Saw the five-star rating. Just thought I'd walk around a bit. You don't mind, do you?"

"I manage the B&B and we're closed at the moment," Brooke improvised. "Unless you're a guest, we discourage people wandering around the property."

"I'm sure a pretty lady like you wouldn't mind giving me a private tour. Who knows," he shrugged a shoulder, "maybe I'll decide to stay."

"Unfortunately, I've given the staff the night off and I'm busy at the restaurant. I don't have the time for a tour right now."

Bobby stepped closer, loomed over her. "Not a good attitude to attract a prospective guest."

Brooke raised her chin, gave him a frosty stare. "Look, I think I know why you're here. We have nothing here that would interest you and I'd appreciate it if you would just get in your car and move on."

Bobby jabbed a finger in her face. "I have reason to believe that you're harboring someone important to me. I've come here to take her home."

"I am harboring no one and I'm asking... no," her lips drew back in a snarl, "I'm telling you; you need to leave."

Bobby pulled out his cell phone, showed it to her. "I know for a fact that my girlfriend is inside this house."

Brooke studied the blinking blue dot on the phone. Realized Faith's boyfriend had somehow planted a tracker on her.

"Again, I am telling you to leave."

"Listen bitch," Bobby threatened, his nostrils flaring, spital flying out the side of his mouth, "that baby is my property. Tell me where she is. I know she's here."

"A baby is no one's *property* and Faith doesn't want to have anything to do with you. She has no intention of giving her baby up."

"She has no choice in the matter. Arrangements have already been made."

"Faith never agreed to anything. It's all on your part."

"No matter," he sneered, replacing his phone in the back pocket of his jeans. "Like I said, my property."

"We'll see about that." Brooke turned to leave.

Bobby yanked her around, grabbed the front of her shirt in his fist, "tell me where the bitch is so I can get back. I don't have time for this."

Levi jogged up the hill from the barn.

Knew I should've driven the damn truck, he grumbled to himself as he headed across the restaurant parking lot. He stopped in his tracks when he saw the guy confronting Brooke at the corner of the courtyard.

Trespasser? Unhappy customer? Whoever he was, she didn't look very happy with him. Levi studied Brooke's stiff stance, squared shoulders, fisted hands, wondered how long she'd simmer before she decked him.

He edged closer to eavesdrop but when he saw the guy grab Brooke's shirt, then slap a hand across her face, he broke out into a run.

He drew the line with hitting on women.

No matter how aggravating Brooke could be, she didn't deserve that rough treatment.

Levi charged across the lawn, grabbed the guy by the collar, rammed him against the brick wall. Hands around the guy's throat, elbows pressing him against the brick wall, Levi wedged a boot between the guy's feet, angled his knee inches below the guy's crotch.

"I got a problem with men who hit women." Levi growled inches from Bobby Turner's shocked face. He looked over at Brooke. "Are you okay?"

Brooke nodded, her head reeling from the pain in her stinging cheek, but she refused to rub it. She let out a deep breath when she saw Cameron jump out of his truck, race across the parking lot and her father stepped up beside her.

"Call the sheriff," Finn demanded as he placed an arm around his daughter's shoulder. He had observed everything from the back door of the restaurant after watching Brooke run through the kitchen.

"No," Brooke stated. "Let him go."

"What?" All three men said together.

"I'm okay. It was just a slap."

"Just a slap?" Levi barked. "Brooke, this guy assaulted you. You need to call the Sheriff."

"No." Brooke repeated. "It was just a misunderstanding." She stared hard at Bobby. "But if you ever come back here, I *will* see that the sheriff escorts you to his jail.

"Levi," she gave Levi a pleading look, "let him go."

Levi stared at Brooke for a full five seconds. He was certain she was in shock, didn't realize what she was saying.

"Please," she said, "let him go. He isn't worth it."

"That's a matter of opinion," Levi grumbled giving Bobby one last shove before releasing him.

Bobby threw his chest out as he took in a deep breath, straightened his shirt, tried to regain his composure, after being scared witless.

"This isn't over," he muttered in a dark tone, gave the three men a mocking leer. He jumped and marched quickly toward the parking lot when Finn raised a fist, took a quick step toward him.

"What isn't over?" Levi demanded. "Brooke?" He yelled when she quietly stared at the retreating punk. "What isn't over?"

Brooke turned, studied their faces. "It's nothing," she raised a shaky hand to her forehead, peeked up to her bedroom window, wondered if Faith had seen everything. "Just a misunderstanding."

Cameron turned to watch the guy leave. Snapped a picture of the car. He'd zoom in on the license plate later.

"Looked like more than a misunderstanding to me," Levi continued to study her with eagle eyes, her father with concern.

Brooke squeezed her eyes shut when her knees began to shake, and a heavy feeling settled in her stomach. She couldn't think straight, she'd been so shocked that Bobby had found Faith.

"Brooke," Finn gave his daughter's shoulder a slight squeeze. "No father wants to see what I just witnessed. Who was that punk and why are you protecting him?"

"I'm not protecting him," Brooke rounded on him, "I'm protecting- "She almost said Faith's name.

"Who are you protecting?" Levi demanded.

Brooke stared at the three men, unable to find the words.

"Me," Faith called out from the corner of the building. "She was protecting me."

*T*hey had a family meeting around the long dining room table in the B&B. Angelina had ordered that Brooke remove the tall arrangement of flowers that sat on the mirrored tray in the center. Something this serious, everyone needed to be able to see one another.

Angelina sat between her mother and her husband at one end of the long table, upset that Brooke had put her life in danger. Kristina and Faith sat at the opposite end, meekly holding hands under the table amid all the tension. Cameron sat midway near Kristina. Brooke across from him, worried how to explain everything. Jeremy was manning the restaurant and would join them when the last customer left.

Angry that Brooke didn't appear to trust him, Levi paced between the door to the butler's quarters and kitchen, the living room, the front lobby.

"I wish you'd sit down," Brooke complained.

"How can I when someone assaults a friend and that friend just lets him go," he stopped to glare down at her.

"We have important guests coming tomorrow. I had hoped nothing would happen. Nonetheless, we can't afford any problems right now. If we called the Sheriff, that might have led to an investigation with them coming back with questions. We just can't afford any additional problems right now," she repeated.

Levi continued to glare down at her, then he looked over at Faith. Saw the girl was shaking. "And what's to say he won't come back?" Maybe if the girl was scared enough, she'd be more open about things.

Everyone remained silent.

"Brooke, your father and I have tried not to interfere with your management of the B&B, but we have to draw the line with harboring a young girl here. A very pregnant young girl. Why all the secrecy."

Angelina turned to Faith. "Do your parents know you are here?"

Faith looked down. "No, ma'am."

"How did you get here?" Finn asked.

"I brought her," Kristina murmured.

Cameron's eyes blinked in surprise. "*You* did?" He looked past Kristina to Faith. "Are you running too?"

Faith nodded her head. "Bobby wants to sell my baby?"

"He what?" Angelina demanded; her cheeks flushed in anger.

"I'm sorry. Everything's my fault," Brooke interrupted. "This is a delicate situation and I apologize for keeping everyone in the dark."

"Maybe you need to explain this *delicate* situation," Levi commanded from behind her.

Brooke jumped up, turned to squint her eyes at him. "If you would just sit down, I will."

Levi pressed his lips together, marched to the opposite side of the table to sit between her father and her brother.

Brooke felt as if she was on trial – facing the firing squad – with all the faces studying her from across the table.

"Talk," Levi demanded as he leaned back, crossed his arms on his chest.

"Kristina," she waved a hand toward Kristina, "is the Kristina Powell that disappeared from Oklahoma City last Wednesday evening. She was on her way here when she met Faith Henderson," Brooke waved to Faith, "in Nashville. When Myra realized Faith was in trouble and needed protection, we had to change the arrangements."

"Who is Myra? What arrangements?" Finn asked.

"Myra is another of my *Free Spirits*." Brooke cringed, hung her head, realized she would have a lot more explaining to do. "Listen," she leaned forward, threaded fingers through the hair to massage the dull headache.

Thankfully everyone gave her a moment to think.

She raised her head, looked around the table, "a couple years ago, a few of us started a Facebook group to help women and children in abusive situations.

"It was shortly after Connie was here. Remember?" She turned to her parents. "Connie was trying to get away from her stepfather. Anyway, we started connecting with other people in similar situations and the group just grew. I started receiving

146

private messages from people who wanted to help – lawyers, social workers, nurses-"

"Hairdressers, cab drivers, housewives," Kristina blurted out.

"Is that why you are here?" Rita asked Kristina.

"Yes, ma'am."

"And Faith." Brooke added. "We help them to make a break. They meet in designated spots near where they live, then we get them to the next one. Myra taught Faith and knew her father had died a couple years ago. She didn't know about her mother, but when Faith told Myra Bobby planned to sell her baby, Myra knew she needed to do something. Fortunately, I have the room here, so Kristina brought her with her on Saturday."

"Saturday night," Levi stated, his eagle eyes zeroing in on Brooke. "So that's why you drove the delivery to the homeless shelter? They were in the van when you came back."

Brooke nodded. "Yes. Levi, I hated not telling you, but Kristina and Faith needed a safe place to hide. At the time, we weren't sure whether anyone was looking for them."

"Yet you couldn't trust me?" He shrugged a shoulder. "Who am I going to tell?"

"Who was it that wanted to call the Sheriff just now?" Brooke argued.

"He hit you," Levi countered.

"Okay, okay," Finn raised a hand to stop them.

"I'm sorry," Kristina jumped up, her cheeks flushed, eyes wide; embarrassed that everyone was so upset. "I'll leave. I never meant to hurt anyone. I'm just so grateful to Brooke for arranging for me, and Faith, to stay there." She looked down at Faith. "We'll leave. Find somewhere else to stay."

"I don't think anyone has to leave," Angelina interrupted. "Much as I hate being kept in the dark about everything, I understand, and appreciate my daughter's willingness to help

147

you. Kristina, you've been a big help to Brooke and Connie so until we figure this all out and you get your life back on track, I see no reason for you to leave."

Angelina cast soft eyes on Faith. "Faith, I'm sorry your father is no longer around, but I think you need to let your mother know you are okay."

"She doesn't care," Faith sobbed softly.

"Does your boyfriend really plan to sell your baby?" Angelina asked.

"I overheard him talking to some people on the phone. Then when he hit me because I refused to sign a paper, I knew I needed to get away."

"He'd better not show his face around here again," Levi mumbled, "I'll give him a taste of a fist to the jaw."

Brooke tried to ignore him, turned to Faith. "Faith, Bobby knew you were here. He showed me his phone. He apparently has a tracker on you."

Faith gasped; her eyes grew wide, her complexion paled. She turned to Kristina. "Ms. Cooper told me to leave everything behind. That's why we went to the thrift store. I brought nothing with me," she hesitated, "except my purse. Could he have put something inside my purse? Will he come back?"

Kristina placed an arm around Faith's shoulders, hugged her. "He never saw you. Doesn't know for sure that you are here. We will be more careful."

"Yes," Brooke agreed. "We'll check your purse, dispose of that tracker and be more alert."

"Another reason to install an alarm system," Cameron suggested.

"Too expensive," Brooke replied. "But I'll think about it," she amended when all her family began to speak at once. "Just not right now. We have important guests coming tomorrow. That's all I want to focus on for now."

*F*ifteen minutes later, Brooke peeked out the dining room window, watched Levi and Cameron talking in the courtyard. After the family meeting, they had decided to walk the grounds to be sure no one was watching the place.

Kristina and Faith had escaped upstairs. Brooke had escorted her parents and grandmother to the back door on their way to their home.

Angelina enveloped Brooke in her arms. "Brooke, you continue to amaze me with all you do. Your father and I are so proud of what you've done with the B&B, but you've wowed us with these *Free Spirits*. Please, I just ask that you take care. I think this evening is an indication of how dangerous it could be."

Brooke understood her parents' concern and was grateful that things had gone as smoothly as they had. Promised she would be more forthcoming with any future efforts.

Right now, she hated being at odds with Levi, especially after all he has done for her. She needed to thank him for the spice rack, bird bath and turtle; worried he would leave before she could do so.

She jumped back when Cameron headed toward the parking lot, Levi turned to the house.

She listened to the door open, began straightening the linen tablecloth, replacing the floral centerpiece.

Levi stepped into the dining room, paused when he spotted her straightening the chairs around the table. Despite her explanations, he was still upset about being kept in the dark. She should have been more trusting.

"Cameron's going to see about getting some quotes on an alarm system," he stated in a clipped voice.

Brooke opened her mouth to object, changed her mind.

Levi leaned against the door frame, crossed his arms over his chest. "No objections? No arguments?" He taunted her.

Brooke shrugged a shoulder. "I realize we probably need protection. We need other things more. No harm in getting a quote."

Levi studied her quietly. What was it about the woman that could rile him and soften his heart so quickly? She'd just confessed to being part of some big haven network and he's supposed to not be upset. A network that almost blew up in her face earlier this evening.

She could bite his head off one minute, be meek and submissive the next?

No rhyme or reason to the woman, he grumbled to himself. He straightened to leave.

"Levi, please," Brooke needed to stop him.

He turned, just stared at her.

"I'm sorry. I should have told you."

"I guess that explains all the locked doors. And whispers. You really had me going there for a while."

Brooke couldn't stop the chuckle. "Yes. You were all over the place."

He advanced in the room. "Do you have any idea all the extra steps those locked doors caused me? Having to back track?"

Brooke moved away from him, toward the far end of the table.

"Walking all the way around to the other side of the house, then finding that the door has been unlocked in the meantime." He inched toward her.

"We couldn't afford for you to find Faith." Brooke moved away. "She got restless a couple times and might have caused some trouble."

"Couple times?" Levi took more steps.

Brooke stomped a foot, remained in place. She wasn't about to get into a race around the dining room table with Levi Matthews.

"I need to thank you for the spice rack," she blurted. "Connie said you put it there last night."

"Um-hum," Levi smiled.

"The bird feeder is cute and I'm sure the turtle will be a conversation piece. Where did you find them?"

Levi took another step. "Supply store."

"And what's with leaving the Hershey's kisses all around?"

"Problem?"

"Doesn't help my hips," she joked.

"Then maybe I'll just steal the real thing from now on." He grabbed her, covered her lips with his.

"Are we all straight now?" Brooke wrapped her arms around his neck.

"Except for the make-up sex," Levi covered her lips once more.

CHAPTER THIRTEEN

Anna Marshall's personality more than made up for her frail physique. Stylishly cropped gray hair framed her face, sparkling pale blue eyes and wide smile exhibited her enthusiasm.

Brooke decided Anna's daughter Sarah, with her salt and pepper gray hair, would be a carbon copy in twenty years.

Molly, the granddaughter, on the other hand apparently took after her father. Tall, willowy, long blonde hair and brown eyes, she should be a model, not a law clerk as her grandmother described in her email.

All three women brought excitement with them as they marveled at the beautiful setting, quaint courtyard, and comfortable, charming lobby as they studied the long stairs to the left, small parlor on the right. Even the tiny half bath tucked beneath the stairs.

Sarah studied the four framed pictures spaced on the long wall beside the steps. "Those pictures of the gardens are stunning."

"Those are the Victory Gardens at *Victory Hill*," Brooke explained. "During World War I there was a food shortage when the farmers and field workers were recruited to fight in the war. The government encouraged everyone to plant and harvest fruits and vegetables in their yards, community parks anywhere to support the allies.

"At the time, *Victory Hill* was vacant, and my great-great grandmother Wilma Comfort was one of many who planted gardens around the house. She supposedly saw Chelsea, our resident ghost, staring from a window one day when she worked the garden. Grandma Wilma thought that was a sign for her and Grandpa Edwin to buy the house."

Brooke pointed to the other pictures. "The gardens reemerged during World War II and once again *Victory Hill* participated when my great grandmother Elsie Comfort participated. A member of the local historical society discovered the pictures at an estate auction ten years ago and had prints made. I bought some and had them framed. Thought they would add to the history of the B&B."

Sarah had ascended the steps to study each one individually. "Well, they're beautiful. I had no idea the gardens were so large."

"The Victory gardens were all about the community which best describes our small town. It expressed patriotism and fought the food shortage."

Brooke lined their suitcases at the foot of the stairs. "My brother, Cameron will be by shortly to carry these up for you."

"They look worse than they weigh," Anna chortled as she admired the antique grandfather clock standing next to the door into the dining room. "I hadn't put it away after my trip to Alaska, so it was the first thing I grabbed when we decided on this girl's weekend."

Brooke was about to describe the clock when it struck the noon hour. She jumped when the ghost baby cried.

"Oh, is someone staying here with a baby?" Anna inquired. "I love babies. Hope we get a chance to see it."

Brooke pretended not to hear. She knew they were aware of their Chelsea Donovan ghost. Wasn't sure how receptive they would be to a ghost baby as well. And why was the baby crying again? After the usual morning cry at ten o'clock?

"My husband Bill and I travelled through this area many years ago. We honeymooned at Natural Bridge and came back on our twenty-fifth wedding anniversary. Of course, that was many years ago."

"Connie and I weren't sure whether you had eaten," Brooke led them into the dining room, "but we prepared a small lunch if you'd like. Then we can go do a tour of the house and by then Cameron should have your bags in your rooms."

She directed them to one of the smaller tables at the far end of the dining room that looked out on the courtyard.

Sarah brushed the sheers aside, admired the view and laughed. "Oh, look at that adorable turtle," she exclaimed. "And that grin. He looks like he's getting ready to join the fish in the fishpond."

Brooke smiled as she pulled the chair out for Anna. "He's new. A friend put him there yesterday. In fact. I'm trying to think of an appropriate name."

"Maybe you should have a contest on your website," Molly suggested. "Let your followers make suggestions, then have a vote. I've enjoyed looking at the pictures and reading the reviews. This would be another way to keep them coming back to your website."

"Hum, not a bad idea," Brooke said thoughtfully as she set a plate of Cucumber Cream Cheese sandwiches and Chicken Salad sandwiches on the table. Reached for the bowl of Lemon Artichoke Pasta from the side buffet.

Kristina arrived with pitchers of iced tea and water.

"This is Kristina, a friend who is helping. If you need anything she will be more than happy to help."

"Your slave is here," Cameron boomed from the lobby door.

"And that's my brother, Cameron," Brooke grumbled when everyone laughed.

"I'll go help him with the luggage," Kristina offered as she set the pitchers on the side buffet, hurried out of the room.

"Shush," Kristina whispered, a finger to her lips. "The ladies are in the dining room," she scolded.

Cameron grinned, pleased to see her. He studied the three pieces of luggage. "Guess it will be two trips."

"I can help, this one's not too bad." Kristina grabbed Anna's suitcase and started up the steps.

Balancing the other two on either side, Cameron paused a moment to appreciate the sway of Kristina's hips as she moved up the steps.

"They're in *Asher's* and *William Donovan's* rooms," Kristina turned at the landing, frowned down at his bright smile.

"Coming?" She asked tartly.

"Yes, ma'am." Since the ladies wouldn't be available to give tips, he hoped he might get something else from Kristina.

"Faith doing okay after her scare yesterday?" Cameron asked, following Kristina down the hall.

Kristina sighed. "She's okay. Just scared that he found her."

Kristina stopped at *Asher's Room*, studied Anna's name tag on her bag and set the bag inside the room. Originally, Brooke had planned to put Faith in this room but since the secret was out, and this had a single queen bed, Brooke decided to leave the living arrangements as they were. She and Faith would stay in *Harry and Rita's Room* and Brooke wouldn't have to sleep on the cot.

"She's still worried he will come back." Kristina led Cameron to *William Donovan's* room. "Maybe Brooke should have had him arrested?"

Cameron set the two suitcases at the foot of the twin beds.

"Probably," Cameron agreed, "but I can see Brooke's side too. Levi took care of stopping him, but she doesn't want the publicity either. I'm getting some quotes for an alarm system. In the meantime, we'll just have to be more careful."

He stood, studied her. "How about you? Are you okay? I didn't realize all you went through to get here."

"I'm scared Gary will find me like Faith's boyfriend did yesterday," she crossed her hands over her waist. "But since I filed for the divorce, it seems a little easier. He should have the papers by now. I just pray he agrees to everything, and I don't have to relive any of it."

She brushed her face with her hands. "I want it all behind me. I just want a fresh, happy life. To feel safe again."

"Hey," Cameron pulled her into his arms. "It's going to be okay," he hugged her. "You're a thousand miles away. He has no idea where you are. Give it some time and if he's smart, he'll come to his senses. Agree to the divorce."

He rested a cheek on the top of her head. "Then you can move on."

"Promise?" Kristina looked up at him.

Cameron studied her flushed face. "If I have anything to do with it." He covered her lips with his.

*P*iper and Cilla arrived later that afternoon and once again, the baby cried which rattled Brooke even more.

"I was so sorry to hear about Stuart," Piper murmured as she gave Anna a firm, swaying hug. "He was such a sweet man. I'll always remember the day I found him in that daycare center on the ship reading stories to the children. He was so happy, even though he couldn't remember how he got there."

Anna smiled. "He was getting more and more forgetful. Then he caught COVID when we got home, and it just went downhill from there. But the end was peaceful. His daughter and granddaughter were able to be with him in the end."

Anna reached for Molly's hand. "And now, I have a granddaughter about to get married and the more I talked about you, and Aaron, the more she wanted to meet you. Especially after reading your blogs."

Piper blushed. It still amazed her how many people read and were touched by her travel blogs. She was lucky she could do what she enjoyed and bring joy to others as well.

"You know, I think my readership has doubled since I've started writing for Aaron's online paper. It just amazes me how much people use their computers."

"Speaking of computers, is your laptop still haunted?" Brooke asked.

"No, thank God. But we'll see after this weekend when I stay in James *Donovan's Room*."

"I didn't know computers could be haunted," Molly said.

Piper laughed out loud. "I didn't either. But when I stayed in *Chelsea's Room* before my cruise, he somehow latched on. Scared the devil out of me the first time."

"Wonder what Chelsea has in store for me," Cilla asked.

*A*nna leaned against the sofa cushions, stared out the window at the front fields. "It's so relaxing here. Quiet."

Sarah sat to Anna's right in a wing chair next to the sofa, Molly in the other wing chair at the opposite end of the sofa. Piper relaxed in the recliner near the grand piano in the corner next to the steps up to the library, Cilla on the loveseat between the two windows.

Brooke and Connie occupied chairs on either side of the fireplace, taking a minute to visit with their guests before heading into the kitchen to clean the dinner dishes.

Faith paused at the door into the dining room. "Oh, I'm sorry, I didn't think anyone was here," she turned to leave.

Anna smiled. "Please join us."

"Are you sure?" Faith asked, looked to Brooke for guidance.

"Of course," Anna patted the sofa cushion beside her. "When are you due, dear?"

Faith leaned into the side of the sofa as she sat, adjusted a pillow against the small of her back. "When I saw my doctor last week, he said another month. But things are changing every day."

"I'm sure you and your husband are getting excited."

Faith looked down, rubbed her belly. "I'm not married," she murmured.

"Oh. Are your parents going to be able to help you?"

Faith shook her head. "My Dad died a couple years ago. My Mom has sorta disowned me."

"Oh dear, really?"

"Yes, ma'am. It's just me."

"What about the baby's father?"

"He's not interested." Faith stopped, realized maybe she shouldn't be talking too much about her situation. She looked toward Brooke a second time for guidance. As before, Brooke nodded her head.

Faith cast a look at Anna. "I thought he was, at first, then I found out he plans to sell my baby. That's why I'm here."

"Sell it," Molly exclaimed, "as in black market? Without your approval? Did you sign any paperwork?"

"No."

"You know," Anna placed a hand on Faith's arm, "you remind me of my grandmother. She was in the same situation as you are."

"She was?"

"In fact, she was about your age when she had twins – my mother and another baby that died."

Brooke and Connie sat up straighter, exchanged looks.

"This was the early nineteen hundreds and back then, my grandmother had no choice in the matter. You see, she was living in an orphanage and the baby was taken away from her, given to a family to raise." Anna shook her head, stared out the window. "I didn't know any of this until I was about ten years old when a man claiming to be my mother's uncle came to visit her. He said his name was Henry Cooke and he had a sister, Grace Cooke who was my mother's biological mother."

"Was that how you found out your mother was adopted?" Faith asked.

Anna smiled. "Yes. I was being naughty at the time, eavesdropping. When my mother caught me peeking around the door, she told me to come inside, sit quietly and listen. She didn't believe in keeping secrets. Was open and honest with me about everything. She explained to this Henry Cooke that she always knew she was adopted and had tried to find her real mother before she married my father."

"Did she ever meet her mother?" Faith asked

"Unfortunately, no. That was why Henry Cooke was visiting. He explained that their parents had died of some illness, and he and Grace had lived in an orphanage almost half of their early life. He was three years older than Grace and when he turned eighteen, he continued to work at the orphanage until Grace was old enough to leave.

"One night, Grace was raped. She soon learned she was pregnant and many months later she delivered twins. She refused to tell Henry who raped her.

"A midwife came when she went into labor, wouldn't let Henry anywhere near the room. One of the babies died shortly after birth but the other baby, my mother, was immediately taken out of the room and adopted out. The next day, when Grace confessed to Henry that the minister had raped her, Henry confronted the minister. They argued, fought and Henry killed the minister. He was tried and sentenced to thirty years in prison."

"That's awful," Piper said, "the man deserved to be killed."

Anna nodded. "It seems he had raped other girls as well. After the minister's death, the orphanage was shut down."

"What about the rest of the children?" Faith asked.

"I guess they were put in homes in the community. When they took Henry off to jail, Grace managed to run away. Henry never heard from Grace again until nineteen-fifty when he was released from prison and found her in a sanitarium being treated for tuberculosis. By that time, she was on her deathbed. She told him how she had somehow found the couple that adopted my mother. Regretted never coming forward but knew my mother was getting better care with the couple that adopted her.

"My adoptive grandparents had passed by then, but Henry was able to locate my mother because she and my father had settled in the same town."

Listening to Anna's backstory, Brooke began to see a correlation with the history of *Victory Hill*. "Did you ever learn the name of the orphanage?" Brooke asked.

"No. And Henry didn't want to talk about it. Just said it was somewhere in Southwest Virginia."

Brooke's stomach dropped. Too close to home. "You know *Victory Hill* was once an orphanage, but I've never researched it."

"I just goggled Henry Cooke," Piper stated, "but nothing really comes up. Could be the murder isn't big enough to warrant interest, but I bet we could do some research in the local papers."

Everyone jumped at the sound of the baby crying.

Brooke and Connie exchanged looks, checked the clock on the mantle.

"I don't know about you but I'm getting goose bumps. We have a baby ghost that cries every day at ten in the morning," she explained. Everyone looked up at the clock on the mantle that read eight in the evening.

"Too bad we don't have better records," Brooke said. "I can't decide if that's the time the baby was born or died."

"I'll check vital records for that time period," Piper suggested. "With this new digital age, you never know what might have turned up between then and now. Maybe one of the midwives kept records."

Cilla shivered. "You know, it's really a small, small world. I just learned a few months ago that I am descendent of Chelsea Donovan."

"Really," Sarah is shocked.

"When I visited the restaurant months ago, I somehow happened to lock eyes with Chelsea Donovan as she stared down at me from an attic window. I began having dreams of her life – her marriage, her wedding night, when her husband, James left for war, the birth of their son. It was all so vivid. I even dreamed about the soldiers that raided the house, the doctor that forced her to help him treat the wounded.

"Come to find out, Chelsea was the sister of Seth Hall, my great, great, great grandfather. My grandmother had the family Bible that documented everything and to this day I think I must have been meant to come to *Victory Hill* and see her." She shivered. "Since I'll be staying in *Chelsea's Room* these next two nights, maybe she will shed some light on the situation. Maybe she's somehow crossed paths with this ghost baby."

CHAPTER FOURTEEN

Saturday morning, Brooke, Piper and Cilla relaxed on the side porch with mimosas. Anna, Sarah and Molly were still sleeping. Said they would be up mid-morning.

"How was your night in *Chelsea's Room*?" Brooke asked Cilla.

Cilla laughed. "Slept like a baby. If she came into the room, I must have been dead to the world."

Piper shivered. "Can't say that about my stay. I'll never forget the chills that went up my spine when I saw her pass through the door to the attic."

"You didn't tell me about that," Brooke scolded. "Only that the door to your room came ajar, and you saw the curtains move when you were in bed."

"That too," Piper pointed a long, slender finger at Brooke, "but when I went up the stairs to my room after having dinner with Aaron, I saw her pass through the door to the attic as I was coming up the last two steps. Believe me, I had serious second thoughts about staying in the room."

"What about last night in *James Donovan's* room?" Cilla wondered. "Did he haunt your laptop?"

Piper looked sheepish. "I purposely left my laptop in the suitcase."

"Chicken," Cilla chuckled.

Brooke set the Crab and Swiss breakfast quiche on the table.

"Oh, my goodness, this is delicious," Piper rolled her eyes after her first bite.

"Thanks," Brooke smiled. "I experimented with the recipe. First time I made it, I thought it looked too bland, so I added a handful of spinach to give it color. And some chopped onion with a dab of cayenne pepper for some kick."

"I want the recipe," Cilla crooned. "I can see Jake devouring a whole pie."

Pleased that they liked the quiche, Brooke decided to broach another topic that had been nagging at her.

"You know, Anna's backstory and our ghost baby are almost too coincidental. I half-way wonder if there is a connection. Especially since the baby seems to be more vocal since all of you have arrived. Do you suppose the baby is trying to tell us something? Does it sense a connection?"

Cilla took a bite, pointed her fork at Brooke. "It is odd that the baby should all of a sudden cry more."

"I've been so wrapped up in the romance of Chelsea and James Donovan, I never gave the orphanage murder or baby ghost a thought. I mean, who would want to promote a murder?"

"Let me do a little research, see what I can find," Piper suggested. "I really do like Anna and if there's a connection, I would love to be able to give her some closure. And you, too of course." Piper grinned at Brooke.

Brooke frowned when she looked over, saw Levi approaching with another man wearing khakis pants and button-down shirt with a bright red logo on the pocket. She narrowed her eyes at Levi when she recognized the name of the security company.

"Excuse me a minute," she jumped up, stepped down from the porch. Smiled at the other man while nudging Levi aside.

"Really? Now? When I have a house full of guests?"

Levi paused, waved to the women, didn't realize he'd be facing the music so soon. Thought everyone was still in bed. "He was free, so I asked him to come."

"But I thought Cameron was taking care of it."

"Called in a favor. Brooke, just let me show him around, no one will know the difference. It's not like he's going to install it this afternoon."

His nose went up as he sniffed the quiche. "What's that you're eating?"

"Quiche. Men don't like quiche."

"Matter of opinion," he called to her retreating back. "I'll eat anything that smells that good."

"You'll eat anything that smells good," she called over her shoulder.

Brooke was still unnerved when she joined Piper and Cilla.

"Everything okay?" Cilla asked.

"Oh, yeah," Brooke waved a hand, "Levi's just getting an estimate on an alarm system."

"I'm surprised you don't already have something in place," Piper commented. "You can't be too careful these days."

Brooke shrugged a shoulder. "We've been lucky so far."

"What if Faith's boyfriend should decide to come looking for her?" Cilla asked.

Both women perked up when Brooke's eyes opened wide.

"Spill," Piper ordered as she reached for the bottle of sparkling wine, refreshed her mimosa.

Ten minutes later Brooke had finished her condensed story about Bobby Turner's visit to the B&B.

"Lucky for you, Levi was so close," Cilla exclaimed. "No telling what else that guy might have done."

"Exactly, he, my dad and my brother were there in the nick of time." Brooke agreed. Then she chuckled. "You should have seen his eyes when Levi grabbed him from behind, backed him up to the brick wall." She laughed. "And when my father raised his fist, it was like he couldn't get to the car fast enough."

"He still might come back," Piper warned.

"Yeah, that bothers me, but we're trying to be cautions. I haven't ruled it out; I just like to give Levi a hard time."

A loud noise drew their attention to the front lawn, and they observed two motorcycles coming up the long drive.

"Hmm, if I didn't know better," Cilla murmured, then smiled when the cyclists waved as they rounded the curve toward the back.

"Was that Jake," Piper inquired. "Who was the other guy?"

Moments later, they heard the humming bikes approach the porch from the back of the house.

"Aaron," Piper squealed. She ran and jumped into his arms when he and Jake got off their bikes, removed their helmets.

"What are the two of you doing here?" Cilla wrapped her arms around Jake's neck, kissed his cheek.

"Wanted to be sure your ancestor didn't terrorize you during the night," Jake said, his lips covering hers. "Umm," he licked his lips, "that tastes like more. I'm starving."

Aaron pulled Piper tight, offered her a sensuous open-mouthed kiss. "I missed you." He lifted her wine flute, finished off her mimosa.

"Lucky for everyone, I made two quiche pies," Brooke announced.

"*T*he gazebo looks good," Aaron complimented Levi later that afternoon. "Nothing like a fresh coat of paint to brighten things."

Levi smiled. "You realize I'll probably have to do it all over again next spring. Isn't going to last forever," he mumbled under his breath.

Aaron smiled, gave Levi a pat on the back. "Yeah, but we won't tell the ladies."

James and Chelsea Monroe had arrived mid-morning and once settled, they joined in on the tour of the grounds with Aaron and Piper, Jake and Cilla, Anna, Sarah and Molly.

"Is it too late to plant tulip bulbs?" Piper asked as she stood back, imagined the gazebo next spring. "I just think a border of tulips around the gazebo would be spectacular backdrop for the wedding."

"I don't see why not," Brooke assured Piper. "Even if it is late, I can force them in pots."

Brooke studied Levi when he got a strange look on his face. He had made a mental note to include extra pots in the current side project he was working on in the barn.

As they worked their way through the gardens, Jake reached for Cilla's hand, nodded for everyone to follow as he wandered beneath the long pergola that traversed the center of the lawn. It ended at a simple frame trellis with a bench that overlooked the expanse of the yard.

Jake stopped at the bench. "You know, when we were here a few weeks ago, I saw this magnificent site and thought it would be the perfect spot."

"Perfect spot for what?" Cilla asked, then covered her mouth with her hands when he knelt in front of her.

"To ask you to marry me," Jake looked up, adoration and hope glowing in his eyes as he opened a small velvet box. "Will you marry me? Here? In this very spot? Next June?"

Everyone cheered as Cilla jumped up and down.

"That was another reason I came here this weekend," he spoke against her lips when she fell into his arms.

"That's it," Molly exclaimed, tears in her eyes. "*Victory Hill* must be the most romantic place ever. This is the place for me as well." She turned to Brooke. "Can I please get married on your front lawn?"

Brooke stared at everyone, her eyes brimming with tears. "You know, I worried that no one would want to consider *Victory Hill* as a wedding venue and already I have three for next year. I just can't believe it," she whispered.

They spent the rest of the afternoon and evening celebrating Cilla and Jake's engagement, sharing ideas for the perfect weddings. Even the tour of the bare honeymoon suite couldn't dampen the joy as Levi offered a very descriptive overview of the final product with every assurance that it would be finished well ahead of schedule.

After a meal of Rosemary Beef Tenderloin, Broccoli and Cauliflower Gratin and Apple Spice Cake, everyone settled in the living room to wind down.

"What's going on with the school grant?" Jake asked. "Did the beginning of the school year go smoothly; have any kinks that needed working out?"

Brooke nodded her head. "So far, so good. We started the breakfast routine, decided to go simple first. You know, fruits, dry cereal. Volunteers have been recruited from parents, grandparents, even some vets in the community."

Jake smiled. "Good to hear."

"I guess you heard about the Rotary Club holding a wine festival a few weeks ago. They donated the proceeds. And the local wineries that participated in the festival also donated a percentage of their sales. All total, we've raised five thousand just from the wine festival."

Jake pulled an envelope from his shirt pocket. Handed it to Brooke. "Another reason for my visit."

He watched Brooke's eyes grow round when she opened the envelope, read the ten-thousand-dollar amount on the check.

"Part of the grant agreement was we would match whatever the town raised. Five thousand to match your five thousand. Ten thousand for the first quarter is a pretty good start, wouldn't you say?"

Brooke shook her head as she let the donation sink in. "You know, we're a small town but we take care of our own. With this ten thousand, we'll be able to equip most of the classrooms with mini kitchens – small fridges, toasters, two-burner stoves.

"The Garden Club and Women's Club have set up a schedule to visit the younger classrooms to help the smaller children put together sandwiches, open yogurt. The children are learning to be self-sufficient. Older children are learning about preparing the food – using toasters, even boiling eggs, peeling them. Haven't had any accidents yet." She laughed.

"But keep the checkbook handy," Brooke advised. "The Ruritan Club will be selling Brunswick Stew at the Christmas Bazaar in December. And the Garden Club has also said their next Spring Garden tour will support Williamtown. If successful, the Garden Club will help another town that decides to do the grant."

"Sounds promising," Cilla smiled. "We enjoy spending our money wisely and giving back to the communities."

"The community has become aware of our needs and everyone is working together. There is a strong sense of camaraderie that wasn't here before."

"All because of you," Cilla praised Brooke.

Brooke shrugged a shoulder. "I didn't really do anything but make people aware."

Levi cornered Brooke in the kitchen. Massaged her shoulders as she bent over the sink cleaning the pans from the meal.

"What's this about a mystery man coming tomorrow?"

Brooke gave him a slanted look. "Have you been snooping in my register again?"

"No. I overheard Connie and Kristina talking about it this morning. Said you had a lot on your plate with all this company, then this mystery guy coming tomorrow. Maybe you can contact him, see if he will reschedule."

"No," Brooke decided as she wrung the dish cloth out. "He insinuated it was for a special occasion and I don't want to spoil it for him. Everyone will be leaving tomorrow. I'll have plenty of time."

"I didn't know about the grant. Between that, the B&B, your *Free Spirits*. You do too much already. You can't make everyone happy all the time. Keep them safe."

CHAPTER FIFTEEN

Brooke set the charcuterie cheese board on the small table next to the wine chiller, turned the bottle of Sauvignon Blanc twice, lit the candles as requested. The sun had set thirty minutes ago so it was dark outside. The lamp was on, but she planned to turn it off once mystery man arrived.

She was exhausted.

Her parents had given her the day off from the restaurant so she 'd given Connie the day off from the B&B. Decided they could clean the rooms and get the house back in order on Monday.

Kristina offered to substitute for Brooke in the restaurant; said it would be good training if she was going to be on her own soon. Reminded everyone she had a huge debt of gratitude to repay.

Faith promised to be careful if she could spend the afternoon in the gazebo. She was currently covering the lobby downstairs – waiting for their mystery guest – while Brooke took care of final preparations.

All the weekend guests were gone by two. James and Chelsea Monroe had left after brunch, promising to return soon. Anna, Sarah and Molly departed shortly afterwards, once again confirming Molly's wedding next June, date to be determined.

Aaron and Jake departed on their bikes, followed by Piper and Cilla in Cilla's car, all hinting of a possible return for Thanksgiving.

As soon as the house was empty, Brooke had spent the afternoon preparing *Edwin and Wilma's Room* for her mystery guest. Took extra care cleaning the room, dusting the furniture, added an extra spritz of lavender to the fresh sheets. Wondered who would be sharing the sheets with him.

She'd decided she would prepare the meal – prosciutto, cheese, crackers and nuts for light snacks, chicken wraps with dipping sauce if hungry for more – then retire to her room once he and his companion arrived.

She wore a white oversize button-down shirt over black leggings with black pointed toe ballet flat shoes – semi-professional but casual too. Linked and unlinked her fingers as she turned in a circle, examined the room one last time. Couldn't understand why she was so nervous. Maybe it was the strange circumstances with the reservation. She worried it might be a false reservation and no one would show. At least he'd paid for it she reminded herself.

And if this was a special event, she might have another wedding to add to the calendar next year, she tried to be positive. It amazed her how Piper's blogs about her stay here had inspired so many people to want to come.

All she needed to do was keep Levi motivated to finish the renovations.

A smile tugged at Levi's lips as he took the steps to the second floor two at a time.

He had arrived minutes earlier, found Faith sitting in the chair next to the grandfather clock in the lobby. Told her he'd keep watch for the guests if she wanted to head on up to her room. Faith needed no convincing and as soon as she'd cleared the dining room and turned into the kitchen toward the back stairs, he grabbed the gift box he'd hidden on the porch, locked the entrance doors.

He then checked the register, saw Brooke had blocked Monday closed after the long weekend and thrust a fist in the air. They would have the entire house to themselves.

Except for Kristina and Faith.

He strolled down the long hall toward *William and Elsie's Room*. He knew her parents had given Brooke the day off. And just to keep her suspicious mind guessing, he'd stopped by to say goodbye to Aaron, Jake and the girls, then asked Brooke if she'd like to go to town for pizza and ice cream this evening. The corner of his mouth curved up when he recalled her polite refusal.

She might be a handful – opinionated, bullheaded, and stubborn – but he found he enjoyed keeping her guessing. Tossing out the little gifts during the week kept her wondering who was doing it. Then when she realized it was him, she'd mellowed some.

He gazed down at the gift box. Wondered what she would think of what was inside.

*B*rooke paced between the left front window around the bed, past the bathroom door to the right front window; turned to give the wine bottle another twist in the chiller, checked her *FITBIT*.

Mystery man was five minutes late.

Not a good sign, she worried. Had it all been in vain? Was someone playing a sick joke?

Her heart skittered when she heard footsteps on creaky boards in the hall. Held her breath the closer the steps came to the door. Was he finally here? She frowned when she realized she heard no voices, only one set of footsteps. Why didn't Faith escort him up as planned?

She inched forward. Her eyes widened as she let out a breath when Levi peeked around the door frame.

"Levi?" Her lips parted in surprise. "What are you doing here?" She took two quick steps toward him. "I hope you're not planning to do any work this evening," she panicked, wanting to hurry him along.

Then it occurred to her he wasn't dressed for work. Rather, he had cleaned up since this afternoon and now wore khaki pants and blue plaid shirt. He'd even replaced his boots with brown loafers.

He was also carrying a gift box.

Levi's eyes gleamed as he stepped inside, shut the door behind him.

"Levi, I can't talk now. And you can't be here. You know I'm expecting a late arrival. I still have a few things I need—"

Levi switched the lamp off. Gave the bottle of wine a turn.

"What are you doing?"

A smile danced on his lips as he silently walked around the room, checked the rose buds on the bed. Helped himself to prosciutto wrapped cheese.

"Levi," she exclaimed, "you can't just come in here"

"I can, if I made the reservation." He reached into his shirt pocket, handed her a sheet of paper.

"You?" Recognition dawned on her face as Brooke studied the email receipt. "*You're* mystery man?"

"In the flesh." He reached for a cracker and cheese.

"But why?"

He shrugged a shoulder, set the box on the bed.

"Why not?"

"You asked me out this afternoon. Why go to all this trouble? All this expense?"

"Never can seem to be alone with you." He stood in front of her, brushed a finger along her cheek. Lowered his head to kiss her other cheek. Pulled her closer, zeroed in on her lips.

Brooke felt his hand fist her shirt at the small of her back, leaned in as he deepened the kiss. Enjoyed the taste of the cheese. Couldn't resist the soft sigh as she wrapped her arms around his neck.

Wait, she thought, what was she doing? She was used to arguing with this guy, not locking lips in the master bedroom of the house.

And what was he doing? Why had he made this reservation a week ago?

She nudged away from him. Stared up at him. "Are you serious? You're mystery man? With some special event?"

"Does make-up sex qualify as a special event?"

Brooke stepped back. "I haven't said I'd have make-up sex with you."

"That's why I reserved the room. Been mellowing you all week, figured I'd have tonight to convince you."

An eyebrow shot up when Brooke spied the box on the bed. "What's this? Something else to," she formed quotation marks with her fingers, "mellow me?"

"Open it. Has your name on it."

Brooke flipped the card, read her name. Gave the box a shake and cast him a surprised look when it felt so light. "What did you do?'

"Open it," he repeated as he twisted the screw cap on the wine bottle.

She nudged the bow aside, lifted the lid, parted the tissue. Her eyes grew round when she saw the navy-blue gown. Filigree lace covered the top that would cover her breasts, a narrow strip formed the hem. She gave him a questioning look.

"Thought maybe you would model it for me." He poured wine into the glass.

"Hmm," she lifted the short gown with narrow straps and very little back, stared at him through the sheer material. Tried to hide the grin when his eyebrows waggled.

"Ever since I caught you cleaning *Asher's Room*, I've wondered what it'd be like to make love to you in each of the bedrooms of this mammoth house." Levi handed her the glass of wine, sat on the bed. "Figured I'd start here. Tonight. With that."

"Really? How novel," Brooke teased.

"Seriously," he placed his hands on her hips, nudged her between his legs. Affection glowed in his eyes as they travelled over her face, "much as I enjoy teasing you, I realized I've been too hard on you too. Accused you of thinking you're the lady of the house – although I guess you are in a way. And after the big family meeting the other night, I realized you do too much for others, and not enough for yourself.

"So, tonight is about you. And me. Tonight, you and I are the only guests in the B&B. I'm going to go down, help myself to some of the Jameson in the library." He nodded his head to the small bottle of Lavender bubble bath. "The girl that helped me with the gown suggested the bubble bath. Said it was very relaxing. You've got thirty minutes to relax, then we're going to eat and enjoy each other."

Brooke's heart swelled as warmth spread through her body down to her toes. "Promise?" She threaded her free hand through his hair, leaned in to cover his mouth with hers.

She was still fanning herself five minutes later when she added the scented bubble bath to the water. She felt rejuvenated; like doing a happy dance. No one had ever gone to so much trouble for her. Made her feel desirable.

Much as Levi irritated her, she realized she also enjoyed their altercations. Now, she looked forward to savoring his romantic side.

She took another sip of wine, studied her reflection in the wide mirror above the double sink. Brushed long fingers against her tight cheeks. Leaned closer. Did her eyes look softer? Was she more relaxed? She smiled in anticipation and dashed down the hall to her loft for her makeup while the tub filled.

Thirty minutes later, Levi wandered back into the bedroom the same time Brooke stepped out of the bathroom. His heart stopped as he studied the vision across the room. The spunky, argumentative, body of nervous energy was replaced by a creamy, gorgeous, flushed face, pinkened cheeks, wide eyes full of apprehension.

He knew the blue would look good on her; didn't realize how vivid it would be against her creamy skin. Her loose auburn hair fell past the thin straps on her slender shoulders. The lace in the design of two flower blooms covered perky breasts, aroused nipples. The sheer fabric continued past her flat stomach where another strip of lace grazed her narrow hips. It occurred to him he had never seen her shapely legs, small feet in the flesh.

Desire flickered to life and heat coursed in his veins as he watched her step toward him. He knew she was nervous by her walk. The thin fabric brushed against her as she inched her way toward him.

There was a sudden bright flash and Levi saw another woman. She wore a long white gown. Her long blonde tresses were pinned atop her head, flowed down her back. Her blue eyes glazed with desire called to him, as she smiled, held out a hand to him.

Levi blinked, saw Brooke frowning at him, concern in her eyes. A second later, the blonde vision reappeared, then flickered like bad television reception. He blinked again and found Brooke's arctic blue eyes focused on him.

"Levi, are you okay?"

"Yeah," he shook his head, "I think my multiple times great grandmother was trying to intrude on our evening. Not happening," he stated as he brushed a hand through her hair, cupped the back of her head, pulled her in for a kiss.

"I think dinner can wait," he murmured as he leaned down, gathered her in his arms and carried her to the bed.

Levi gently lay her on the soft covers, settled beside her, the sweet aroma of rose petals surrounding them. Brooke's heart raced as he simply studied her, brushed her hair from her face. "Beautiful," he murmured as he leaned down, kissed her forehead, cheek before settling on her mouth, his tongue dipped between her lips, elicited a moan from Brooke as she brushed a bare foot along his leg.

Brooke arched when his fingertips skimmed her chest, edged beneath the lace to cup her breast, brushed her aroused nipple. Slid down the sheer fabric that covered her flat stomach to cup her hot, moist center. She gasped, bucked at the orgasm that overwhelmed her when that same finger dipped inside her.

She pulled at his belt, tugged his shirt loose, unbuttoned several buttons until Levi stood, bypassing the buttons, jerked the shirt over his head. His eyes on her, he quickly undressed, then settled beside her on the bed. His mouth clasped on hers, angled along her jaw, down her neck, nudged the sheer material aside to latch onto her breast. She arched, moaned softly as an electrifying thrill overwhelmed her, one hand grazing up and down his back, the other pulling his head closer to her breast.

Levi shifted, pressed his aroused flesh against her center.

"Look at me," he whispered. Watched her eyes glaze, heard her soft gasp as he entered her, felt her tightness around him. For a single moment, they were still, accepted their coupling, recognized the attraction that had been simmering, was meant to be. He captured her soft moans with his mouth as he slowly thrust again and again, each thrust edging her up and over the hill to ecstasy until he followed her.

*L*evi rested his head against the headboard, Brooke nestled beside him. He brushed his fingers up and down Brooke's arm, waited for his beating heart to return to normal. She feathered her fingers up and down his stomach, inching lower with each sweep.

"You go any lower, you'll be asking for another round," he warned only to have the threat diminished when his stomach growled.

Brooke smiled.

"What did you fix to eat? Obviously making love to you takes a lot of energy. I'm famished."

He stood, transferred the tray of food to the wicker bed tray which he set in the middle of the bed. He lifted the lid, studied the bright green wraps. "Those are the darkest green cabbage leaves I've ever seen."

"Not cabbage leaves," Brooke chuckled as she settled across from him. "Swiss Chard."

"Never heard of it," Levi reached for a wrap, bit into it. "Not bad, though," he decided appreciated the grilled chicken spiced with a touch of chili sauce and coconut.

"Dip it in the honey-ginger peanut sauce." Brooke showed him.

"Where do you come up with all these recipes."

"Cookbooks. Internet. Facebook. My *Free Spirits.* We also trade recipes in our posts."

"Your entire family shares a passion for cooking," Levi noted as he added wine to their glasses. "Except Cameron."

"Oh, he cooks too. Just enjoys munching off my parents more."

"I've noticed he hangs around the B&B a lot. Seems smitten with Kristina."

"Yeah. Has me worried."

"He's a big boy," dipped his wrap in the sauce.

"Yeah, but he's also rebounding from a broken engagement."

"Hmm. But like I said, he's a big boy."

"I just don't want to see him hurt again. And Kristina has some problems of her own she needs to settle."

"Seems like Faith has some things she needs to settle as well."

"I just hope her boyfriend got the message and stays away."

Levi frowned at her. "If he's smart, he will. Don't plan to give him another chance to assault you. You should have had him arrested."

"I can't afford the publicity and I don't want to spend my evening talking about him."

Levi washed the last of his wrap down. Noticed that she had stopped eating so he carried the bed tray to the dresser.

"Publicity or not, no man should be hitting women." He climbed back on the bed, reached for his wine. "Especially you." He nudged her back against the pillows, nibbled at her lips as he tilted the wine across her chest. Swallowed her yelp when the cool liquid dripped on hot skin, then proceeded to lap up the wine, following the trail that had dribbled down her breast.

*H*ours later, when Brooke and Levi were both in a deep sleep, sated from lovemaking, they never heard the locked door open. Feel the brush of air as Chelsea stared down at them, tears streaming down her cheeks. She lovingly brushed both their heads. Maybe now, they would work together, find her deepest darkest secret.

Bring her peace at last.

Levi stirred after Chelsea disappeared. He'd dreamed he was in the completely renovated honeymoon suite. The floors were sanded and polished, ceiling and walls painted white. Candles glowed all around the room.

Brooke was there, dressed in white. He carried her to the massive bed. Looked down and saw her, not Chelsea. Her red hair laying across the pillows, eyes staring into his.

Levi jerked awake, worried James had once again tried to meddle with his dreams. Smiled when he recalled seeing Brooke, not Chelsea. Felt Brooke's warm body, snuggled next to his and hugged her closer.

"It's cool," she shivered. "Did you open a window?"

"No," Levi answered, half asleep, "just Chelsea."

Brooke's eyes popped wide open. "Chelsea?"

"Um-hmm, that's how I know she's near," Levi murmured half-asleep.

"Levi," Brooke leaned over him, "do you think she saw us making love?"

Levi's eyes popped open at the absurdity of the question. Couldn't stop the grin. "She might not have been here before," he commented as he reversed their positions, "but we can certainly give her a show now," he bragged as he claimed her lips, slowly slid inside her.

"*D*oes it bother you that James and Chelsea try to take over our thoughts? Our dreams?" Brooke asked, once again feathering a finger up and down Levi's tight stomach.

Levi frowned at the ceiling. "First of all, I want it understood that it was me just now making love to you. Not James."

Brooke couldn't stop the giggle. "Yeah, but that first kiss we shared. In the attic? That was Chelsea kissing James."

Levi continued to frown as he was sure the second kiss in the attic, after they found the dress and gun, was James's kissing Chelsea.

"Yes, it bothers me. Some. I've gotten used to the air brushing my face whenever she seems to be around. It's the visions I have a hard time with. It's like an out of body experience and I don't like not having control of my body."

"Why do you think they do it? Is there something more we're supposed to do? I mean, we found their treasures. The book, the dress, the money. We've determined he died on the battlefield. What more is there for us to do?"

"There must be something else. Something that's preventing her from crossing over. Keeping her prisoner in this house. And what about the crying baby?" Levi added. "Why are we suddenly hearing it more? Not just a ten in the morning? Do you suppose the baby has something to do with them?"

"Honestly? I think the baby has an attachment to Anna. It started crying almost as soon as Anna, Sarah and Molly arrived. And to hear Anna's story, it's almost too coincidental. Do you think there could be a kinship? Are we meant to find the baby? And if so, where is it?"

"And what about the little girl you've seen."

"That's another thing," Brooke exclaimed as she jumped up to rest her chin on her hand on his chest, "I never saw her before and now I've seen her three times. I'm really getting worried. We have so many ghosts, people won't want to stay here."

Levi ran his fingers up and down her smooth back. "I know you want to get this honeymoon suite done asap, but maybe we need to slow down some. Take a closer look at the root cellar. Cameron and I can move some of the stuff out. I might have a few contacts in Richmond that could check it out."

"I just don't want too much publicity. We have so many projects going between Aaron funding the renovation, Jake and Cilla the grant. The school project is running so smoothly, and we have the Christmas Bazaar coming up, I hate to see everything stall."

"Understood," Levi kissed the tip of her nose. But we need answers too. Not right away," he added when she sighed, "but we need answers."

CHAPTER SIXTEEN

Levi's eyes widened when Brooke set the egg casserole beside the plate of croissants, bowl of fruit.

"All that for me?"

"Comes with the overnight reservation," Brooke reminded him as she sat across from him at the kitchen table. They'd decided to eat in the kitchen rather than the formal dining room.

"When did you find the time to make it?" He helped himself to a heaping spoonful.

"Yesterday afternoon. It needs to set overnight so I figured it might be a good breakfast for 'mystery man' since I didn't know who his special guest was or how hungry they would be."

"You realize you're going to have to marry me now. Just kidding," he added when Brooke blinked. "Going to miss all this good cooking when this job is finished."

"You keep working on the extra side projects," Brooke freshened his coffee, poured some for herself, "you'll never get the job finished."

Not a bad idea, Levi thought as he watched her serve herself. Once he finished the glass greenhouse project, he'd have to think of something else.

"So," Levi broke a croissant in two, "you going to tell anyone I was your mystery man?"

"Haven't decided yet."

The corner of Levi's mouth turned up. "You know they're going to ask. And if they're like my sisters, they'll want to know all the details."

Brooke raised an eyebrow. "I could always say he didn't come."

Levi leaned forward, squinted his eyes. "And that would be a lie."

"Well, if we get finished before anyone wakes up, it'll be my little secret." She winced at the sound of the back door opening.

"Not happening," Levi smiled as he reached for the fruit bowl. "And I think I hear someone else coming down the steps."

Brooke took a deep breath when the Dutch door opened, Connie and Kristina walked into the kitchen.

"Good morning, ladies," Levi winked as he scooped fruit onto his plate, chuckled to himself when Connie and Kristina stopped, looked at Brooke, him, then each other, as if putting two and two together.

Levi knew the healthy glow to Brooke's cheeks wasn't from his lovemaking but from having her friends find out. It was bound to come out soon enough, he decided. Why not face it now; he'd have some fun with it.

"I knew it," Connie's face lit up. She studied the humongous egg casserole. "You plan on sharing that?" She elbowed Kristina. "It's one of my favorites."

"Help yourself," Levi offered. "I was just telling Brooke she was going to have to marry me. I don't know what I'll do when I finish this job, she feeds me so well."

"Keep it up, you won't get any more," Brooke handed Connie and Kristina plates. "Eat up. We have a full day of cleaning after our busy weekend. Thankfully, we don't have any guests coming in today. Kristina, I hope you're up to helping."

Kristina did an eye roll when she tasted the casserole. "SO good. All the cheeses. Is there something hot in here?"

"Sausage has a little heat," Brooke offered.

"Um," she crooned. "Of course, I'll be glad to help with the cleanup."

"Hopefully, Cameron won't be getting in the way," Brooke teased. "I've noticed he seems to come by more often than usual."

"He has an appointment in Richmond today," Kristina offered. She looked up when everyone was silent. "I, uh, he and I went to town for dinner yesterday."

"I see," Brooke smiled.

She looked over at Levi who was leaning back in his chair, enjoying the conversation. "Don't you need to get to work?" She added his empty plate to hers, carried them to the sink. "The sooner you get this job finished, the sooner you can move on to another job, find another cook."

"Or marry you," he joked as he followed her to the sink, cupped her chin, kissed her lips soundly. "Thank you for breakfast."

He turned, exchanged smiles and a wink with Connie and Kristina. "Enjoy your breakfast ladies," he called over his shoulder as he closed the Dutch door.

They listened to him whistle as he wandered across the porch and out the back door.

Brooke shook her head as she glared at the door.

"Soooooo," Connie reached for a second helping, "do tell. Was Levi the mystery man?"

Brooke settled in her chair, crossed her arms over her stomach and smiled.

"I knew it. I saw him last night as I was leaving to visit my mom. Thought it was too coincidental that he happened to be coming by the same time mystery man was due to arrive. Tell us, did mystery man live up to your expectations?"

Kristina poked Connie. "Maybe it's none of our business," she suggested.

"Of course, it is," Connie waved a hand. "As much as we've watched him aggravate her. Come on girl, tell us. Did he live up to it?"

"More than," Brooke blurted out before thinking. "All right," she threw her hands up when the women exchanged smiles. "And he came bearing gifts. This short, short gown, bubble bath. Told me to relax, enjoy a bubble bath, model the gown. We were in bed before he even thought about eating."

"Ohhh," Connie did an eyeroll. "And his performance?"

"Superior, and that's all I'm going to say." Everyone giggled. "We even had a visit from Chelsea."

Kristina dropped her fork. "Chelsea?"

Brooke nodded. "Couple times."

"Wait," Connie's eyes went wide as she picked up her fork, "are you saying she was there when you and Levi were" she turned her fork in circles.

Brooke laughed. "No, of course not. But Levi did say she appeared to him as I stepped out of the bathroom. And then later," she swallowed, "later she must have come into the room while we slept. A cool breeze woke us."

"Whoa," Kristina whispered, "I think I would have been out of that room so fast."

Brooke shook her head. "I don't think she would ever hurt us, but it was unsettling." Brooke thought of the passionate kisses she and Levi experienced in the attic. "I think she misses James, but something is keeping her from crossing over. Then, there's the mystery of the baby ghost."

"I know, right?" Connie exclaimed. "I couldn't believe it when the baby started crying as soon as Anna and her daughter and granddaughter arrived. Again, when Piper and Cilla arrived. Are they trying to tell us something?"

"After finding the treasure in the attic the other day, Levi and I have decided we're going to check the root cellar. See if anything is there. Piper has offered to research the murder in the orphanage, see if there might be some connection there. One way or another, we need to bring some closure to these ghosts before they run our clientele away."

Levi strolled around the attic, checked his notebook, made a list. Smiled as he reflected on his night with Brooke. She'd looked so beautiful when she stepped out of the bathroom. His heart swelled; joy filled him from within when he recalled her sigh the first time they'd made love. The way her eyes had stared into his as if she also sensed the connection, bonding of souls he'd experienced.

Booking that room was the best investment he'd made in a long while he decided. Satisfied the craving he now realized had plagued him since he first laid eyes on Brooke. Looked forward to fulfilling his fantasy to have her in each of the bedrooms over the coming months.

He turned the page in his notebook, listed all the rooms in the B&B, put a check mark beside *William and Elsie*.

He looked up when he felt the brush of air against his cheek. Remembered how Chelsea had tried to interfere, then visited the room later. Realized he now understood the need she might have to be with her husband. Wondered why she couldn't pass over and be with him.

He studied the bare walls of the attic. He might have been joking when he told Brooke he was going to marry her but decided at that moment, he would get the honeymoon suite finished ahead of schedule and he and Brooke would be the first to christen the room.

He turned to another blank page, drafted a plan from beginning to end then reached for his cell phone to call in a few favors.

Levi and Cameron lifted the root cellar doors and were immediately hit with the cool, stale air.

"Heard you had a date with Kristina yesterday." Levi rested his door against the ground.

"Uh, huh," Cameron agreed, doing the same with his door. "Heard you were mystery man."

Levi grinned. "Nothing's sacred around here, is it?"

"Not when there are so many women in the household. That's what Gran whispered in my ear just now." He and Levi had just come from a late lunch in the restaurant. Decided to check the root cellar before getting back to work. "And it's obvious from watching the two of you that things are much more friendly."

"Indeed," Levi agreed, saying nothing more.

The two men stepped down the three steps onto the dirt floor. Stared at the disarray of equipment and building supplies left over from when Cameron's grandfather had enclosed the porch.

"Guess the first thing is to move all this stuff out," Cameron suggested.

"Yeah." Levi stared at the clutter; thought about all the balls he was suddenly balancing. He was pleased that his plan was coming together.

His first call had been to a plumber friend who was sitting at home, bored after a cruise was cancelled due to his wife testing positive with COVID. He didn't hesitate to take up Levi's offer to check the attic.

Levi's second call had been to a contractor who happened to have a two-hour window of time available that he could stop by to consider the job for a new electrician he was hiring.

After an hour of inspection by the three men, Levi's plumber friend determined it would only take him two days. He'd get it done before going back to work. Levi and the contractor would supervise the electrician.

Since Levi needed both men on both floors, one would work in the attic while the other worked in Brooke's new bathroom, then they would switch. If all went well, Levi could start his work by the end of the week.

Encouraged by the way things were coming together, he'd waited for Brooke to leave for her shift in the restaurant then enclosed the shell of her bathroom with sheetrock, nailed a temporary door in place. Deciding he wouldn't let her see the new bathroom until it was finished, he tacked police tape across the entire wall.

"Before I forget," Levi remembered meeting the security guy on Saturday, "Tad said he'd send us a quote on the alarm system."

"Great," Cameron started tossing tools into a wooden box. "The sooner we get it done the better. Can't be too careful these days."

Levi lifted an old two-by-four, held it up, turned it right and left, decided it was straight enough for the project he had going in the barn. "I can back my truck up, load the lumber and equipment, take it to the barn."

"I can't believe Granddad just left all this stuff here. Maybe this is why he always told us to stay out of the root cellar. Didn't want Granny to see all the mess he left."

They shifted things, made their way toward the back of the cellar, deeper under the house where the dirt floor sloped toward the joists of the floor above.

"At least it's a dirt floor," Levi breathed a sigh of relief. "We don't have to remove any concrete floor."

"Tight quarters, though," Cameron said.

Levi picked up a wooden handled trowel. Studied it. Old but useful.

"Your grandfather might have used this to lay the bricks for the addition. We'll use it for the excavation. Odd how it is handy."

It occurred to Levi that maybe they were finally on the right track. As if everything was starting to come together. The treasure, renovations, baby ghost, Chelsea.

*B*rooke almost stumbled up the steps to the loft. She was exhausted. She, Connie and Kristina spent the morning changing beds, vacuuming, cleaning bathrooms, dusting, getting everything back into shape.

Faith helped where she could, but they didn't want her overworking herself. Now that everyone knew she was there, she was able to move around the house more.

Brooke smiled. No more confusing Levi with locked doors.

He had come to the restaurant for a late lunch, and she couldn't help but notice how everyone seemed to smile whenever he joked with her.

She never intended to say anything. Hadn't even mentioned to her family that a mystery man had made the reservation and was surprised when Granny said something.

"I understand Levi was your mystery man."

"How did you know?" Brooke had almost

"Little birdie mentioned it when she came by this morning for the tablecloths."

Brooke cringed. All she needed was to have her family watching her every step from now on.

Then Jeremy had the nerve to comment about how much nicer and friendlier she'd been since mystery man visited the night before. Laughed when she threw a dirty napkin at him.

Right now, she wanted nothing more than to fall into bed and sleep for ten hours.

She hesitated when it occurred to her that her loft area seemed a little smaller. Smiled when she realized Levi had enclosed the framework. She looked over to see the yellow police tape across the wall to what would be her new bathroom. The tape almost glowed in the light from the porch.

She tried the door and found it locked.

"What's with the police tape?" She texted Levi, then checked her FITBIT figured he was probably fast asleep.

"Stay out" Levi texted back almost immediately.

"The door's locked."

"Now you know how I felt." He added an emoji.

CHAPTER SEVENTEEN

Brooke hummed to herself as she cleaned the table, carried the drink glasses to the back. "What?" she asked when she turned, caught her grandmother smiling at her.

Rita Comfort lifted her shoulders. "You seem happy," she called out as Brooke carried the glasses to the drink station.

"Why not?" Brooke returned. "It's a beautiful day. It's also hump day. Not that that means anything to me, I work every day. But the customers have been happy. We've been busy and our happy customers have been generous tippers. Who wouldn't be happy?"

Rita patted her granddaughter's cheek, kissed the other. "It's just nice to see you smiling, that's all. If I didn't know better, I'd think Levi had something to do with it. You two haven't been arguing as much."

"Oh, Gran, he'll always be a jerk. Maybe I've just gotten used to him."

"Maybe," Rita agreed.

They both looked up when the bell above the entrance jingled and a couple wandered it. Brooke guessed them to be in their late fifties. She was tall and slender, short salt and pepper hair. He was tall as well but more stocky, slightly receding hairline.

They paused just inside the foyer, stared around with smiles on their faces.

After her grandmother seated the couple at a booth, Brooke wandered over to take their drink orders.

"Welcome to *Victory Hill*. Can I get you something to drink while you look over the menu?"

The woman smiled, asked for unsweetened iced tea, the man water.

"This is the loveliest place!" the woman gushed when Brooke returned with their drinks.

The corner of Brooke's mouth curved up.

"We were driving up that long, fenced driveway and I commented to Sidney, I could just imagine the soldiers camped out in the front fields." She laughed. "My name's Monica. Monica Warren. And this is my husband, Sidney. I taught U.S. History. Sid was the PE coach. We both retired this June and have been spending our children's inheritance, we like to say."

"The farm is beautiful, especially in the spring and fall."

"I thought the mansion was a private residence then we noticed the bed and breakfast sign. Do you suppose there might be any vacancies? I know it's late in the day, but we thought we would ask. Take a chance."

"I happen to manage the B&B and as a matter of fact, there are a couple rooms available. Two other couples arrived this morning. I can give Connie a call, let her know you'll be checking in."

"That would be wonderful," Monica smiled. "Maybe we'll get something light here and then have dinner at the B&B."

"**A**re you sure you don't mind helping Connie?" Kristina asked Faith as she combed her hair into a ponytail. "I feel so bad leaving her in a lurch like this."

Possessed by Love

"You helped with the dinner meal. I don't mind helping with the clean-up. Been feeling a little energetic today."

Kristina turned to study her young friend. "Some of my friends have said they went through a cleaning phase before they went into labor. Maybe you're getting that burst of energy."

"I hope so," Faith followed Kristina down to the kitchen.

"You're sure you don't mind?" Kristina cast nervous eyes towards Connie who was packing a box with left over rolls and a tub of butter beans.

"No problem. You helped serve dinner. Just need to set this on the porch for Jeremy to take to the homeless camp, finish loading the dishwasher and wash the pans."

Connie looked at Faith.

"Everyone is in the library. I've prepared the cart with the tea and scones. Do you think you can handle the two steps into the library?"

"I believe so," Faith affirmed. "Just take my time. Are they as friendly as Ms. Marshall and her daughter and granddaughter?"

Connie and Kristina exchanged looks.

"They're okay. Between you and me, the one woman never seems to stop talking."

"Oh, okay. I'll try to slip in and out then."

Faith navigated the cart to the two steps in the lobby that led to the parlor. She transferred the plate of scones and tray with the tea pot, cups and saucers to the long bench outside the door to the library. Figured the closer everything was to the room, the quicker she could set it up and leave.

She smiled at the three couples as she set the plate of scones on the oval marble-top table that stood in the center of the room. Returned moments later with the seeping tea.

"Oh, you work here too?" Monica asked Faith.

"I'm just helping until I have my baby," Faith smiled as she rubbed the side of her stomach. "Can I help anyone with some tea?"

"You don't look like you have much longer," Monica continued while Faith poured the tea. "I'm sure you're excited to be so close to the due date. Do you know what it is?"

Faith decided this was the woman Connie said talked too much.

"No, ma'am," Faith turned to hand a cup to her. Her hand shook slightly, it had been so long since she'd been around people. She didn't feel as comfortable with these people as she had with Ms. Marshall.

"We have two grandsons," Monica gushed, squeezed Sid's hand. "And another on the way. I hope you have a happy and safe delivery."

"Thank you," Faith backed out of the room, anxious to get away. "I seem to have forgotten the cream and sugar. I will be right back."

"I love the selection of books," Bess Armstrong said as she reached for a scone. "Will have to compliment Brooke on her well-rounded selection – John Grisham, David Baldacci, James Patterson, Robert Parker, Sandra Brown even Nora Roberts."

"Even have some about ghosts," Ed Armstrong added.

"I'm sure you heard we have a ghost here," Connie rushed in with the creamer and sugar.

"Of course," Bess chuckled. "That's one of the reasons we came. Do you think we'll see her?"

"Maybe," Connie smiled. "Chelsea was a little scarce for a while, but I believe Brooke said she thought she saw her sitting at her desk in *Chelsea's Room*."

"Ohhh," Bess rubbed her hands together, shared a look with her husband. "Our room."

"So, how old is *Victory Hill*?" Monica asked.

"Well," Connie paused by the door, resigned to giving a quick history of the house. "The original house was built in seventeen-eighty by William Donovan, founder of Williamtown. It served as a hospital during the War between the states when his great grandson, James Donovan, was killed in the Battle of the Crater. Chelsea was James Donovan's wife, she died here of a broken heart. After her death, their son was taken to Richmond to live with his uncle and the house was empty for many years.

"The house was sold in eighteen ninety-two by James and Chelsea's son and turned into an orphanage. There was a murder here in nineteen fifteen and once again, the house was empty for many years until Brooke's great, great grandparents bought it in nineteen twenty. So, it has been in the Comfort family for almost one hundred years. Next Spring, they plan a centennial celebration here and in the restaurant."

"Well, it is certainly a charming place," Monica gushed, "I'm so glad we decided to stop by the restaurant."

*F*aith realized she was fighting a losing battle trying to get comfortable with the book. After escaping the library, helping Connie put the dishes away, she'd returned to her room. She tried sitting in the wing chair next to the window, but the baby took up most of her lap, the confining seat caused her lower back to ache.

She stretched out on the bed, leaned the paperback against her swollen stomach. Tried to read but thought of the conversation with the guests in the library instead. Didn't know why they made her uneasy. Maybe it was their questions about the baby.

They didn't comfort her like Ms. Marshall; talking to her was like talking to a grandmother. These people were just making conversation. Conversation about her baby which made her nervous.

She tried to focus on the book, but once again, her mind wandered. Images of Bobby flickered in and out of her thoughts. She recalled watching him argue with Brooke the other day then slapping her. Felt the sting on her cheek when she remembered the day he'd slapped her.

Faith jumped, cast a quick look at the door to the main hall, listened intently for more noise. Was someone outside her door?

Maybe it was the guests returning to their rooms after their tea.

Ten minutes earlier, she'd heard the downstairs porch door open and shut. Found herself counting the steps coming up the stairs; hoped Kristina was home from her date with Cameron.

She had smiled when the footsteps continued past her door toward Brooke's loft. Figured it was Levi as Brooke had come in from the restaurant thirty minutes earlier.

She smiled, happy that Levi was the mystery man and he and Brooke were getting along better.

Another noise in the main hall alerted her.

Was it Chelsea? Would she finally get to meet the ghost?

Maybe it was the guests returning to their rooms after their tea. She wondered if they might need help. Should she let Brooke know?

Faith got out of the bed, cracked the door to the main hall, jumped when she saw Bess Armstrong standing three feet away looking over the books in the glass front bookcase in the hall.

"Oh, I'm sorry," Bess apologized. "I hope I didn't awaken you." She nodded to the bookcase. "Anytime I see a shelf of books, I *have* this need to check it out. See what's offered."

Faith smiled. "I'm sure Brooke wouldn't mind if you took one to your room. In fact, I'm reading one right now. Help yourself."

Faith closed the door, leaned against it. Decided she liked it better when she lived behind locked doors and didn't have to deal with people.

*L*evi watched Brooke stare at the locked door to her new bathroom.

"It's still locked," he whispered smugly. Two could play the game.

Brooke jumped. She'd just showered downstairs, was dressed for bed in her comfortable PJ's. "Don't do that," she complained. "It's almost midnight, what are you doing here?"

Levi studied the oversized tee-shirt. "Funny how the simplest outfit can be just as sexy as the skimpiest." He studied her slender legs.

"What do you have on under there?"

"None of your business. I repeat, what are you doing here?"

"Cameron was out," he stepped toward her, "I got lonely." He brushed a fingertip up and down her arm, gave her a puppy-dog look. "Wondered if you might be feeling the same."

The corner of her mouth quirked up as Brooke stepped toward him. "I might be," she walked her fingers up his biceps, wrapped her arms around his neck, offered her mouth to his.

When his hands skimmed over her bottom, she jumped up to tighten her legs around his waist as he carried her into the bedroom, kicked the door shut with a foot.

*F*aith shifted in the bed. She was sure she felt something on her shoulder. She reached for her phone and sighed that she'd only been asleep thirty minutes, hated that she couldn't just sleep eight straight hours.

She looked over to see that Kristina's bed was still empty.

She fell back on the pillow and closed her eyes, willed herself back to sleep but they suddenly flew open when she was certain she felt a nudge on her shoulder.

An alarm rang in her mind when she saw movement, heard the soft step across the room.

Was someone in her room?

CHAPTER EIGHTEEN

Kristina stepped softly up the steps, a smile on her face, her heart almost bursting with joy. She hadn't felt this happy in a long, long time. And all she and Cameron had done was grab some fried chicken dinners in town, brought them back here and sat in the gazebo. Talked for two solid hours.

He told her about growing up in Williamtown, going off to college, setting up his practice in town. Hinted he needed help in the office.

She'd shared how she had taken business classes at her local community college and wanted to open a flower shop. Gary had hired her to manage the office but after they married, insisted she stay at home. Said he didn't want his wife working outside the home. He didn't replace her either, continued to man the office himself. When she didn't get pregnant, she'd wanted to take more classes, but once again Gary refused. After the abuse, she'd been scared to leave.

They had watched Brooke wander over from the restaurant after her shift.

"You know, I always knew my sister had a big heart but never realized how big until the other night when she told us about her *Free Spirits*. And helping you."

"I wouldn't be here if it weren't for your sister," she had answered.

They'd chuckled softly when they observed Levi sneak in the back door thirty minutes later. Watched the light go out in Brooke's bedroom shortly after he arrived.

"I guess that's my cue," Kristina had commented. "After a house full of guests, tomorrow will be another busy one cleaning up."

She stopped at the top of the stairs, pressed a hand to her lips remembered how Cameron had held her hand as they walked toward the B&B, kissed her like she'd never been kissed before saying good night.

Kristina opened the bedroom door off the landing, glanced over to see Faith's still form in her bed. She knew Faith had a hard time sleeping and didn't want to awaken her, so she quickly stepped into the bathroom to change and brush her teeth.

Moments later, she came out of the bathroom, paused when she heard a sudden noise to her left then fell to the floor after being struck from behind.

Faith sat upright in her bed, watched Kristina fall, started to scream but a hand suddenly covered her mouth.

"You scream, you die, bitch." Bobby Turner whispered in her ear.

Faith's eyes grew wide in fright. The bedside lamp clicked on, and she stared at an equally surprised Monica Warren.

"What's she doing here?" Monica pointed a long finger at Kristina's still form. "You said she was by herself."

"Who the fuck cares, we got what we came for don't we?" Bobby answered.

"But what are we going to do with her?" Monica turned to Sidney, who pulled black zip ties out of his pocket.

Sidney turned Kristina over on her stomach, bound her hands and feet.

"Get a washcloth from the bathroom," Sidney ordered, "stuff it in her mouth. She's starting to come around."

Kristina tried to scream as Monica rammed the cloth in her mouth. She rolled on her side in time to see Bobby bind Faith's hands in front of her swollen stomach.

She and Faith stared at one another with wide eyes filled with fright. Tears streamed down Faith's cheeks as Bobby pushed her past Kristina toward the door to the front hall.

"Get her downstairs," Sidney ordered, slapped Kristina when she tried to scream, began to pound her feet on the floor. "If you know what's good for her," he pointed to Faith, "you'll keep your mouth shut."

*B*rooke snuggled closer to Levi's warm body. Suddenly the overhead lights and bedside lamp come on and they both sat upright.

"What's going on?" Brooke shielded her eyes from the brightness.

The lights went out, came back on, went out again.

"Something's wrong," Brooke jumped out of the bed, grabbed her robe. "I need to check on Faith."

Levi tugged on his jeans, followed her into Faith and Kristina's room.

They both almost stumbled over Kristina's mumbling body.

Levi switched the overhead lights on.

"Kristina," Brooke exclaimed as she bent over her. "What happened?" Brooke tugged the cloth from Kristina's mouth. "Where's Faith?"

"They took her," Kristina whispered, afraid the man would hear them.

"Who? Who took her?"

"I'm sure it was her boyfriend. Faith looked so scared. And there was a man and woman with him. Brooke, I think they are one of the couples that's staying here," she added in disbelief.

Levi yanked and broke the ties confining Kristina's hands and feet.

They opened the door to the darkened hall made their way past closed doors toward the front stairs. Turned at *Asher's Room* headed toward the dim light shining from *William and Elsie's Room*.

Brooke knew Monica and Sidney Warren were staying there, cautioned Levi to hesitate. He peeked around the door frame, found the room empty.

Suddenly the lamps in the little parlor outside *Chelsea's Room,* on the small tables at each corner of the landing and the chandelier in the lobby flickered on and off.

Brooke and Levi exchanged looks, realized Chelsea was trying to warn them.

Levi's head jerked when he heard the creaks and startled whispers on the stairs. He peeked through the windowpane that overlooked the landing to see Monica and Sidney Warren at the top of the stairs, Faith between them. Bobby Turner was two steps ahead of them.

"Call nine-one-one," Levi ordered as he moved toward the steps. He didn't want to make his move too soon for fear Faith would lose her balance and fall.

Half-way down the steps, the ghost baby began crying. Monica and Sidney visibly jumped.

"What the hell is it with this place?" Sidney growled. "First the lights, now a baby? There's no baby staying here."

"Should've thought twice about breaking into a haunted house," Levi shouted as he raced down the long stairs just as Cameron came barreling through the lobby door from the courtyard.

Levi pushed Monica into the wall causing her to bang her head against the wall and collapse on the step. He side-stepped Faith who had grabbed hold of the railing with both hands, punched a startled Sidney who had turned at the commotion behind him. Keeping up his momentum, Levi tackled Sidney to the floor; they rolled toward the dining room.

Cameron launched himself like a missile at Bobby Turner, and they slid through the doorway into the living room.

Faith heard the thuds of bare knuckles against skin and moans of the two men being apprehended. There was a loud commotion behind her on the landing, and she looked up at the shocked faces of the other guests, staring down in awe at the activity downstairs.

Faith groaned, doubles over in pain.

Brooke and Kristina dashed down the steps, helped Faith into the chair next to the grandfather clock next to the dining room door.

Minutes later, Bobby Turner, Monica and Sidney Warren were seated in the middle of the living room floor, each with their hands and feet zip tied. The men's lips were puffy and bleeding, eyes beginning to swell; Monica had a big goose egg on the side of her forehead.

"I didn't know what was going on," Cameron accepted a small bag of ice from Kristina, placed it on his bleeding knuckles. "I was in my truck, heading home and suddenly the house just lit up like a Christmas tree. In the attic, your room. On. Off. I didn't know what was going on. Then they came on in the lobby downstairs and I decided to investigate."

"Ours too," Bess Armstrong spoke. "I texted the Parkers, then we all peeked out our doors, just as all the commotion started down here."

"My room as well," Connie added as she rolled the cart, loaded with fresh brewed coffee into the living room. "When the baby started crying, I knew something was wrong."

"Same for me," Brooke agreed. She turned to her guests. "I apologize for everything. I've never had anything like this happen."

"Do you think Chelsea was trying to warn you?" Kristina asked.

"And the baby?" Connie added.

Suddenly the lights went out, came on again seconds later. Everyone stared at one another in silence.

"Well, I have to say we've certainly gotten our money's worth," Ed Armstrong stated.

Brooke couldn't stop the smile. "Do you think"

Everyone jumped at the sudden loud knock at the courtyard door.

"This is too much," Brooke grumbled. "I realize Chelsea might be able to make the lights come on, but why the knock?"

Levi shook his head when the knock sounded again.

"I think that might be the Sheriff," he headed to the lobby to answer the door.

*B*rooke tried her best to answer Sheriff Thompson's questions, explain why two missing women were staying at her bed and breakfast.

He'd encouraged Connie to shepherd the guests back to their rooms so he could question Faith and Kristina further.

He studied Kristina. "I recall seeing your missing person alert; believe it has been cancelled?"

"My lawyer has been in touch with my husband so yes, I hope it has been cancelled."

"I'm surprised you're so far away from home. Have no plans to return?"

"No, sir."

He noted the way Cameron sat next to Kristina, his arm resting on the back of the loveseat. Turned to Faith, studied her nervous hands that clasped and unclasped in her lap, or rubbed her swollen stomach from time to time.

"Can you tell me where you're from, young lady?"

"Nashville, sir."

"How old are you?"

"I'm sixteen, sir," she whispered.

"Haven't had a missing report for you cross my desk. Do your parents know you are here?"

"No, sir. My father died two years ago; my mom kicked me out of the house."

"She did, did she?" He looked to the deputy who was making notes. Pointed to Bobby, Monica and Sidney who had been handcuffed but were still sitting in the middle of the living room. "Do you know these people?"

"He used to be my boyfriend?" Faith pointed a finger at Bobby.

"Used to be?"

"Yes sir. I thought we were going to get married. Then I heard him talking to someone about selling my baby and I knew I had to get away." Faith cast a quick look at Brooke. "I saw Kristina at the *Wendy's* and she invited me to join her."

The Sheriff looked at Kristina. "That so?"

"Yes, sir. She looked so alone I asked if I could sit with her. We started to talk. I realize I probably should have encouraged her to go home, but she said she was by herself. And scared."

Sheriff Thompson turned to Brooke. "Don't know what your arrangements are with this young lady, but I suggest you contact her mother. What they do after that is between them."

"You three," he nodded to the deputy to help Bobby, Monica and Sidney stand. Studied the paper a deputy had just handed him. "You'll be spending some time in my jail. I see, here, each of you have been in trouble before. We'll let the judge decide what he wants to do with you."

"Sir," Faith spoke as the Sheriff stood, "can I ask a question?"

"Of course."

Faith looked at Bobby. "How did you find me? I left everything behind."

Bobby sneered, "I've been tracking you ever since you started whining about keeping the bastard." Faith looked down embarrassed. "You may have dumped your phone but that stupid pocketbook you love so much?"

Faith thought about the purse tucked under her bed. "I haven't looked at it in days."

"Check the side zipper," Bobby snarled. "Tracker's still putting out a little blue dot on my phone. That's how I knew which bedroom you were in."

Kristina stiffened. Her hands moved to the pierced earrings in her ears.

Something for you to always remember me by, Gary had said months after they were married. *I'll always be a part of you*. The earrings had been a part of her attire for so long, she never thought to leave them behind.

Could he have put a tracker in them? She wondered.

She immediately removed them; decided she would flush them down the drain as soon as possible.

"You okay," Cameron brushed a finger across her bruised cheek. "You've been quiet."

Kristina turned frightened eyes toward him; handed the earrings to him.

"Please take these. Do what you want with them. Gary gave them to me and after what happened to Faith, I worry he may have a tracker in them."

Cameron studied the small studs. "I don't think"

"Would you just check them" Kristina interrupted. "I don't want him showing up here just like these three did. And even if you don't find anything," she rested her head on his shoulder, "I don't want them back."

"I'll have them checked, but Kristina, they're kind of small. Why would he have a tracker on you anyway? Is he that paranoid?"

Kristina nodded toward Bobby. "Would you have thought he would put one on Faith?"

"Hard to believe that he would go to the trouble, but he did have a reason for wanting to track her. Would your husband go to that extreme?'

"I have no idea. I don't care. I just don't want them anymore."

*B*rooke had been watching Faith the entire time Sheriff Thompson questioned them. She was grateful that Kristina and Faith had thought to withhold Myra Cooper's part in her escape from Nashville. Now she worried the evening's shock would trigger an early labor.

"Are you okay?" She asked when Faith stood after the Sheriff's departure.

"I think I might be in labor."

"Well," Brooke rubbed a hand across Faith's shoulders, "you did have a scare."

"Yeah, but I've been feeling off all afternoon." Suddenly, her eyes grew wide in embarrassment when she stared at the little puddle at her feet. Bent over, her hands hugging her stomach when a sharp pain jolted her body.

"What are we going to do?" Connie worried. "That was a pretty strong contraction. Do we want to risk a trip to the hospital in Roanoke?"

Brooke had been worried something like this would happen.

"Go call Nancy Hughes," she suggested to Connie. "I texted her the other day when Faith started having the pains. She knows the situation, said to call her if anything happened."

Connie reached for her phone; speed dialed Nancy's number.

Brooke led Faith to the stairs. "Can you handle the stairs?"

Faith's complexion is pale, eyes large with worry. "I think so," she started up when another contraction hit her.

Brooke's heart swelled, knew she was in love when Levi raced over, scooped Faith into his arms, carried her up the stairs.

CHAPTER NINETEEN

It was two in the morning before they could get Faith settled in the bed. She had pillows behind her, around her as they waited for Nancy Hughes to arrive. Nancy was part of the delivery team at the Roanoke Hospital and had been one of Brooke's *Free Spirits* for a year. She often answered questions posted to their Facebook page from concerned mothers in difficult situations.

The contractions eased off some but by lunch time the next day, Faith's contractions were coming hard, and Nancy confirmed it wouldn't be much longer.

Cell phones were pinging as everyone from the restaurant requested updates.

Faith feared the pain and the way her body was reacting – her stomach stiffening then the unbearable cramps. Nancy tried to help her work with the breathing techniques and riding out the pain.

"I want to push," Faith sobbed.

"Can't, it's not quite time," Nancy vetoed that option.

"But I want to. I want to get it over. Why does it have to take so long?"

Nancy gave Faith's hand a little squeeze of support, sorry there wasn't more she could do for this child who was having a child.

"Your body is getting the baby in place, honey. Just a little while longer," she encouraged.

Nancy studied the worried looks of the other girls in the room.

"There are too many mother hens and cell phones in here. If you can't stop making faces, exchanging looks, answering texts, you're all going to have to leave. You're not doing Faith any good being here."

"They can't leave," Faith demanded. "They brought me here. They must stay with me." She paused when another contraction wracked her body; tried unsuccessfully to hold her breath until it was over. "If I was at home, in a hospital I could have all the drugs I wanted."

"Not necessarily," Nancy argued. "If you'd let everyone know sooner, maybe. But you waited too long. Once you reach a certain point in labor, it's too risky for the baby to insert an epidural."

"But I was trying to be strong," Faith sobbed, feeling a crying jag coming on. "So much was going on with Bobby and that couple. Everybody's been so nice to me, I didn't want to be a bother." She looked from one to the other. "I'm so sorry I snapped at you."

Everyone exchanged worried but understanding looks. Brooke reached for Faith's hand, Kristina, the other, Connie wiped Faith's forehead with a washcloth.

Nancy chuckled. "It's normal, honey. You ask any woman that's had a baby and she'll tell you she went through a range of mood swings near the end. I'm a perfect example. When the nurses told me they thought I was ready and they'd see if Dr. Smith was ready, I ordered them to tell Dr. Smith he'd better be there. They must have told him as a few minutes later he marched in and stated, 'Dr. Smith reporting for duty.'"

Faith tried to smile, then frowned as another contraction hit.

"Pant," Nancy commanded, showing her how to do it. Encouraged Brooke, Kristina and Connie with her eyes to do the same.

"Good teamwork," Nancy cheered as she checked Faith's progress. "And looking great," she looked over the top of her bifocals. "The baby is crowning. That means I can see the top of his head." She looked up, pat Faith's knee. "Next time you can push. When you feel the urge, grab your knees, lean forward and push."

Forty-five seconds later, Faith let out a loud cry. Connie helped her lean forward, Brooke and Kristina each held a knee offered their encouragement.

It took two tries before the baby was out.

"And we have a fine-looking baby boy," Nancy cheered as she accepted and cradled the baby in her hands.

Everyone jumped when the ghost baby sounded followed by the humming of a lullaby.

"Oh, he's beautiful," Connie crooned.

"Look at that head of hair," Brooke remarked.

"Listen to that yell," Kristina laughed.

Nancy lay the baby on Faith's stomach, let him rest a moment before she clamped the umbilical cord in two places. She handed Faith the sterile scissors to cut it. "Normally, we let the father do this, but since you did all the work- "

Once the cord was cut, Nancy turned the baby on his side, rested him on Faith's chest so mother and son could study each other.

Brooke, Connie and Kristina watched as Faith studied her baby. Tears filled everyone's eyes as Faith whispered, "My beautiful baby. I want to name him after my daddy."

"To Matthew James Henderson," Connie raised her wine glass to toast Faith's baby. Mother and son were both bathed and sleeping soundly upstairs. Connie, Brooke, Kristina and Nancy were enjoying a glass of wine along with Levi and Cameron.

"I don't know about Cameron, but we just met the girl and all day, I felt like the nervous father." Levi looked at Brooke, "*Her* father," he clarified.

"I seriously doubt Faith will be giving that baby up," Kristina stated.

"We'll need to get them both to the doctor tomorrow for an official checkup. She's so young. What about her parents?" Nancy asked.

"Her father's deceased. They must have been close, she wanted to name her baby after him," Brooke explained. "At the moment, things are strained with her mother. Seems she has a boyfriend who tried to get a little too friendly with Faith."

"Faith needs to at least tell her mother about the birth," Nancy advised. "Needs to look into insurance."

Brooke nodded her head. "I agree. *Free Spirits* can only do so much. At least the boyfriend is out of the picture so she can focus on getting her life back to some sort of normalcy. We'll keep everything low-key for a little while longer. Maybe in a day or so, Faith will be up to a discussion or making a call."

"Did you hear the ghost baby?" Connie asked, "after Faith's baby was born?"

Brooke cringed when she saw Nancy's eyes widen.

"We have a ghost baby in the house," Brooke explained. "It used to cry every day at ten in the morning but since we had a few guests stay here last weekend, the baby has been more vocal. Cries more often."

"Do you know anything about this baby?" Nancy asked. "How it died?"

"No. Only thing we know is *Victory Hill* was an orphanage before my family bought it. Then it was shut down in nineteen fifteen. The guests that were here last weekend may have had family that stayed in the orphanage. Her grandmother was a twin and the other twin supposedly died. We're still researching it."

"I think I remember reading an article about the orphanage," Nancy remarked. "Something about a murder?"

"Yes, the minister that ran the orphanage supposedly abused the girls. Just so happens the uncle of the lady that was here served time for murder. We're trying to verify the murder took place here. Regardless, we have a baby ghost here and no idea where he or she might be buried."

"You know," Connie refilled everyone's wine glasses. "I happened to be in my room one morning when it cried. I know it's crazy, but it did seem like it was a little louder in my room – you know like hearing a signal from a metal detector. How it's louder the closer you are to the object." Connie looked at Brooke. "You've seen the little girl outside the root cellar door. And the root cellar is near my room."

"Another ghost?" Nancy exclaimed.

Brooke shook her head. "Right? It's like suddenly, they're coming out of the woodworks."

"What I'm trying to say is maybe the baby is buried in the root cellar," Connie said. "I just don't understand why though."

"Well, hospitals didn't really get started until the nineteen twenties." Nancy explained. "Up until then they didn't even have doctors delivering babies."

"Yeah, most were done by midwives or mothers of the mothers," Levi added. "I read of a woman who had fourteen children and twelve of them were delivered by her mother. She delivered the last two in the hospital and hated it. This was before anesthesia and epidurals. Back then, women just preferred having their babies in the homes." He shrugged a shoulder. "Riskier, but the way things were done."

"With the added risk of hemorrhaging, and all the secrecy, you might find more than babies buried there. Some of the girls might not have survived the childbirth. Lots of vital records noted childbed fever as the cause of death back then."

"But how did they get away with it?" Kristina complained.

"If this minister was supposedly abusing the girls," Nancy explained, "they probably kept the girls secluded, isolated so people in town never knew about the babies."

Kristina thought of Bobby Turner, Monica and Sidney Warren. "Who knows, he may have been selling the babies."

"Whatever the circumstances, I don't want to publicize things right now," Brooke stated. "At least not until we know for sure."

"Cameron and I started clearing the root cellar the other day, I'll give it another check. I've also studied anthropology, participated in a dig, know a little of what to do if we find something."

"What about metal detectors?" Connie asked.

Levi shook his head. "Wouldn't detect much if they are babies. Now, if it were an older person, say someone who had a gold tooth filing or hip surgery with nuts and bolts, it might set off a signal. We're just going to have to take our time, start scraping away and see what we find."

*B*rooke collapsed across her bed. It had been almost twenty-four hours since she'd slept so soundly in Levi's arms then been awakened by the flickering lights, attempted kidnapping, arrests, and Faith's labor.

She was exhausted.

Nancy said she would be back in the morning to help Faith prepare for the doctor's visit, then take her for the checkup.

Seconds after her head hit the pillow, Brooke was fast asleep. She didn't feel the brush of air across her forehead, hear the ghost baby cry and be consoled by Chelsea's lullaby.

Hours later, Brooke turned her head side to side, her body stiffening and shaking as if in pain.

"It hurts," she murmured, "Mamie, it hurts so much."

"Don't you fret, Miss Chelsea, you're going to be okay. You did this once; you can do it again. It won't be much longer now."

Brooke felt a wet cloth on her forehead, turned her head to see Mamie's round ebony face, gazed into concerned brown eyes.

"I want it out of my body," she shouted, "I can't stand it anymore. I want it gone."

Brooke's body arched up as if overcome with a convulsion. "Oh," she bellowed a long, drawn-out scream, felt as if something had been ripped from her body.

Brooke heard a baby cry.

"It's a girl, Miss Chelsea, it's a beautiful baby girl."

She looked over, watched Mamie wrap the baby in a linen cloth.

"Take her away," Brooke heard herself order. "She's a devil-child. I don't want it near me."

"But she needs to nurse," Mamie begged.

"I don't care. I don't want that devil-child near me again.

Brooke's eyes flew open, she stared up at the ceiling.

What had just happened? She wondered. Was Faith's baby so much on her mind, she dreamed she had one?

Then she recalled the dream. The words that came out of her mouth but were not her words. The woman, Mamie – was she a servant – trying to get her to nurse the baby.

Did Chelsea have a second child?

Brooke grabbed her cell phone. It might be six in the morning, but she was sure Cilla was up.

"How did you do it?" Brooke demanded as soon as Cilla answered the phone.

"Do what?"

"Chelsea's dreams? How did you handle them?"

"Are you having them?"

"Yes, I just had one. Apparently, Chelsea had another baby. Didn't you dream of Richard's birth? Did you feel everything?"

"Oh, my. I believe I had my dream in the back of Jake's SUV, so I was already uncomfortable. We were stuck in traffic and had pulled over to rest. Whenever I had the dreams, it was like I was Chelsea. She had hallucinated, saw James, wanted him there. I remember feeling upset and the pain from the delivery woke me up."

"You felt the pain too?"

"Oh, yes. You're saying Chelsea had another baby?"

"Yes, it was so vivid. Didn't you say a Union soldier tried to rape her?"

"Yes, but the doctor saved her. I remember him ordering the men to stay away from her. He made her assist him with the patients. But Chelsea and James had only the one child – Richard."

"Well, I just dreamed she had another. A girl. And she didn't want to have anything to do with it. Did she have a servant named Mamie?"

"Yes. Two servants – Mamie and Violet. They were with her the whole time. Took care of her after James left for war. Hid in the root cellar with her. I believe the doctor made them cook for the patients."

"Well, Mamie delivered the baby. I could see her so vividly. I don't know what she did with the baby, I was so shocked to have experienced the delivery. Maybe I have babies on my mind because Faith just had her baby"

"Faith had her baby. That's wonderful. What did she have?"

"A boy. A lot of excitement in this house the past two days but that's another long story for another time. I don't know what to think about this dream. Do you suppose Chelsea might have decided now was the time to drop another little secret in our laps?"

"We need to talk to Piper," Cilla suggested. "See if she knows anything about another baby."

CHAPTER TWENTY

Brooke studied her phone for the third time, saw she had no new text messages. She'd texted Piper as soon as she finished her call with Cilla but that was three hours ago.

She'd been up since the crack of dawn thanks to the dream about Chelsea's second baby. Wondered if the ghost baby could be Chelsea's second baby but when she recalled how Chelsea often hummed a lullaby for the ghost baby, quickly discredited that idea. It was obvious Chelsea had no feelings, attachment or love for the baby she'd carried full term.

So, who was ghost baby's mother?

The little girl outside the root cellar flickered through her thoughts. Too young to be the mother Brooke decided, but where did the little girl fit into the scheme of things?

And what happened to Chelsea's baby girl? Did she survive? Did Mamie take care of her? Was she left on someone's doorstep?

Is she the little girl she keeps seeing outside the root cellar?

So many questions, so many ghosts!

Brooke peeked into *Chelsea's Room* wondered if she would once again find Chelsea sitting at her desk composing another letter to James.

And where were these letters? She pondered.

Brooke studied the room. After the fiasco with the attempted kidnapping, then Faith's labor and delivery, today had been declared another major clean-up day. Connie was working on the kitchen and downstairs, Kristina the bedrooms at the other end of the hall.

She had already cleaned *William and Elsie's Room* with a fine-toothed comb. Wanted no evidence of the Warren couple in her B&B.

At least the Armstrong's weren't messy guests, she thought as she studied their room. Gathered the sheets and towels, carried them to the door.

She had just changed the bed and was getting ready to clean the bathroom when her cell phone chimed.

"Congratulations on the baby boy," Piper exclaimed first thing.

Brooke laughed. "Thanks. Mom and baby are doing great and Nancy Hughes, the nurse slash midwife is coming by later this morning to take them for an official checkup with the doctor."

"Heard you had a little excitement as well?"

Brooke sat on the commode, took a couple minutes to update Piper on the attempted kidnapping.

"And then you had your own dream baby. Cilla says she appreciates passing those dreams on to you."

"Yup," Brooke sighed. "Weird. I don't know how Cilla got through it. But at least the dreams have offered answers. We've been able to piecemeal all Chelsea and James went through."

"I hadn't forgotten you. And I didn't mean to put you off after your text, but I wanted to finish my research. I also wanted to talk some more with Anna; just got off the phone with her.

"Managed to find a couple articles about Henry Cooke and his murder trial. Not a lot though. Believe it or not, the articles were in your local paper which I found online. All this took place during the First World War so the major articles were about the war. What I found was in the community columns of the smaller local newspapers. Back then the papers were more than just about the news. It was how everyone kept up with their neighbors. There were columns for the different towns and localities written by ladies, and men, that talked about people visiting friends and family in other towns, going to church, who was sick, marriages, births of babies, stuff like that.

"There was mention of the minister's body being found on the front lawn of the orphanage. Then I stumbled upon a brief article about the case. Seems some of the other children witnessed a fight and identified Henry Cooke as the one that murdered the minister but nothing else. I got the feeling there was a shroud of secrecy over everything."

"The poor children probably described what they saw," Brooke said, "not realizing the extent of what the man was doing to them and how Henry Cooke had done them a favor."

"Probably," Piper agreed. "Because there was no real evidence other than the body, and word of the children, they had a brief jury trial that lasted one day. It took the jury two hours to find him guilty. Then they apparently, shipped him off to the state penitentiary in Richmond.

"I kept looking and found mention in another issue that after the trial, some of the smaller children were taken in by families in the community. One family took five brothers and sisters, ages three to twelve."

"Seems such a shame that Henry Cooke had to suffer when the minister was so cruel, almost deserved it."

"Yeah, but now we know that Henry and Grace Cooke were at the orphanage before it was *Victory Hill*."

"So, Anna wasn't mistaken about the special feelings she experienced."

"No, she almost seemed relieved when I shared what I'd found."

"Now, we need to determine where the baby ghost is buried and if it was a twin to Anna's grandmother. Levi and I are going to check the root cellar today."

*L*evi once again experienced the chill of the underground room as he stepped down the three steps onto the dirt floor. He'd left the doors open to allow the musty air out, fresh air in, felt the moth bump against his arm as it was drawn to the light.

He shook his head at the clutter.

He and Cameron had moved the bulk of the lumber, tools, equipment to the barn but there were still wood shelves filled with bottles, jars of nails, cans of paint, boxes filled to the rim stacked on top of each other or scattered about.

He scuffed the dirt floor with his boot, reached for the trowel he had left on the shelves. Leaned down to scrape away the soil to test the hardness, brushed it between his fingers to test the dryness.

He glanced over his shoulder when a shadow fell across the floor.

Brooke peeked inside, wondered what she would see. Found modern-day clutter rather than antique jars of canned vegetables and fruit, crates of wine.

"Just heard from Piper," she accepted Levi's hand as he stood, helped her down the steps. "Looks like Henry and Grace Cooke were here when it was the orphanage. She found a short article about the murder. Trial took less than a day, jury less than two hours. Piper talked to Anna who is somewhat relieved to have a little closure. Now we just need to prove the baby or babies are buried here and that one of them was a twin to Anna's grandmother."

"Like I said, if babies are buried here, it's going to be slow going."

"I realize that. A little at a time, whenever we can. That's all we can do."

They shifted and stacked boxes, sectioned off an area closer to the back of the cellar, where the ceiling was lower.

It was dark. Levi had brought an extension work light, plugged it into an outside outlet next to the laundry room door, carried it as far inside as it would go, and suspended it from a nail he'd hammered into a floor joist.

"Can't imagine that we will find any tiny objects so no reason to bring in a sifter," Levi commented as he reached for his bucket of tools. "But we might need a wheelbarrow before long."

Brooke studied the contents of the bucket — small pick, trowel, old paint brush, straws, dustpan — as he removed them. He handed her the older trowel. "Cameron and I found this the first time we came in here. It belonged to your grandfather. I brought my own but thought you might want to use his."

Brooke smiled, brushed her fingers lovingly across the flat surface of the triangular blade.

Levi gently tapped the dirt in several places with the pick. "We're going to start slow. You start on that side, I'll start here. Just take the trowel, scrape it through the soil, work it loose. If it looks like we've found something, we'll take the paint brush to sift the dirt aside. Just take it nice and easy."

Brooke got on her knees, put on her gloves, began brushing dirt aside.

"I had a strange dream this morning," she said as she nudged the trowel through the dirt. "I dreamed Chelsea had a little girl." She peeked over at him to gauge his reaction. "Do you know anything about her having another child?"

Levi sat back on his heels as if giving it some thought. "To my knowledge, she and James had only the one child, Richard."

"Well, I dreamed she had another. A girl."

"Maybe you had Faith's baby on your mind."

"Nope. I pretty much felt every contraction, the delivery, heard Mamie pleading with her to nurse the baby but Chelsea wouldn't have anything to do with it. Called it a devil-child."

"Nothing else?"

Brooke nodded her head. "That was enough. Not the best way to wake up to a new day."

They continued to work in silence.

"If we find something, how is it going to help us. I mean," she paused to look over at him, "suppose we find bones. What happens then?"

"We send it off, have a familial DNA test done."

"Familial, as in family?"

Levi nodded. "It's new. They match the DNA with potential relatives to make a connection."

"I know they've used it to solve a lot of cold cases."

"Yes. Michelle McNamara advocated for it when she was trying to discover the identity of the *Golden State Killer*.

"She was a writer that specialized in unsolved crimes and was working on a book about unsolved rapes and murders in California in the seventies and eighties. This guy would break into people's homes while they were sleeping, tie the man up, make him watch while he raped the wife. Did that to over fifty couples. Then he began killing them. He got away with it for so long in the beginning because he moved around. Some occurred in Northern Californa, some in Southern California, the police never saw a correlation. But when he started killing them, and they started collecting DNA and evidence, they began to find similarities. Michelle nicknamed him the *Golden State Killer* and worked with the detectives while she researched and wrote the book about him.

"Unfortunately, she died in 2016 but they caught him two years after her death."

"They caught him," Brooke asked, mesmerized in the story.

Levi nodded his head as he applied the pick to a couple more spots.

"Turned out he was a policeman that had been fired early in his career for shoplifting a can of dog repellant and a hammer."

"A policeman," Brooke exclaimed. "Shoplifting?"

"They think he didn't contest the firing because that would have brought attention to him. I guess he was buying the dog repellant because his next victim had a dog, the hammer in case he needed to overpower the husband. Anyway, he moved away, continued to steal, rape and kill for the next twenty, thirty years."

"How do you know all this?" Brooke had stopped digging. Thought of how much he was like Jeremy.

Levi shrugged a shoulder. "I read a lot. It's what I enjoy.

"After Michelle McNamara's death, they decided to reopen the case, uploaded his DNA profile into *GEDmatch*, a national database. Apparently, they found some connections to distant relatives and through a process of elimination with places of residence, family dynamics, employment, they narrowed it down to him. Arrested him in twenty eighteen. He later confessed to other burglaries and rapes. They tried him and he's now in prison for life."

"So, if we find something, we could have it processed through this *GEDmatch*?"

"That, or we could just compare it to some specific DNA samples."

"Like Anna Marshall's because of her backstory?"

"Mm-hmm. Maybe me, being a Donovan descendant."

"But all this happened after your family sold the home."

"True, but you never know."

"What about Cilla? Chelsea was one of her ancestors. We might even find this baby girl Chelsea supposedly had."

"That too. We'll have to see what we find."

They worked for an hour, but strained backs, aching knees and work dictated that they take a break.

"Tomorrow I'll bring my knee pads," Levi suggested as he closed and locked the doors. "Should make it easier. Probably be too big for you, though."

"Levi," she leaned against the brick wall, gave her back a break, "are we wasting time? Do you really think there might be babies buried here?"

"Won't know till we check some." He leaned down, brushed her lips lightly with his. "If you get discouraged, I can handle it. This is what I enjoy. Archeology. Genealogy. I know," he put his hands up backed away when Brooke opened her mouth. "We have a renovation deadline. We'll just take our time."

Levi also had another project to get finished. Brooke's birthday was in three days.

CHAPTER TWENTY-ONE

Levi scraped a hand through his hair, rubbed the back of his neck as he paced from the restaurant kitchen's back door to the drink station. How should he do this, he wondered.

He looked up, opened his mouth to speak when Brooke wandered in with a tray of dirty dishes. Deposited them on the counter at the sink next to the commercial dishwasher.

She gave him a curious look as if to say, *shouldn't you be at work somewhere else.*

Like I'm not working my ass off as it is, he brooded. Staying two steps ahead of the electrician and plumber who were finally done; the barn project; digging and sifting through two more feet in the root cellar which she seemed to have forgotten about. With a newborn baby in the house, he'd put his part of the attic renovations on hold, but now that the basics were done, he planned to start first thing Monday morning – baby or no baby.

Brooke slid him a guarded look when she circled back to the main dining room only to reappear minutes later at the drink station.

Levi marched over to shut the swinging door. Time like this, a man needed a little privacy. He caught Finn's curious look at his wife. Great, he sighed, they're probably wondering the same thing.

Levi cleared his throat. "I want to marry your daughter," he blurted out.

Finn almost dropped the tongs as he prepared to turn the chicken breast on the grill. Didn't see that one coming, he thought to himself. Eyebrows raised, he paused, rested the tongs on the edge of the grill as he studied the boy who had started walking back and forth again. Wondered if Levi knew what he was taking on.

"She's aggravating, bossy, annoying, confusing, infuriating..."

Maybe he did, Finn decided. "Okay," he answered, gave his wife a lopsided grin. God help him if he could live with a woman with those qualities. He'd lived with one for over thirty years.

"She erupts at the drop of a hat, badgers you till she gets her way, then never seems to appreciate anything I do," Levi continued as if trying to convince himself.

"Okay," Finn repeated.

"And if that weren't enough – "

"Levi," Finn interrupted him. "I said OKAY. You have my blessing. Much as I love my daughter, believe me, you're going to need a lot more than my blessing."

Levi turned to thank him, amazed it had been so easy when a squeal sounded from the swinging doors.

Everyone looked over to see Brooke swaying backwards through the swinging door from the dining area. Her arms full of dirty dishes were raised as she tried to keep her balance and not drop the dishes.

Levi jumped to catch her under her arms before she fell on her backside; Rita raced over to catch the dishes before they crashed on the floor.

"What happened to that door?" Brooke barked as she stepped away from Levi to right herself. "I almost broke my neck."

Anger swelled up in him as Levi stared down at her in dumbfounded fury.

"You complain when the door sticks, you complain when the door is fixed," he griped.

"The least you could have done was tell someone you fixed the blooming door." Brooke fisted her hands at her waist, gave him a frosty look. "I almost dropped all the dishes."

"If you wouldn't be in a such a hurry all the time, you might've noticed," Levi argued. Mirroring her stance, he hovered over her, almost nose to nose.

Undaunted, Brooke pointed to the swinging door. "Do you know how many times I've had to push that door open? If you'd just said something, I would've been more cautious."

Levi stared into her blazing squinted eyes. Did I just ask this woman's father if I could marry her, he pondered in disbelief.

"That's it," he threw his hands up in frustration, bent to toss Brooke over his shoulder, turned to Angelina and Finn. "I have honest intentions where your daughter is concerned, believe me, and we will finish our conversation, but there are times when she just tests my patience. I really need to handle this first."

Angelina's amused eyes watched Levi stalk past them with her angry daughter pounding his backside. Young love, she chuckled to herself. They had so much to look forward to. She looked over at Finn who was shaking his head, as he plated the butterflied chicken breast. "You never did that with me."

"You always seem to have a knife in your hand," he called over his shoulder.

Levi kicked the screen door open, continued to the small patio where he set her on her feet.

Brooke tossed her braid over her shoulder as she braced herself, ready for battle.

"You don't ever seem to appreciate anything."

Brooke stared up at him noted his flattened mouth, blazing eyes. She'd never seen him so angry. It occurred to her maybe she'd been a little rash in her reaction. What was wrong with her?

She'd missed him, that's what. She hadn't seen him since their dig in the root cellar two days ago. She'd heard him going up and down the attic stairs or outside her bedroom when she awoke in the mornings, but he never ventured downstairs for a snack or to follow her from room to room to talk like he used too. And in the evenings, it was like he disappeared.

Her own nerves seemed more intense, uptight this past week. With the attempted kidnapping, birth of the baby, realization that the ghost baby might be a relative to Anna Marshall and buried in the root cellar, and that Chelsea had a second child. What else could happen? How had things gotten so crazy?

She worried she may have pushed Levi too far with her latest temper tantrum. She should have sought him out more. The electrician's and plumber's trucks had been here for two days, but she'd been so busy she'd never ventured up the steps to check on the progress of the renovations or tried to sneak a peek into her own bathroom.

"I fixed that door for you so it wouldn't wear you out." He paced five steps away. "I put that damn herb rack on the porch, so you'd have your herbs handy to the kitchen," he stated as he returned to glare down at her, his muscles tense.

Brooke was silent, decided to let him vent. Understood his anger and frustration.

"I'm building" he almost blurted out about the glass greenhouse but caught himself as he turned abruptly, brushed his hands through his hair then down his face as he stared out at the garden.

Brooke stepped behind him, wrapped her arms around his waist, held on tight as she rested her cheek against his back. "I *do* appreciate you. So much it scares me."

She tightened her arms again and they both stood silent, willing their frantic hearts to calm.

She stepped around to face him, stared up at his frustrated expression. Cupped his face in her hands.

"I do care," she kissed his lips lightly, then wrapped her arms around his neck, pulled him down to kiss him with a passion that took his breath away.

Cameron smiled as he headed down the back drive on his way home. He'd just left Kristina at the B&B after giving her a tour of his office and introducing her to his two patients – an unhappy black lab named Jack who'd just been neutered and Jill, a tired golden lab who'd delivered five pups that morning. Both belonged to a college friend who decided seven dogs was his limit.

Kristina had been impressed with both the setup and patients and he hoped he'd finally convinced her to consider staying in Williamtown to help him in the office.

He saw the lights in the barn, detoured toward the rough wooden doors, decided to check things out. He heard the electric nail gun, figured Levi was making progress with his project.

It was a big open room on a concrete slab with vacant horse stalls and a chicken pen on one side, tackle rooms and more stalls on the other. His grandfather's old tractor was parked in the far corner, a more modern one in front of it. A wooden ladder led up to a hay loft, that now held plastic storage bins of Christmas decorations. Metal ladders, shovels, pitchforks, and other farm tools hung from hooks on the walls.

He looked to his left, saw that Levi had stored the equipment and boxes of building supplies from the root cellar in one of the tackle rooms.

Two bare light bulbs were suspended from the rafters and an additional extension bulb hung over the project Levi was building.

Various sizes of windows – small square windows, large rectangular windows, some with one big pane, most with four divided panes – were spread through the big open room. Now that he studied them, Cameron began to see a pattern to the layout, figured Levi had determined the best pattern to accommodate all of them on the three walls of windows. An old door was leaning against the wall, four smaller panes on either side.

Levi stood atop the hay trailer beside a stick building with four corner studs nailed to a square frame mounted on wheels.

Cameron decided he had to give Levi credit for his creativity.

"You're burning the candle at both ends, aren't you? The attic during the day, here at night?"

Levi lined a window with a corner stud. "Better than arguing with your sister."

Cameron chuckled. "Heard about the swinging door."

Levi smiled, recalling the makeup kiss. Wondered if Finn mentioned his request for Brooke's hand in marriage.

"Aren't those two-by-four studs from the root cellar," Cameron observed.

"Yup." He nailed the window to the stud.

"These wheels look old."

"Found a bunch of rotting wheelbarrows when I moved the equipment from the root cellar in here. Added the wood to the wood pile at the fire pit, attached the wheels here. Will make it easy to move. Figure I'll drive the trailer over to the garden, roll it off and into place. Will you be available to help?"

Possessed by Love

"Sure. Given any thought to where you're going to put this thing?" Cameron held another window so Levi could nail it in place.

"Planning to do that before hitting the sack tonight."

Later that evening, Angelina and Finn wandered toward their home. Less than a mile down the back drive toward town, past the gardens and through the woods, they always enjoyed the transition from the hectic workday in the restaurant to the quiet of their home.

Sometimes they talked about the day – crazy customers, specials for tomorrow, supplies that needed replenishing. Sometimes they said nothing at all.

Finn reached for his wife's hand, tucked it under his arm. "Were you surprised with Levi this evening? Asking to marry our daughter?"

"Nope," Angelina responded, happy that her daughter had found someone that loved her. "They've been nipping at each other since the day they met."

They looked over, saw Levi wandering the garden, head down, hands in his pockets.

Finn chuckled. "There's the poor boy now. Probably having second thoughts. Wondering what he's about to get himself into. I don't know what they said to each other outside, but they obviously ironed out their differences. Brooke was a different person when she came back in."

Angelina smiled up at her husband. "He loves her. And will be a good husband to her." She nudged him with her shoulder. "Has a lot of patience; like someone else I know."

Finn gave her a lopsided grin. "He's going to need it." His eyes gleamed as he gave her hair a quick look. "Takes a lot of patience to be able to live with a redhead."

He swooped down to kiss her when she would have made a comment.

"Did you notice how protective Cameron was of Kristina the other night?" Angelina rested her head on her husband's shoulder when they started walking again. Approached the bridge her father had built over the creek that ran along the back edge of the property.

The path ended at a Y. Trailed to her parents' house on the left, hers and Finn's house on the right. She cast a quick look to be sure her mother had left the small lamp by the living room window on, their sign that she was settled in bed.

"Um hmm," Finn answered. "They seem to be spending a lot of evenings in the gazebo."

"That worries me. She's obviously running away from problems."

"He's a big boy." He recalled seeing Cameron and Kristina at the back door of the B&B when he'd carried some trash out to the barrel.

"But he's just getting over Lisa. I'd hate to see him hurt again."

"Like I said, he's a big boy. Right now," Finn leaned down, tossed his surprised wife over his shoulder as they entered the house, "I've got other things on my mind."

*B*rooke wasn't far behind her parents leaving the restaurant. She looked over to see Levi walking in the garden. Wondered what he was doing out there so late.

"What are you doing out here?" She called out to him.

Levi jumped, he was so intent on studying the lay of the land, trying to decide where to put the glass greenhouse, he never heard her approach. Now, he had to come up with a reason why he would be walking out in the garden at nine in the evening.

Possessed by Love

"Look up," he raised a hand to the clear night, stars shining, full moon glowing. He reached for her hand. "Too tired for a walk with me?"

Yes, she was tired, but the sight of him buoyed her spirits. She walked into his arms and smiled up at him.

"Thank you for fixing the swinging door," she kissed one cheek. "And the herb rack," she kissed the other cheek.

Levi grinned, rested his forehead to hers. "You're pretty generous with the thank you kisses."

"Thought maybe I'd show you," she took his hand, led him away from the house toward the tall weeping willow midway down the back lawn.

She brushed the long branches aside and Levi was surprised how lush the grass was at the base of the tree. Almost as lush and thick as a putting green.

Brooke kicked off her shoes, reached for her hair, began unbraiding it.

"Cameron and Jeremy used to play here as kids. This was their fort. Just like they tried to scare me in my castle in the attic, I would try to scare them here."

She threw her head back.

"They always looked for me to come down from the house," she continued as she threaded fingers through her hair, let it hang loosely down her back.

"One time," Levi's eyes followed her fingers as they unbuttoned her blouse, "I rode my bike down the back drive."

His body came to attention when she removed her blouse, dropped it at her feet. He swallowed when she unhooked the front clasp of her bra, added it to the shirt.

"I attacked from behind."

Levi was grateful that the moon offered enough light to appreciate her perky breasts as she unzipped and stepped out of her khaki pants and panties.

"Got them good," she brushed her hands through her hair as she lay on the lush grass, extended her arms, inviting him to join her.

"Got me good too," Levi responded as he quickly undressed.

CHAPTER TWENTY-TWO

Levi was exhausted. It was Brooke's birthday and he'd been up until two in the morning putting the finishing touches on the greenhouse. Touching up the interior cabinet, painting the lumber for the shelves, installing the hardware on the door.

Cameron had been a big help, spent a good portion of his Sunday afternoon holding the windows in place so he could connect them to each other. Levi stood back, pleased with the result. He hoped Brooke would like it.

He was surprised how easily it came together considering it was such a mixture of items he had found around the property. Nothing like refurbishing an assortment of windows of all shapes and sizes, overhauling the legs of a discarded dining room table, renewing an old cabinet.

He hoped the attic would be the same. At least the electrical and plumbing work was done. The heating and air guy would be upgrading the system, adding the attic, installing the ductwork today. After that, he would be free to do what he did best. Bring the attic back to life.

He'd decided to put the greenhouse in line with the shed between the restaurant and B&B but closer to the gardens so every time Brooke looked out, she would see the weeping willow tree.

His body still tingled two days later; knew he would never be able to look at that tree the same again.

He would never forget how Brooke had so nonchalantly stripped, offered herself to him. How her pale skin almost glowed in the moon's brightness that filtered through the long overhanging branches. And later how she'd straddled him, tossing her head back, threading her hands through her long flaming mane, her arms stretched above her head as she rode him, drove them both as if galloping up the hill over the fence of desire before collapsing on him.

They had laid on the lush grass, stared at the back of the B&B each of them holding their breath when they thought they caught a glimmer of Chelsea staring at them from an attic window.

"Do you see her," Brooke had asked in awe.

He recalled looking over and shivering, certain he felt the gaze of his multiple times great grandmother on them.

Levi shook his head as he opened the Dutch door to the kitchen. Right now, he needed to keep Brooke busy so he could put the greenhouse in place.

"You need to pick the color for the honeymoon suite," he stated as he grabbed a muffin from the tin.

"White," Brooke answered, unloading the dishwasher.

"Do you know how many shades of white there are? Twelve."

"I want white. Bright white."

"I know if I pick a color, you'll want something else. You need to pick it."

"Levi, I don't have time"

He tossed three brochures on the counter. Added five narrow strips, each strip with three different shades of white.

"There's even an ethereal white."

"You're kidding, right?"

"Nope," he opened the brochure, pointed to page two. "And on the next page you have pure white, even divine white."

He strolled to the door, called over his shoulder, "Pick the color and get back to me."

*B*rooke ignored Jeremy as she passed through the restaurant kitchen later that evening headed toward the back door. Not even Jeremy took the time to wish her a happy birthday, she fumed. Just focused on cleaning the grill in preparation for closing.

Wait till he turns twenty-five.

No one had said anything all day. All. Day. Not even Connie. She'd simply asked her which room she wanted to clean, then disappeared.

Right before she was going to announce she might take the day off.

Her parents were busy all day but the icing on the cake was when her grandmother called to see if she could come to work earlier. She didn't know why; they were no busier than usual.

Brooke stepped outside turned toward the B&B, figured no one could stop her from having a long luxurious bubble bath. In fact, she knew *Chelsea's Room* was vacant, she just might take a long soak in the clawfoot tub she'd worked so hard to refurbish.

She stopped when she found her parents and grandmother sitting around the table on the patio.

"Come join us," Angelina held a glass of wine out to Brooke. "Happy birthday," she added when Brooke sat in a chair.

"You mean you remembered?" Brooke almost wept.

"Of course, I remembered. You're my only daughter. A mother never forgets her child's birthday."

"Came two weeks early in fact," Finn recalled.

Brooke heard the back door to the B&B open, watched Cameron, Kristina, Connie and Faith walk their way. Faith carried the baby tucked in the split oak basket Levi had set on the bottom shelf of the herb rack. It was a perfect fit for the newborn cocooned within the soft blankets.

Jeremy stepped out of the kitchen, locked the door behind him. He headed toward the patio, nabbed a beer out of the cooler.

"Happy birthday," he gave her a kiss on the cheek.

Only person missing was Levi, Brooke thought.

"I wondered. No one said anything. Not even you Gran."

Rita chuckled. "Believe me, it was hard. And this year it's special."

"Yeah?" Brooke wondered. "Twenty-five? Quarter of a century?"

Gran winked. "I'll be three quarters of a century in a few weeks."

"No cake? No ice cream?" Brooke feigned disappointment.

"That and more," Angelina raised her glass in the direction of the gardens.

Brooke looked over to see a tiny glass house maybe six feet square, settled on the lawn twenty yards away. Three of the walls were made of a hodgepodge of windows with three square windows on each side of a tall pane glass door for the entrance. Atop the little house was a small A-roof made of connected windows to allow the sun inside. A square copula in the center of the roof was made of windows on two sides, solid panes on the other two sides.

All the wood was painted white which gave it a surreal look beneath the full moon.

As she approached the edifice, Levi stepped from the shadows of the tree, to open the door. She stepped over a ledge onto the grass and dirt floor. Inside was a long counter on the left for workspace supported on what appeared to be legs of a discarded dining table. Two big tubs rested on another discarded table frame on the back wall. On the right side was an old cabinet with a drawer for her gardening tools, storage space for supplies.

Clay pots lined wood shelves – high on the two sides, lower on the back – attached to block supports strategically mounted where window frames connected. Candles glowed everywhere – skinny ones on the cake, pillar ones of varying height scattered along the shelves.

Brooke could see the rows of flowers in the garden beyond gleaming under the moon's rays. Saw the weeping willow tree where she and Levi had made love two nights earlier.

"You can use the tubs for fill dirt." Levi said behind her. "And the extra pots? For the tulips for Piper's wedding."

"You did this?" She turned, gaped up at him.

He nodded.

"When? You've been working full steam."

He shrugged a shoulder. "When you said you wanted a greenhouse, I remembered a blog I'd read. I hit gold that day I went to Richmond to get the replacement windows for the bedrooms. Steve was glad to see me drive away. It was a matter of designing and juggling the windows."

"It's beautiful."

"It's set on wheels so you can move it if you want. Find the best spot for sun."

Everyone wandered over. It wasn't big enough for more than two people inside, but the windows made it easy to peer inside from all sides.

"That's why we needed you to work in the restaurant this afternoon," Rita apologized. "So, Levi and Cameron could bring it up from the barn."

"You were in on it too?" Brooke turned to her brother.

"Just the moving part. And maybe I held a few windows in place," he added.

"I think it's adorable," Connie gushed as she pulled Brooke out, stepped inside to grab the glowing birthday cake. "We'll have to share the cake around the patio though."

"Thank you," Brooke grabbed Levi's hand as everyone headed back to the patio. She leaned in to kiss him.

As she turned to join the rest of her family, she saw the little girl at the root cellar.

*H*e was wearing toffee brown wool pants, white silk shirt with full sleeves. She wore the long-sleeved cornflower blue dress with the fitted bodice that accentuated her narrow waist. He stood tall and stern; she small and dainty. Situated slightly behind her, his right hand rested on her arm, his left hand was just visible at her waist.

They both tried to maintain their smiles while his eyes had a haunted look, tears shimmered in hers.

They stood for a long time while the artist chatted, trying to cheer them, dispel the gloom. Chelsea was upset because she knew James would be leaving the next week for war. James was concerned about what to expect.

Suddenly things seemed to fast forward and Chelsea's hand was pulling back the cloth that covered the finished portrait.

Brooke and Levi opened their eyes at the same time, turned to look at one another.

"Did you "

"Yes." Levi grumbled. "They did it again. This is getting ridiculous." He jumped up, paced her bedroom in the waxen glow of the moon.

Brooke sat up, wrapped her arms around her knees. "Were they having a portrait done?"

They both jumped when the bedroom lamp flickered on then off.

"First the dream. Now this. Is she trying to tell us something?"

The lamp flickered again.

Brooke lay back, lifted the sheet to invite Levi back to bed.

"I've been over every square inch of this house in my lifetime," Brooke stated. "I have no recollection of any portrait. In fact," she lay her head on his shoulder, "I don't even recall finding anything that would have belonged to your family here. Well, except for the dress, book and gun. They were hidden.

"Could George, James' brother have taken it? Do you recall seeing it among any of your ancestral paintings? Do you even have anything that might have belonged to James and Chelsea?"

"Don't recall anything but will have to check with my mother."

"Levi, these dreams are scaring me, I'm almost afraid to sleep any more. I don't know how Cilla managed it."

"Just close your eyes," Levi skimmed a finger up and down her arm. "Try to put it out of your mind. We can't let it consume us."

"But it's so hard," she sighed as she closed her eyes. "She won't let us."

Levi stared at the ceiling, listened for her breathing to settle. Worried his multiple times great grandmother's mystery would take its toll before they found answers. It was a long time before he finally closed his eyes.

*O*nce again, hours later when Brooke and Levi were both in a deep sleep, they didn't feel the brush of air as Chelsea stared down at them, tears streaming down her cheeks. She lovingly brushed both their heads. Soon...

Soon they would find her deepest darkest secret. Bring her peace.

CHAPTER TWENTY-THREE

Kristina hummed as she set the vase with two fresh Magnolia blooms on the pedestal table in *Edwin and Wilma's Room*. She had put a smaller arrangement in the bathroom, hung fresh towels on the racks. She turned to brush a hand across the bedspread, gave the room one last check before returning to the lobby.

Connie had the day off and since they had only one couple checking in later that afternoon, Kristina offered to watch the B&B for Brooke. Levi was working upstairs in the attic; Faith was with the baby, so it wasn't like she was alone in the house.

Kristina was pretty sure she just heard the chime of the lobby door so maybe the couple had arrived early.

After Bobby Turner, Monica and Sidney Warren had tried to kidnap Faith, then Faith had the baby, Levi and Cameron insisted the alarm system be installed. Now, the door chimed whenever anyone entered the lobby or back door of the B&B.

They had also installed panic buttons – in the lobby next to the registration desk and kitchen on the underside of the bar – where Brooke or Connie could alert the restaurant if they had an issue.

Kristina smiled as she headed down the hall toward the front stairs and lobby. It occurred to her that for the first time in a long, long time, she was happy. Relaxed. Looking forward to another day. She'd been at the B&B for two weeks and two days and found herself worrying less and less about Gary. Chuck had emailed to say Gary never responded to his email about a divorce so he had proceeded with the paperwork and Gary should have received the papers by now.

She hoped Gary was reconciled to the fact she no longer wanted to be married to him and would let her go.

She enjoyed helping Brooke with the B&B but after two weeks, she needed to be making other living arrangements. Cameron has been so considerate, attentive and patient; she was seriously considering Cameron's job offer.

Faith had also started making plans and called her mother over the weekend. It had been a tearful conversation as her mother realized she had misjudged her daughter, kicked the boyfriend out of the house and was coming tomorrow to meet her grandson who would be one week old. If all went well, Faith hoped to return home with her mother and finish out the school year.

Kristina paused at the top of the stairs, listened to the quiet. I know I heard the door chime, she thought to herself.

"Hello," she called out, figured it she was mistaken, no one would answer.

When the ghost baby answered, she looked at the clock at the bottom of the stairs and smiled when it chimed the tenth hour.

"I certainly doubt you and Chelsea had anything to do with that chime," she murmured softly to their spiritual residents.

"Hello, darlin'." Gary Powell stepped out of the living room, leaned on the door frame next to the antique registration desk.

Kristina's stomach lurched, tightened, felt as it if it was chained to a cinderblock that fell to her feet. She grasped hold of the banister as she tried to control the sudden shaking, held back a sudden frantic cry that had lodged in her throat. She didn't want him to know he still frightened her.

"Gary," she whispered to the ghost from her past.

"Thought you'd seen the last of me?" He laughed up at her, but his squared shoulders, tense body and tight eyes told Kristina otherwise.

She cast a frantic glance at the alarm's panic button inches from his hip, knew she had to somehow get to the one in the kitchen.

"How did you find me?" She slowly made her way down the remainder of the steps, kept her left shoulder close to the wall as she inched toward the dining room door.

"Wasn't hard. You should know by now I keep close tabs on what's mine."

"But didn't you get the divorce papers?"

"Like that's going to stop me," he mocked her, "you don't leave till I say you can leave."

When he pushed away from the door frame, Kristina turned and sprinted through the dining room toward the kitchen. She heard his heavy footsteps behind her, managed to step into the kitchen before he grabbed her arm and slapped her with the back of his hand. She felt the sting of his ring on her cheek as she stumbled backwards toward the bar.

With beads of sweat on her lip and forehead, knees shaking, she edged toward the panic button on the side of the bar. Flinched when he lunged, his hand raised for another strike. She managed to press the button as she fell into the corner between the refrigerator and stove.

"You thought I wouldn't know you had searched my desk?" He loomed over her. "Thought I wouldn't notice how things had been rearranged."

"Your desk?" She crawled past him toward the back door, reached for the door knob. "I've never been near your desk." She cried out, when he grabbed her hair, pulled her upright.

"You lie." He slapped her again.

She fell against the table, bounced toward the wall.

"You won't live to tell anyone about me."

*L*evi was pleased with the way things were progressing in the big room of the attic. He set the sheetrock in place on the half-wall between the two dormers, reached for the nail gun to attach it to the stud. Would get this sheetrock up, spackled and sanded, then he'd be ready to paint. Now that Brooke had picked the shade of white that pleased her.

The first two nails thudded in place, then the lights went out. It was overcast outside as thunderstorms were predicted for later that afternoon, so the attic was almost pitch black.

"What the hell?" The battery-operated nail gun might be charged but he couldn't see.

He debated the best way down. Both stairwells would be dark, but he was closer to the main part of the house. He realized he'd left his cell phone in his truck, so he didn't even have that as a flashlight. Doubted he could find the secret panel to the storage room above Brooke's loft in the dark.

He made his way to the front of the house. Stepped carefully down the stairs to the door to the second floor. Hoped there were no visitors today, he'd forgotten to check the register.

He inched the door open, listened to silence.

It was a little lighter on the second floor as he inched his way down the long hall toward *Harry and Rita's Room* and the stairwell to Brooke's loft. He would check the fuse box mounted in the laundry room – Connie's bedroom – of the back porch.

Faith answered his knock right away her eyes wide with concern. He looked past her, saw the door to the landing open.

"Is everything okay?"

She nodded quickly. "But I think somebody's in the house," she whispered. "I heard a man's voice. He was loud. And I think I just heard Kristina cry out."

Levi raced to the other door and listened, heard some rambling as well.

"Lock your doors. And call Brooke, get her to call nine-one-one. I'll go down and check."

"Be careful," Faith pleaded.

Levi slowly descended the back stairs, listening for any more voices.

Cameron studied the man sitting in a chair at the table in the courtyard. He was burly, too heavy to be angling the small café chair on the back legs.

The new alarm system was in place and there was no need to worry but after the attempted kidnapping, he was more suspicious. Something nagged at him.

He knew Connie was off and Kristina was manning the B&B by herself, but she always carried her phone, he was sure she would call if she had a problem.

He was about to suggest the guy move on when the guy looked his way, got up and headed for his car where he got inside but sat behind the wheel.

Cameron thought he'd seen that car in the parking lot another time.

Still feeling uneasy, he decided to call Kristina. When she didn't answer, he began to worry.

"Why are you doing this?" Kristina pleaded with trembling lips, tasted the acidic blood in her mouth. "I don't know anything."

"You lie," he yelled, his face red, nostrils flaring, spital flying from his mouth as he raised his hand again but turned in disgust when she flinched. "I should have taken care of you when I realized you snooped."

"But I didn't do anything," Kristina shouted. "I don't know what you're talking about." She took advantage of his back to her and jolted out of the kitchen. Almost made it to the door to the side porch next to the butler's quarters before he caught her, plowed a fist into her face.

"Did you think I wouldn't find you?" He loomed over her, breathed loudly.

"But how? We were so careful."

"Cameras, you bitch. They're everywhere. We tracked you at the bus station."

Gary grabbed a handful of her hair. "Did you really think a different hair color would trick me? We got you getting on the bus in town. Just a matter of checking the stops, asking a few questions. Got you going in the shopping mall, picked you up in Nashville."

Suddenly her phone rang. Gary reached into her pocket, threw it across the room.

"I warned you that you were mine. You will never be free of me."

Cameron looked over to see Brooke racing out of the restaurant, their father close behind.

"The alarm went off," Brooke hollered. "I tried calling Levi, but he doesn't answer. Goes to voicemail. Then Faith called, said a man was in the house."

"Wait for the Sheriff and watch the guy in that car," Cameron ordered Brooke before he turned to race inside the house.

"I'll go in the back door," Finn called out.

Cameron eased the lobby door open, listened for a moment. Thought he heard a loud voice in the back of the house. He eased around the stairs toward the door to the dining room, paused for a quick look to be sure the room was empty.

Crept across the dining room past the long table and side buffet toward the kitchen.

As he listened to the man's tirade, he quickly ascertained it was Kristina's husband. He peeked around the antique cupboard into the butler's quarters, felt his blood boil when he saw Gary Powell's bulky form hovering over a bloody and battered Kristina.

Cameron glimpsed Levi charging into the kitchen from the back porch just as he launched himself across the butler's quarters, knocked Gary off balance, so they both collided with the table and lamp at the end of the settee.

Kristina screamed, crawled away from the two men as they rolled further into the corner of the room. Cameron managed to straddle Gary Powell and began to pummel him with hard, angry fists.

"You will never raise a hand to her again," Cameron shouted.

He managed to deliver a good number of punches before Levi and Finn each grabbed an arm to pull him off the bleeding and shocked intruder.

Suddenly, Brooke raced into the room followed by Sheriff Thompson and a deputy. A second deputy stood guard over the man in the car outside.

Minutes later, a handcuffed Gary Powell was escorted out of the B&B. His nose was bloody, would probably need to be reset, cheeks cut and red, left eye beginning to swell shut.

A crowd had gathered in the parking lot as soon as the Sheriff's cars came barreling up the back drive, sirens going full blast.

Cameron followed to watch the deputies put Gary Powell and the other guy in the back of their cruisers.

"Kristina and I will be there shortly,"

Cameron paused when two men stepped out of a dark sedan, advanced toward him and Sheriff Thompson. One held up a badge.

"I'm Christopher Hunter, this is Ashby Stewart with the Federal Bureau of Investigation. We're here to arrest Gary Powell."

"Get in line," Cameron barked.

"You took your sweet time," Cameron complained minutes later as everyone assembled in the living room at the B&B.

Sheriff Thompson sent the deputies and prisoners to the jail, decided there was more room in the B&B than his office for the growing group of witnesses – Kristina, Cameron, Levi, Brooke, Finn O'Connor, and now two FBI agents, Christopher Hunter and Ashby Stewart.

"You were outside here the whole time he was inside beating his wife," Cameron growled.

"Sir, we had no idea his wife was here. We've been watching Powell for two months. Waiting for him to make a move. Followed him here."

Sheriff Thompson raised a hand to interrupt the ensuing argument. "Let's all calm down. Get some answers."

He studied Kristina Powell, her lip swollen, cheek bruised, black shadows beginning to form under one of her eyes. She was obviously distraught, wringing her hands, shifting as if unable to get comfortable, knee bounding repeatedly. Once again, he examined Kristina's drivers' license, this time verified she was Gary Powell's wife.

"Ms. Powell, in light of what has just happened, I'm afraid I have to ask why you are here and not in Oklahoma City."

Kristina looked at Brooke who nodded. "I left my husband a little over two weeks ago."

"So that would explain the missing person report?"

"Yes, sir."

"And you had your reasons?"

"Yes, sir."

"Ma'am," Christopher Hunter interrupted, "we need to ask you about your husband and the sooner you open up, the sooner we can clear you."

"Clear me?" Kristina turned wide eyes toward him. "But I haven't done anything. All I did was run away."

"My point. Your husband has," he paused, looked at his partner, "let's just say we need to know what you know."

"I don't understand. My husband was a CPA. What else is there to know?"

Agent Hunter turned to the Sheriff. "Is it okay if I proceed from here?"

When the Sheriff nodded his head, Hunter continued. "Ms. Powell, it seems your husband, Gary Powell, led a double life. Ma'am, did you know he was a hitman?"

Kristina's mouth fell open. "Hitman? As, as in killing people?" She stammered. "I can only say he liked to beat me. Sometimes I wondered if he intended to kill me."

Sheriff Thompson studied her. "I remember the missing person report. I take it that's why you decided to disappear."

Kristina bobbed her head.

"We've been watching your husband for several months," Agent Hunter continued.

"But he told me he was a CPA."

"Well, he was a CPA. Of sorts. Have you ever heard him mention a client or family by the name of Tribecka?"

Kristina shook her head.

"They are a family in New Jersey. Your husband managed their accounts. He also laundered money for them with a few side jobs eliminating competitors, people who owed them money. We've been tracking the Tribecka family for years and when a series of murders occurred last year, we began to piece together a deal gone wrong. Your husband popped up on surveillance cameras in all instances, so we started tracking him."

"He went out of town a lot, but he always said he was auditing a particular company. He wasn't very forthcoming about anything."

Agent Stewart pulled out a notepad.

"We need to verify some dates with you, not right now," he added when Cameron opened his mouth to argue. "Soon. It seems your husband used you as an alibi on two of the instances. And to make a long story short, someone — we don't know who — broke into his office, discovered the laundered books. He apparently suspected you did it and when you suddenly disappeared, things began rolling."

Kristina studied the three men. "Last week I told Sheriff Thompson that I've recently filed for a divorce from my husband. Will he be charged? Convicted? Will that hamper the divorce in any way?" She worried she might never be free from Gary.

"I will be glad to answer any questions you might have but I would appreciate some guarantee that it won't hamper my efforts to end my marriage to Gary Powell."

Agent Hunter studied Kristina's battered face, saw the concern in her eyes. "There shouldn't be any problems."

CHAPTER TWENTY-FOUR

The following day, Brooke, Connie and Kristina stood outside the courtyard, waved to Faith and her mother as they left to return to Nashville. It had been a bittersweet morning. Everyone was sad that Faith and the baby were leaving but happy to see a family coming together.

Amber Henderson had arrived in time to be greeted by the ghost baby followed by a condensed explanation of its backstory. She took one look at her daughter and burst in tears, apologized profusely for setting such a bad example. She took another look at her grandson and fell in love again.

"I named him after Daddy," Faith had announced, wide-eyed, worried about her mother's reaction.

Amber smiled. "I think that is perfect. We will have to see that he knows all about his grandfather and the good man he was."

Amber also shared that Bobby Turner's trial would be soon. "They will probably subpoena you to testify but I will be there to help you through it. It's the least I can do since I wasn't there in the first place."

"Maybe they can do it by deposition," Brooke suggested as she watched Faith stiffen, "and you might not have to go to the courtroom. Either way," Brooke advised, "just tell the truth."

She covered Faith's hand, looked her in the eye. "You did nothing wrong."

Kristina sighed heavily when Amber Henderson's car rounded the curve toward the front drive.

"Are you okay?" Brooke asked as she studied the dark bruises beneath Kristina's eye and on her cheek.

Kristina nodded. "I'll be better when I know Gary is a long way from here."

"Sheriff Thompson said he would be in touch sometime today. Guess we need to let the wheels of justice move. And be patient."

"I'm sorry I wasn't here yesterday," Connie apologized for the third time. "Maybe if I'd been here things might have been different."

"It could have been worse," Kristina said. "Gary never liked any of my friends. Never wanted them to come to the house. You might have been harmed before it was all done."

Kristina covered her face with her hands. "I had no idea he was involved in so much crime. To think that I was married to a murderer, I don't know how long it will take me to get over that."

"Don't think about it," Brooke placed an arm around Kristina's shoulders to comfort her. "Just take it one day at a time. Let things settle down." She looked over to see her brother heading their way. "I think I see part of the solution coming now."

Kristina lowered her hands, followed Brooke's gaze. What must he think of me, she wondered. She wouldn't blame him if he didn't want to have anything to do with her.

Cameron approached them, studied Kristina as if she were a scared rabbit ready to bolt any second. He cupped her face in his hands, softly kissed the bruise under her right eye, the cut and bruise on the left side of her mouth then lingered on her forehead.

Brooke and Connie exchanged looks, decided to head back into the B&B when Kristina wrapped her arms around Cameron's middle and leaned into him, rested her head on his shoulder.

"I'm sorry," she whispered.

"Sorry for what?" He murmured in her ear.

"For bringing all this trouble to your home. Your family."

Cameron hugged her closer. "Only thing that matters is you're safe and the bastard is out of your life. Probably be spending the rest of his life in prison."

"I hope so," She raised her head to kiss him.

Levi ambled across the wide planks of the attic floor, studied the ceiling and walls, pleased with the progress. The heating and air system had been upgraded, new ductwork completed, and all had been tested that morning. It had been a tedious process, but they managed to attach the new ductwork alongside the rafters.

He had used his air compressor to clean the rafters of cobwebs and grime before they came, planned to give the ceiling another quick compressor sweep, then use it to spray paint the entire ceiling white. The ductwork would blend with the rafters and the white color would add depth and character to the room. He planned to do the same with the walls with exception of the half wall between the dormers he finally finished yesterday after Gary Powell's arrest.

What a day, he thought as he shook his head. The girls had put up a good front the rest of the afternoon but when night came, nerves erupted everywhere. Even the baby was more upset than usual, probably picked up on Faith's tension. Ended up he'd offered to stay with Brooke, Cameron in *Asher's Room*.

Brooke had a rough night, blamed it on dreams but wouldn't talk about it. When he and Cameron met up in the kitchen at six this morning, they decided to sneak out, let the women sleep longer.

Levi opened the dormer windows to take care of the dust and grime. Figured a cross breeze would help to dry the paint job. He studied the middle dormer that looked down on the courtyard on the back side of the house.

Steve Johnson with *Relics of the Past, Inc.* had texted him last night to say he had found two antique wood glass lite French doors to replace the window. Once the doors were installed, he'd worry about the semi-circular balcony. It was going to be for looks only so there was no urgent rush to get it done.

He turned back to the room, gave it another look. Next on the list was sanding the floors and steps from the second-floor entry. Maybe by the end of the week, he figured.

But first, Levi decided maybe he'd go downstairs, raid Brooke's fruit bowl and cookie jar. He had descended the stairs to her loft and was headed toward the stairs down to the kitchen when he walked by *Harry and Rita's Room*, spied Kristina sitting on the side of her bed.

"Hey," he called out, then stopped when she looked up and he saw the tears in her eyes.

Levi cringed. He wasn't good with women and tears, but she'd had a rough day yesterday and deserved a little TLC. He stepped into the room, sat beside her on the bed.

"Are you okay?"

She nodded toward Faith's bed. "Faith just left. Seems so quiet with her and the baby gone."

"Yeah, I guess so, but look at the bright side, now you can at least get a good night's sleep."

Kristina tried to smile, winced at the sting on the corner of her mouth.

"I just feel so useless. Cameron asked if I wanted to help him in his office but look at me," she pointed her fingers at her face, "I'm all bruised. I don't want to scare his customers away. Probably even frighten the animals."

"Hmm," Levi thought about the work he wanted to get done. Munchies he planned to swipe from downstairs.

"Connie said she could handle the B&B today, suggested I take a nap. Levi," Kristina turned to face him, "I can't continue to stay here, sponge off Brooke. I need to do something."

Levi studied her face, understood her embarrassment, frustration; her need to keep busy. If she wouldn't work with Cameron because of the bruises, she certainly wouldn't work with Brooke in the restaurant.

"You haven't heard from the Sheriff?"

"No, and that's another thing. It's driving me crazy not knowing anything."

Levi thought about the root cellar – another mystery that needed to be solved but nobody had the time to do the tedious work.

"Have you got a sweater? Sweatshirt?"

Fifteen minutes later, Levi had settled Kristina in the root cellar. He'd shown her what to do, marked off a section for her to work and left her on her knees, smiling as she slowly scraped dirt aside.

"Just take your time," he suggested. "And if you get cold, or bored, it's okay. Much as we want to get it done, there's no rush. I'll tell Connie where you are in case the Sheriff comes by looking for you."

"I hope I find something," she called out as he left.

*B*rooke carried the tray of food – burger, fries, slice of blueberry pie for Levi, Chicken Caesar Salad for her – up the stairs to the attic. Blaring music competed with the hissing of the air compressor, Brooke wondered if he even heard the tunes.

It was seven in the evening, and she'd missed him. Hadn't seen him all day. When Kristina came bouncing in the back door of the restaurant, full of smiles, told everyone what she had been doing, Brooke felt a need to show Levi her appreciation.

The smell of fresh paint greeted her, and she was immediately struck with how much brighter the big room was. He had suggested the *Reflective White*, for the ceiling. Said it would capture the natural light from the windows during the day. She didn't know how it looked earlier in the daylight, but right now, it added so much depth to the room. The rafters stood out so vivid and wide, she was reminded of a cathedral ceiling.

She flicked the light switch to let him know she was there, raised her eyebrows when he turned to frown at her. The frown was immediately replaced with a smile when he glimpsed the tray of food.

Levi looked out the window and realized it was dark outside.

"Sight for sore eyes," he cheered as he shut down the compressor, closed the windows.

"Levi, the ceiling looks beautiful," Brooke congratulated him as she set the tray on a gallon bucket sat Indian style in front of it. "I'm in awe of the difference." She handed him a beer. "Kristina said you were up here. Figured if it was this late, you probably hadn't eaten."

His eyes grew round. "Kristina, yikes, I should have checked on her." He sat across from her.

Brooke chuckled. "She's fine and thank you."

"For what? I forgot about her."

"For putting her to work in the root cellar. She was full of smiles when she came to the kitchen. Said you felt sorry for her and decided to put her to work."

"Can't say I felt sorry for her. She was desperate for something to do."

"Well, I appreciate it. She plans to go back tomorrow. Is determined to find something for us."

"Your artist friend is coming next week to paint the mural on the stairwell." He slid a sheet of paper across the floor toward her. "What do you think?"

Brooke studied his sketch which was basically symmetrical lines to resemble a large wide stone wall. He had added water lines to mark a history of flooding. The wall next to the bottom steps was shaded a dark blue green to portray a moat. The next few steps were bare, with the stones running parallel. Sporadic vines were sketched growing up the wall. At the top step and along the frame of the half-wall was the side of a door to make it appear as if you were entering a castle.

"Nothing fancy," Levi explained, "but it might give some character, style to the stairwell."

"I love it. I had no idea you could draw like this."

Levi shrugged a shoulder. "Sort of comes with the trade. When you study enough old buildings, I guess you just pick up on it." He leaned back on his elbows. "I'll paint the wall that gray shimmer color to give it the concrete, stone look. Your friend can take it from there."

He tapped his knuckles on the wood floor. "These are next. Staining and sealing them. Should be able to do that in a day, maybe two. Will have to stay off them so I figure I'll join Kristina in the root cellar."

*B*rooke tossed and turned. After yesterday, she'd been exhausted, hoped to get a good night's sleep. But the dreams wouldn't stop. One after another, they flashed through her mind like lightning in a thunderstorm. It was almost like Chelsea wanted her to know everything; was giving her important pieces of information.

She dreamed of Chelsea overhearing the soldiers talking about the Battle of Petersburg, worrying that James might have been killed. Then Dr. Fleming was there. Comforting her. Kissing her.

Brooke sat upright, shocked to realize Chelsea had enjoyed the kiss, missed a man's touch. She fell back, rolled into another dream.

The Doctor was more persistent, but Chelsea always managed to evade any more personal contact. She argued with him when he insisted James was dead and she needed to forget him, move on.

Brooke awoke, found herself crying. She gaped at the ceiling through glazed eyes, drifted into another.

This time, Dr. Fleming was angry that she still clung to the notion that James was alive. He grabbed her, shook her, then kissed her. She tried to stop him, but he was stronger. He persisted, his hands all over her, she found herself giving in. Before she knew it, the doctor had overpowered her, pinned her to the floor and was inside her.

Brooke fell out of the bed.

Oh my God, Brooke swallowed hard. He raped her. That last dream had been so real; Brooke was sure she felt the penetration. Even now, her heart was racing, her skin tingling, her arms felt so stiff and tired as if she had fought him herself.

Dazed and too scared to go back to sleep, Brooke brought her knees to her chest, covered her head with her arms and rocked back and forth. Her heart ached as she felt Chelsea's embarrassment and shame that she had let the doctor take advantage of her.

No wonder Chelsea wanted to hide. Wanted nothing to do with the baby.

CHAPTER TWENTY-FIVE

Brooke struggled to get through the next day. By early evening, she was dragging so her grandmother ordered her to leave and go straight to bed.

But I don't want to dream any more, Brooke thought to herself as she stumbled toward the B&B. She rounded the corner of the shed and came face to face with the ghost of the little girl.

Are you Chelsea's devil child? Brooke wondered. What happened to you?

The child turned, disappeared into the wall above the doors to the root cellar.

Brooke raced over, tried to unlock the doors but they wouldn't give.

Levi found her struggling with the padlocks. "Brooke, what's wrong?"

"She's in there. I need to get in there."

"Who? Who's in there?" His heart skipped. For a brief second, he worried he might have locked Kristina inside.

"The little girl. Chelsea's devil-child. I just saw her disappear into the wall. We've got to find her."

Levi grabbed her arms, turned her to face him. Leaned closer to study her face. He didn't like the circles beneath her eyes, or the pale complexion.

"Levi, please, open the door. We've got to"

He caught her in his arms when she began to crumple to the ground. Carried her around to the back door.

"Put me down," Brooke protested, "I'm okay, really. I need to find her."

"You need a bed, is what you need." He kicked the door shut behind him, started up the steps toward her loft and bedroom.

"I'm not in the mood to make love with you right now."

"And I'm not either," he gave her a tight squeeze. "We'll get you changed, in bed and I'll stay till you fall asleep."

"I don't want to sleep," she argued. "The dreams will come back."

"What dreams?"

"Chelsea's dreams," Brooke sobbed as he set her on her feet beside her bed. She swat at his hands when he began to undress her.

"Brooke, you're dead on your feet. Your mother and grandmother are concerned. Sent me to check on you." He reached for her belt a second time, was pleased when she didn't object. "Let's get you undressed, in bed, then you can tell me about those dreams."

Brooke knew when she was bested. She gave in, let him undress her, accepted the oversize tee shirt he tossed at her, then let him tuck her under the covers.

"Will you stay with me?" She pleaded.

Levi stripped to his drawers, joined her under the covers. Leaned against the headboard, took her into his arms held her close.

"Now, tell me about those dreams."

"He raped her."

Levi's heart skipped a beat. "Rape? Who?"

"The doctor. He raped Chelsea. I dreamed it. Felt it."

Levi stiffened. "You felt it? As in, he was here?"

"No, he wasn't here but it seemed so real; it was like I experienced it. Levi, I fell out of the bed. It upset me so much I couldn't go back to sleep. Was scared to."

"What else did you dream?"

"She heard the talk about the Battle of Petersburg, refused to believe James was killed there. The doctor may have been in love with her, I don't know, but he kept telling her she needed to accept that James was dead. I think he wanted her to move on with him. Then they argued and he kissed her. He had his hands all over her and she found herself giving in. When he penetrated her, I was so shocked, I fell out of the bed."

Levi's gunmetal eyes turned almost black when he thought of his multiple times great grandmother taking over Brooke's dreams, exposing her to her grim memories.

He'd noticed that Brooke's words were slurred, listened as her breathing slowed, wondered if she would have a night free of nightmares.

Decided he'd be here if she didn't.

Brooke snuggled closer to the warmth, listened to the steady beat of his heart. He was so good to her. Looked out for her. Protected her. She drifted further and further into the cozy cocoon of warmth.

"You need to pack. Your things, Richard's things. Enough for the next few days. We'll get more clothes when we arrive up north."

"Up North?"

"The war's over, I'm going home. You and Richard are coming with me."

"But what about Mamie and Violet? They belong to me. They've taken care of me. I must look out for them."

"They're free now. They can look out for themselves."

"No," Brooke mumbled, stirred in Levi's arms.

"Shush," she heard him whisper in her ear. "Go back to sleep." Brooke felt his fingers stroke her cheek, up and down her arms as she drifted back to sleep.

Suddenly Brooke jerked, found herself running across the fields towards the woods. Her heart raced, felt like it would burst. She carried the crying child, he was heavy and upset, tried to squirm out of her arms.

She knew he searched the house for her, had heard his shouts when she escaped to the back side of the outdoor kitchen. The soldiers had gone, few remaining patients were being transported to hospitals up north. He'd wanted her to go with him, but she couldn't. She wouldn't leave her home, Mamie and Violet. If the war was over, she had to be here when James returned.

Like the whirlwind of the previous night's dreams, Brooke found herself in the attic once more, staring across the fields where the soldiers had camped. Everyone was gone, except Mamie and Violet. And her dear little boy. She vowed to wait for James to come home.

Then she felt movement in her belly and was ashamed that she carried a devil-child inside her.

Brooke cried out, felt Chelsea's pain. She jerked when she heard the man's voice, worried she was still trapped in what felt like a never-ending nightmare.

"Shush," Levi soothed her.

"Levi," she hugged him close when she recognized his voice, "make love to me, Levi, please. Make these terrible images go away. Please," she almost begged.

Levi's heart ached to hear the pain in her voice. He brushed his lips over hers, then her chin, forehead, shoulders, back to her lips, while his hands softly massaged her body, relaxed her, slowed her racing heart.

He felt the quiver as she accepted him, answered her soft sigh when he entered her, slowly kindled the passion he knew they shared, carried her toward their private paradise.

*B*rooke awoke relaxed, refreshed and alone. She didn't know where he'd gone but knew she owed Levi Matthews big time.

She stretched her arms above her head and smiled. She felt ready to take on anything today. Then she looked at the clock and yelped. It was eleven o'clock!

"Someone definitely got a good night's sleep," Connie smiled when Brooke raced into the kitchen. Connie handed her a heaping serving of egg casserole warm from the microwave.

"Levi said to let you sleep and considering you look a whole lot better than you did yesterday, I have to say it was a good idea."

"Where is he anyway?" Brooke gulped down a mouthful.

"In the root cellar. Said he stained the attic floors and would be working there today. Also said for you to stay away. Something about catching you trying to go in the cellar last night?"

Brooke winced. "Yeah, I saw the little girl again. Connie, I asked her if she was Chelsea's devil child and she just looked at me. Then she turned and disappeared into the brick wall. Next to the root cellar."

"So, you think besides babies, the little girl is buried there as well?"

Brooke shrugged a shoulder. "Who knows. But I hope we get some answers soon."

Little did she know her prayers would be answered when Levi wandered into the restaurant later that afternoon. Signaled he needed to talk to her.

"We found something," he announced when she joined him next to the drink station.

It was going on four o'clock in the afternoon, but Levi made the call anyway. Sheriff Thompson had been notified immediately but Levi knew the Richmond forensics lab needed to be here as well.

He'd already alerted Gill Phillips when he and Brooke realized they might find something in the root cellar. Gill had been his go-to person whenever he started a project that might involve excavation.

Gill had taught him signs to look for, proper procedure, answers to problems. Hinted that the root cellar would be a suitable place to preserve remains. He was also an expert on familial DNA and might be able to get them fast answers. He said he and his team would be there first thing the next morning.

Even though it was a dark, grimy and cold site, there was excitement too. All the women had cried – Kristina because she found something, Brooke because she might have answers for Anna Marshall, Connie because she was sure this was the ghost baby.

Kristina had found the first small bone and almost fainted from the shock. Levi was grateful he'd been there and had moved closer to help her brush more dirt aside, uncover the entire sixteen-inch skeleton.

"It's so small," Kristina had sobbed.

They decided to broaden the search and discovered another small skeleton several feet away.

"We need to turn this over to the authorities and a more experienced team," Levi decided.

"You've had quite a bit of excitement here this past week," Sheriff Thompson stated as he stared at the upended dirt in the dark corner of the cellar.

"Yes sir," Brooke agreed. "Much as I hate the publicity that will come with it, I'm hoping this find will bring some closure for people."

CHAPTER TWENTY-SIX

Victory Hill was a hub of activity. Although the television stations weren't there, word had spread throughout Williamtown that human bones had been found at the B&B. Business was booming in the restaurant as people decided to eat there in the hopes that something would happen while they were there. Angelina and Finn were concerned about their food inventory, considered closing the restaurant for the day.

Brooke was thankful that there were no expected guests in the B&B and had decided they wouldn't take any new reservations for the next several days.

The Sheriff had placed bright orange cones between the root cellar doors and the small shed, connected those cones with bright yellow police tape.

Gill Phillips and his team arrived in time to be greeted by the baby ghost and had set to work removing the uncovered bones, digging further to be sure there weren't more.

Levi was grateful the attic floors were dry as he had a full day ahead of him. Once Brooke departed to work in the restaurant, he left explicit instructions that she go nowhere near her loft area for the remainder of the day.

"What do you mean I can't go to my loft," she'd argued when he dropped by the restaurant for lunch.

"I'm working on your bathroom, and I don't want you snooping. Or interrupting."

Her eyes grew round. "You mean it's finished?"

"Not quite," it wasn't a complete lie he thought to himself, "but it will be. You'll just have to use the bathroom you share with Connie a little longer or stay in one of the other rooms this evening."

"Not sure about that. Your friend asked about my room rates." She leaned closer to Levi. "He and his team found two more. He seems to think this project is going to take a few more days."

Levi shook his head, headed back to the kitchen. He wanted answers as much as she did but right now, he had other things on his mind. He'd raided her closet, quarantined her loft and gotten her off his back for a short while, now he needed to take care of the next phase of his plan.

*B*rooke had just deposited a tray of dirty dishes beside the commercial dishwasher and was headed back to the main room when her mother stopped her, handed her a note.

"Levi wanted me to give this to you at six o'clock." Angelina nodded her head toward the wall clock. "You've been served," she announced with a bright smile.

Brooke opened the envelope, studied the plain white card inside. *Meet me in the honeymoon suite at seven for a business meeting and blessing ~ Levi* was scribbled on the card.

"He also said your loft is still off limits, but Connie will tell you where to go."

"What is he up to?" Brooke wondered out loud.

"Go, go, go," Rita Comfort appeared at the drink station, shooed Brooke out the kitchen door.

Connie met her at the back door of the B&B, told her everything she needed was in *Chelsea's Room*. "Levi said you can go up the attic stairs from there."

"And not before seven," Connie added as Brooke headed around the corner of the B&B, past the sectioned off root cellar for the lobby and front stairs.

She turned into *Chelsea's Room*, found her denim Savanna shirtdress laying on the bed, pearl earrings and bracelet beside it, silver slide shoes on the floor. There was even fresh underwear.

Brooke didn't know what he had in mind – well, maybe she did – but after what he did for her the other night, she figured she'd play along.

At six fifty-eight, she clasped the bracelet around her wrist, stepped into the slides and headed for the attic.

She was immediately struck by the smell of freshly painted walls, soft glow of pillar candles atop the half-wall at the top of the stairs and Enya's instrumental and vocal music that echoed throughout the room.

She mounted the stairs, turned at the top to see candles everywhere – on overturned buckets, stacked boxes, a long board resting on the rungs midway up two ladders. The mahogany floors were sanded, stained, varnished and buffed to a shiny finish. A mattress covered with her quilt and pillows lay on the floor in front of the wall he'd added between the two front dormers. What looked like a square card-table completely draped with one of the restaurant's long linen tablecloths was set in front of a back dormer window, two domed plates, wine glasses and flowers arranged on top.

Levi dressed in jeans, white polo shirt and navy socks leaned against the door frame of the soon-to-be bathroom, watching her as she stared about the room.

"It's beautiful," she murmured softly. "So romantic. Just as I imagined."

He straightened, walked toward her. "Wanted you to have a glimpse of what it could look like."

"So, you didn't finish my bathroom?"

Levi gave her a pained expression. "Not quite. I had something else I wanted to do first."

"All this?" She smiled, waved a hand to encompass the room.

Levi handed her a wine glass. "This."

Brooke looked down to see a sparkling blue sapphire with a diamond halo ring suspended from the wine charm hooked around the stem of the glass.

"Levi," her breath hitched. She felt breathless, her knees wobbled, her heart nearly stopped. She certainly hadn't seen this coming. She looked up at him, her eyes sparkling with tears of joy.

"I knew I wanted you the moment we met but the other night, when we made love under the elm tree," he paused, shook his head. "I thought that first night in *William and Elsie's Room* was the defining moment, but I've decided every day is a turning point with you."

He unhooked the ring from the charm, knelt in front of her, licked his lips nervously.

"Brooke Maureen O'Connor, you can be annoying, exasperating and drive me up a wall at times, but I've learned I can't live without you. Will you marry me? I can promise you our life will never be boring."

Brooke was sure if she didn't do something fast, she would melt on the spot. A tear spilled down her cheek as she set the glass on the table, cupped his face, leaned down to kiss him. "Yes." She kissed him again. "Yes." And again. "Yes."

Levi stood when she wrapped her arms around his neck, held her suspended in the air as he took possession of her lips.

"I decided you and I would be the ones to christen this room, not Aaron and Piper."

Brooke looked over at the single mattress on the floor.

"Didn't say it would be furnished," he gave her a half-smile, "but we will be the first couple to make love in this honeymoon suite."

"Where did you find the mattress?"

"It's yours. You don't want to see your bedroom right now. That's why I said it was off limits."

Brooke shook her head, smiled at the ring sparkling on her left ring finger.

*B*rooke stirred in her sleep, extended her hand to touch the fabric that covered the portrait.

She and Levi had enjoyed the lasagna dinner he had requested her mother prepare, finished off the bottle of zinfandel with chocolate brownies, slowly undressed each other to end the evening in each other's arms. Confirm, seal and commit to the beginning of their life together as lovers.

Chelsea once again trespassed on Brooke's dreams in another attempt to provide answers, find peace at last. Brooke mimicked Chelsea's actions as her hand nudged the fabric aside, stared at the couple painted on the canvas. Skimmed her fingers across the man's face, her heart about to burst from missing him so much.

Brooke felt queasy, sensed that Chelsea was sick, wasting away. Fearful the portrait would be destroyed after she was gone, she struggled to carry it up the attic stairs, found the old trunk and hid it beneath the blankets.

Half-asleep, Levi turned to Brooke, tried to gather her close, comfort her but Brooke sat upright. Stared at him with eyes round as saucers.

"I saw it," she exclaimed.

"Saw what?"

"The portrait. Levi, I watched Chelsea put the portrait in an old trunk."

"Here? You saw her putting it in the trunk here?"

Brooke bobbed her head, remembered the trunk that was always tucked in the far corner of the attic at the top of the steps. She looked over to find the corner empty. "Where did it go?"

"Storage room," Levi jumped up, grabbed his jeans. "I moved it a couple weeks ago when I started working up here."

Brooke reached for her dress, raced after him, found the button to the hidden door to the storage room.

Barefooted, Levi carefully navigated to the light bulb, pulled the string to illuminate the room.

"That's it," Brooke exclaimed, both hands covering her mouth in surprise. She knelt to study the strange lock.

"Yeah," Levi squat beside her, "can't say that I've seen anything like it before." He tugged at the rusted padlock; reached for the hammer he'd been missing from his tool belt. "Do you have a fondness for this old trunk?"

Brooke shook her head, waited patiently while Levi used the claw of the hammer to pry the padlock away from the top of the trunk.

They lifted the lid to find a white dress neatly folded on top.

"This has to be Chelsea's wedding dress," Brooke decided as she stood, lifted the dress out of the trunk. She lay it on the sheet covered sofa, turned back to find Levi removing blankets. There were two more blankets before they found the beige fabric covering the painting from Brooke's dream.

Levi carried the portrait to the big room, leaned it against the wall across from the mattress.

"Levi, look," she reached for the faded envelopes that fell to the floor behind the portrait. "They must have been attached to the back," she exclaimed.

Brooke settled on the bed near one of the candles. Opened the one on top. "It's from James." She studied the envelope, slid the single page out, began to read it out loud.

July 1864

My own dear wife, I am so tempted to just walk away from battle. I miss you and our son and pray you are both well. We have been camped near Petersburg for one week now and nothing has happened. We know the Union troops are near, but no one will make the first move. I have travelled these roads to Richmond enough, I am tempted to simply walk away. I remain your devoted husband, James Donovan

"I dreamed of Chelsea reading this," Brooke sighed. "I remember feeling her hope that James did indeed walk away."

She opened the next letter. "This one is written to James."

August 1864

My Dearest James, I received your letter today, another reason I refuse to believe you were killed in battle. I read it to our son. He listened to every word. I keep rereading it in the hopes that by the time I finish I will look out and see you walking down the long lane to our home.

But it is not safe for you to come at this time. The soldiers are still here, and I worry what they will do if they capture you. I fear your heart would break to see what they have done to your home.

277

"I guess she didn't mail it. Or finish it." Brooke opened another envelope. "Here is another."

October 1865

My dearest James, It has been six months since the dreaded war ended. I continue to wait for you. Atticus said he saw your name on the list posted at the Post Office, but I refuse to believe that you are dead. I miss you so. Every night I pray that you will come home and every day I watch the front drive searching for you.

Mamie and Violet continue to take care of me. Your brother George comes to the house, but I refuse to see him. I know he has feelings for me, but I will not forsake my vows to you.

My dearest James, I miss you terribly. I remain your faithful wife, Chelsea Donovan

Brooke found several individual sheets that were simply folded with no dates.

"These don't appear to be letters. More like diary entries. And no dates."

My dearest James, I am so devastated I have been unfaithful. Dr. Fleming came to me last night, tried to console me when he found me crying for missing you. I don't know what I was thinking when I let him hold me, then he kissed me. I tried to stop it, but he was too strong. I had trusted him because he protected me from the mean soldiers but then in my weakest moment, he violated me. I am so ashamed that I allowed it to happen.

My dearest James, I received the most pleasant of surprises the other day. Mamie brought to me your image! It is the portrait that was done before you left for war. I stare at it and tears fall from my eyes. I desperately miss you, your kind words, loving deeds. As I gaze upon your face, I see that our son has your eyes. It was delivered by the artist's family. He was killed in the war, and they found it when they cleared his studio. George accepted it brought it up to me, hoped I would see him. But I refused. I am too far along with this devil child. I am so ashamed.

My dearest James, I ridded my body of the devil child. It was a girl. I have remained in hiding since I first suspected the doctor's seed had been planted in me. I do not wish to tarnish your family name. Mamie was here to deliver it and I have refused to have anything to do with it. She has taken it away.

Shortly after, George was here, threatened to take Richard with him to Richmond. I fear that might be best. I am in no condition to care for our child anymore. I desperately miss you.

Brooke looked at Levi, set the papers aside, extinguished the candle and climbed into his arms. "It's so sad. She has been a royal pain in the ass interfering in my dreams, but she never asked for any of this. All she wanted was a life with the man she loved." She kissed Levi's neck. "Like I do."

"It's unfortunate the war separated them but that was the life back then," Levi brushed fingers up her arm. "All we can do is continue to share their story, hope someday, something will happen that she will be able to cross over."

"Maybe finding that portrait is the first step," Brooke agreed.

"Maybe."

They both stared at the portrait across the room. The light was dim as many of the candles had burned down but there was a dull glow to the simple frame. They both jerked, came to attention, when the corner of the room suddenly brightened and they saw James and Chelsea standing beside the portrait, posed as they were in the painting.

They smiled at Brooke and Levi before fading away.

EPILOG

Victory Hill was a full house on Thanksgiving. Brooke and Connie had been cooking for days.

The restaurant was closed and Angelina and Finn, Jeremy and Rita enjoyed being on the receiving end of a delicious meal for a change.

Aaron and Piper, Jake and Cilla were there as promised. Wedding dates had been confirmed – April first for Aaron and Piper, May tenth for Jake and Cilla.

Anna Marshall, her daughter Sarah and her husband, granddaughter Molly and her fiancé were also there excited to be returning in June for Molly's wedding.

The day after Levi proposed to Brooke, Gill Phillips and his team found skeletons for another baby plus what appeared to be an older child buried in the root cellar. DNA tests – using samples from Anna, Cilla and Levi – later verified that one of the remains belonged to the ghost baby who was indeed the twin to Anna's grandmother.

The team was still tracking the families of the other babies via *GEDmatch*.

The little girl was a match to Cilla's DNA proving that Chelsea had indeed had a second child. They estimated the child was about four years old and may have died of typhoid fever. There was no determination of the father, but Brooke was certain it was Dr. Fleming. She debated contacting his family in the coming months.

With her parents' and grandmother's approval, Brooke arranged for the remains of the baby ghost and the little girl to be buried in the Comfort family cemetery. No names were assigned to the markers.

Kristina and Cameron had become a couple. She accepted his job offer and had recently moved into his house. Gary Powell was turned over to the Federal authorities and would stand trial for murder and money laundering. Kristina decided not to press charges, preferring to make a clean break from her ex-husband with no affiliation to his criminal activities. Brooke anticipated another engagement announcement as soon as Kristina's divorce was finalized.

Faith and Amber Henderson were also there with the baby. Faith had returned to school and looked forward to graduating the following June. They shared the news that Bobby Turner and Monica and Sidney Warren had been tried, found guilty of running an illegal adoption scheme and were serving ten-year sentences.

Levi finished the honeymoon suite ahead of schedule and was now working on plans for the house that would overlook the meadow.

Everyone had just returned to the B&B after a quick visit to see the family cemetery and site of Brooke and Levi's proposed home.

"Thank you for offering the resting place for my great aunt." Anna gave Brooke a hug after she hung her coat on the hall tree. "It makes *Victory Hill* mean so much more to me now."

"You are so welcome. I'm just happy to have the closure for everyone."

"This dress is stunning. Chelsea was so small," Piper exclaimed as she brushed a hand on the dress displayed on the mannequin in the parlor.

Brooke and Levi decided to display the dress, pistol and *Legend of Sleepy Hollow* book in the corner of the parlor. He had the dress professionally cleaned and looked long and hard to find a mannequin small enough to display it. The pistol now rested in a glass top box on the table next to the mannequin; the book was framed and hung on the wall next to the portrait of James and Chelsea Donovan.

Brooke looked over to see Levi in a deep conversation with Aaron, Jake and Cameron. Suddenly Levi's hands went up with a "poof" movement and Brooke was sure she knew what he is talking about.

She looked up at the portrait and smiled. The B&B had been calm since that momentous night in the honeymoon suite. Brooke was certain that James and Chelsea Donovan had finally found peace.

ABOUT KAY

As a teenager, Kay enjoyed reading Georgette Heyer, Daphne duMaurier, Mary Stewart and Victoria Holt and treasured the ones she collected.

She discovered contemporary romance when she needed something light to read while her children were napping, found herself wondering "what if" and decided to write a story of her own.

Three small children, a full-time job as a Library Director, Little League and civic obligations required that she put the pen away for a while, although she continued to write news articles and library newsletters. She became immersed in the community and made friends with many of the citizens through the library.

In 2007, she and her husband opened a wine shop – Grapes of Taste – and the people she didn't know through the library became friends at their wine tastings in the shop.

In 2013, Kay retired from the library, began reading again, pulled out her old manuscripts. Once again, she found herself wondering, what if I make a change here? A change there? Update things?

She closed the wine shop in 2015 and has been seriously writing ever since.

There are many more "what if" stories waiting to come alive.

Please enjoy her website, www.kaydbrooksauthor.com
Facebook page: Kay Brooks (author)
She also welcomes comments via email:
kaydbrooks.author@gmail.com

Made in the USA
Middletown, DE
21 November 2022

15082047R00172